M000216790

WHISPER OF WITCHES

BOOK 1

NIKITA ROGERS

Copyright © 2021 by Nikita Rogers

All rights reserved.

No part of this book may be reproduced in any form or by any electronic or mechanical means, including information storage and retrieval systems, without written permission from the author, except for the use of brief quotations in a book review.

For Lee
The person who always stands by my side,
holding my hand,
and guides me though my crazy dreams.
I love you.
Too much so.

PROLOGUE

1588

Someone was following them. All around him he could sense movement from somewhere within the darkness of the hill where the ancient monument he knew so well sat proudly. The smell of burning was in the air, of kindling, wood, and peat. There was something sinister in the atmosphere; some unseen dark force that made his skin tingle and the hair on the back of his neck stand at attention. His body shook as he held his sister's hand close to his chest and pulled her up the hill, trying not to look backwards.

"T-they are gone, Samuel," his sister sobbed, clinging to the bundle she was cradling against her chest. "They burned them; they burned them all."

"We need to keep moving, Helena, we can't slow down. If we slow down, they could catch us," he said, trying to pull his sister, but she had stopped walking and was looking down the hill to where the smell of burning was coming from.

He turned his head reluctantly and stared down the grassy mound. Below them, near the wall that surrounded the Raven Hill Monument, stood six glowing pyres. He never realised how rancid a body would smell as it was being burned until he was inside that cart, clinging to the bars and calling out for the magistrate to show his family some mercy. He screamed and screamed for them to stop until his throat was raw, but it made little difference. They burned them all anyway.

"The screams stopped," his sister whispered, tearing her eyes away from the fires, her eyes wide. "They will come for you next; they will know you are missing."

"That is why we must go, Helena. There is nothing we can do for them anymore," he said, taking off in a sprint and climbing the rest of the hill, his sister on his tail.

At the top stood tall ceremonial stones, carved with ancient symbols by their ancestors that lived there long before them. They would be horrified if they could see what was happening just below their sacred site. It was some small mercy that they would never know, he thought. After admiring them one last time, he guided his sister under the stones to a dig spot that had been started and not finished. He had started it the day before, having had the forethought that something like this would happen, but never had the time to finish it before his family was arrested.

"Quickly, place it inside," he said, lifting the shovel that he had left beside the hole and waiting until his sister placed the bundle she was carrying inside. He filled it with soil until the treasure was completely covered.

"Now what?" his sister asked, standing up and brushing the soil from her knees.

He grabbed his sister's hand and gave her a small comforting smile. "Now, we run."

CHAPTER 1

Present Day

The train was crowded that morning. The stench of damp clothing on people who walked too long in the rain filled the small carriage and pressed up against her face like a wall of sticky heat. It was mid-June, and so far, the summer had been too long and too hot and too busy to be anything but unenjoyable. Sitting on the too-old fabric seat of the train, Ana couldn't help but think this story she was chasing for her job with the city newspaper was another dud. A puff piece that readers would undoubtedly glance over on their way to the funnies and the daily horoscopes at the back of the paper. A flop, just like all the other gossip and weirdo pieces she had been tasked with chasing since the end of last autumn when she started working at *The City Herald*.

It was still a job, however, and as boring and tedious as the stories at the bottom of the barrel were, she could hardly say no to easy money. As her editor and boss had told her countless times before, she needed to work her way up the chain of command if she wanted to get anywhere in this business. Deliver, deliver, deliver, right? All those prominent journalists had paid their dues, worked their way up, and shown everyone what they were capable of. They, too, had lived on too much coffee and very little sleep to get where they are. Now it was her turn.

Flicking through the newspaper on her lap, Ana settled on the pink strip at the back and folded the paper so that she could run her finger down the columns.

<u>Virgo (Aug 23 - Sept 22)</u>

You are in the perfect frame of mind to pay attention to detail, dear Virgo. The moon joins Saturn in your business sector and you will feel compelled to take the bull by its horns and take care of business. This month could be a good time to do new things or combine play and work to keep you engaged. With your ruler, Mercury, forming a minor challenging aspect, your message may not go over perfectly. Worries can result from taking in too much information.

Figures.

A shrill metallic ring dragged her mind away from her horoscope and back to reality. Her phone was buzzing and vibrating in her bag on the train carriage floor beside her feet. There was always something a little embarrassing about her phone being too loud in a place where people were trying their very best not to make eye contact or talk to anyone, but she needed her volume to be loud enough to hear it in any situation, just in case the office called. Bringing the phone to her ear, Ana winced at the sound of her editor's voice on the other end, nasally and judgemental but sincere all at the same time.

"Ana, darling, please tell me you have arrived safe and sound, little dove?"

ELIANNA HEARST WAS the shrewd Editor-in-chief of *The City Herald* and had hailed the position for longer than Ana had been alive, making her direct, cunning, and willing to step on anyone like a bug if they displeased her in any way she did not like.

"No, Mrs Hearst, not yet. I am still on the train. One more stop to go and then I will almost be there. The meeting isn't until twelve; I can make it." Ana said, her fingers on her free hand massaging her temple on the side of her head. Talking to Elianna always made her head pulse uneasily.

"You better. The only thing I hate more than rudeness is lateness. You remember what I need for you to get from these people, don't you?" Mrs Hearst asked. The sound of the line cracked a little as the train hurtled under a small bridge.

"We need something to lighten the mood for the end of the month issue. Something for people to laugh at, something to read about these bizarre and peculiar people that make everyone feel a little more normal in comparison. Weirdos, freaks and fanatics, that's what I need from you, Ana. We need a story. We need sales, and freaks sell."

Ana frowned. She wasn't in the habit of making fun of people just because they believed in strange and wacky things, but she needed this job, and Elianna Hearst's recommendations if she was ever going to make it in this industry. She wanted to write about real world issues, not trash like this.

It was then that she realised she hadn't replied, and just as Elianna was coughing her name into the receiver again, she spluttered.

"Uh, yes, yes, I understand what you need, Mrs Hearst. I will call you with an update tomorrow after I have shadowed them and learned more about what they have to offer us. I've really got to go; my stop is coming up," Ana said.

Ending the call, she realised she never really liked talking to Elianna. She had always made her feel icky and gross, like what she was doing was wrong. Maybe that was because she knew deep down it *was* wrong.

The train squealed as it came to a stop, jolting the carriage when the driver hit the brakes and jerking the commuters into each other. She lifted her bag and tucked her newspaper under her arm before she stood and moved to the door as it beeped in warning of them closing. No one had gotten off the train except for her, which said a lot about this sleepy drive-by town. It had taken two hours of sweating and reading columns to get here by train from the city, in which she had tried not to audibly groan when more and more people had filled the carriages.

Out on the platform, surrounded by the smell of the countryside and the breeze that tickled the back of her neck, Ana was starting not to mind being away from the city. As much as a fish out of water she was here, something about the colours of the hills and air filled with birdsong calmed her, instead of the angry honking of deadlocked traffic.

The little shop she was heading to was only a few minutes' walk over cobbled streets and narrow pathways. She finally arrived outside a store with a large wooden door painted in crimson red and black chipping masonry paint on pebble dashed walls. A hand-painted sign hung above the white-paned windows, calligraphed in golds and silvers that read: *'Strange and Unusual Curiosities and Wonders.'*

Ana stifled a groan and tried not to roll her eyes. She was never one for these kinds of fanciful ideas of witches and warlocks, magic and ghosts, and mediums who could contact her great aunt's dead cat from across the veil.

However, she wasn't here for any of that. She was here for a story. A story about the strange people who owned this shop and *did* believe in this kind of thing. She only hoped she could keep her opinions to herself when it mattered. She was never good at that.

Opening the heavy black wooden door, Ana walked inside the shop, glancing sideways at the noticeboard on the wall that had posters and notes with phone numbers for local clairvoyants and palm readers who did parties and call-outs. The shop was bigger than it had looked from the outside, and Ana wandered the aisles of crystals and books curiously. A large wooden table piled with rocks and talismans of all colours rested in the centre of the store. Her fingers settled on the purple rock, and she lifted it gently, feeling the weight of it in her palm. She knew this one. It was her mother's birthstone, amethyst. Her mother always used to joke that it made her sleepy if she touched it. Funnily enough, she was tired, but she chalked it down to the lack of sleep and her early start rather than the mystic powers of the stone in her hand.

She replaced the stone before she strolled to the corner of the store, examining the walls of books and jars of herbs. Symbols were carved into pieces of wood and hung from hooks on the wall. To her left, on the opposite wall, pages upon pages of newspaper clippings on stories about the shop hung. They clearly weren't strangers to some publicity.

"Can I help you?"

The voice emerged from somewhere to her right, and when she turned, she was met with the face of an old lady who was almost nose-to-nose with her and staring at her with steely grey eyes. Wild, curly grey hair sprawled out of her head at strange angles, and she hunched over a little, her eyebrow raised and a quaking hand that held the head of a cane, which she was tapping on the floor beside her feet.

"I said, can I help you, girl?" she croaked.

"Uh, yes! Sorry, your wall, it's quite impressive," Ana said with a small chuckle of embarrassment, tucking a stray lock of hair behind her ear. "I'm here to see Mrs Genevieve Sullivan. Is she available?"

"Oh, it's you" she mumbled.

The old woman sighed and hunched over more as she finally took a step back from Ana and waddled across the hardwood floor. Her cane tapped against the wood, which made Ana wonder how she hadn't heard her approaching before. Perhaps she was too enthralled with the magical items that she didn't notice.

The woman disappeared behind a curtain at the back of the store, leaving her alone again to walk among the display tables of cauldrons and baskets filled with sage. She had always hated the smell of sage; it was potent and invasive, but that was kind of the point, she supposed. Candles sat beside the sage, all different sizes of pillars and spheres, in so many colours that looking at them started to make her eyes hurt. They smelled amazing though, and just as she lifted a beautiful pink one to her nose to smell its rosy scent, the curtain opened again.

The woman who walked into the store was taller, with dark frizzy hair cascading down her back and shoulders, and a white badger stripe in her hair at the front of her head. She had a kind face, round and welcoming, but she had a coyness to her. Perhaps it was in the way she walked.

"Ana Davenport, I presume?" the woman asked with a warm smile as she rounded the side of the counter and across the floor with her hand extended.

"Yes, from *The City Herald*. Thank you for meeting with me. You are Genevieve Sullivan, owner of the store, right?" Ana guessed, quickly putting the candle down again and reaching to shake her hand.

"I am. This is my little slice of paradise, if you will. It's not much, but it's all mine. If you would like to follow me into the back, we can have a chat over some tea and see if we can find a nice story for your article." Genevieve suggested, waving for Ana to follow her.

Genevieve guided her around the counter where a large antique till sat heavily upon it, shining in rusted gold. Through the curtain, Ana found herself in a room with a rounded table in the middle. The table appeared heavy, with a purple cloth draped over the top of it that hovered above the floor with silver tassels. Around it sat six chairs, all of them unoccupied, and the walls were once again littered with bookshelves filled with magical books, crystal balls, weird waxy-looking dolls, and daggers that shone in the dim light of the room.

"Please sit. You are welcome here, Miss Davenport." Genevieve said with a warm smile as she pulled a chair across the patterned carpet and looked up at her expectantly.

Ana gave a bashful smile and nodded, pulling the chair opposite her out from underneath the table and sitting down, then placed her bag at her feet. She pulled out her black leather notebook and set it on the table, opening it to a new page and laying it flat.

"Thank you for agreeing to speak with *The City Herald*, Mrs Sullivan. My editor is hoping to run a piece on you and your store at the end of the month. It may be quite beneficial for your store, and it would be great free advertising. All we need in return is for you to allow me to shadow you for a little while, listen to your stories, and learn about your world," Ana said as she tilted her head, her pen hovering above the page.

"Ah, down to business straight away, I see." Genevieve chuckled, reaching for a china cup that sat in front of her on a saucer and brought it to her lips, sipping at it and watching Ana over the rim. She set the cup down, reached her hand across the table, and wiggled her fingers, "Give me your palm."

"My palm?" Ana asked, looking confused. Her fingers twitched involuntarily, her palm feeling warm at her mention of it.

"Your palm" Genevieve said again, "I can't exactly give my trust and my world over to someone I don't know, can I? Everyone who has ever come here to do a story on my store, and my world, they first must give me their palm".

The room suddenly felt warmer, most likely from the panic that had settled into her stomach. Ana didn't know why she felt this onset of warmth and panic. It wasn't like this woman could actually *learn* anything from a pale sweaty palm, right? Carefully, Ana reached across the wide table and gave Genevieve her hand, which she turned over so that her palm faced upwards.

Genevieve hummed, trailing her fingers over the lines that creased her palm. Ana had never noticed how many there were and how deep they seemed to be in the candle lit room. She could feel her fingers tingling, how her bones and ligaments tensed when she squeezed her skin to get a better look. This was absurd, Ana knew, but her scepticism didn't stop her from leaning in closer, trying to see whatever Genevieve was observing so intensely.

"You are nervous, Ana. You shouldn't be; it's not like I can see your deepest darkest secrets, just generalisations." Genevieve smiled. She paused for another moment before continuing.

"This is your life line. You are a healthy woman, Miss Davenport; your line seems strong and steady. Your head line and your heart line are quite a different story, however. You don't listen to your heart when you should, and your head talks you out of taking chances on things you ought to. You have had loss in your life. A loss deep enough to make you shielded and wary of people, which is a shame. You are living your life at half the capacity of what it could be. Your fate line is harder to read. It's hard to see what your palm dictates your fate to be. Perhaps that is because you are so disconnected from what you understand to be true. Then again, you don't believe in any of this stuff, so I'm not sure any reading I give you would matter all that much."

She released her hand, and Ana retracted it quickly, bringing her hand to her lap and rubbing the inside of her palm, as if she could erase the tingling feeling of those lines on her hand.

"It's not that I don't believe, per se; it's just not really my thing." Ana admitted, heat rising in her cheeks in embarrassment.

"Well, it doesn't really matter if you believe in it or not, if you see what I see or not. I do, and that is what matters to me." Genevieve smiled. "Now, back to our business. I could sit here and tell you the same stories I have told the rest of your kind of people for years. I could tell you of my gypsy blood, my family's magical legacy, our experiences with the occult and things that would make the hair on the back of your neck stand to attention."

"That would be amazing! If you would share that with me, Genevieve, I ha-" Ana started, but she was cut off when the woman across from her raised a finger to silence her.

"Or I could give you something *much* better." Genevieve said with a grin.

Ana heard a sound to her left and saw a tall figure at a door she didn't know was there. She couldn't see their face in the darkness of the doorway, but whoever it was, they held something big and heavy in their hands. Her cheeks burned at the knowledge that someone had possibly been watching her this whole time. Before she had time to process it, the figure stepped into the room.

"This is my son, Ezra. Sit down dear, we have a lot to discuss." Genevieve said as she patted the table gently.

"I heard." Ezra mumbled as he walked to the table.

As he sat down and closed the heavy book, Ana could finally see his face in the candlelight. He was handsome, but serious-looking, with a furrowed brow and dark hair that hid his eyes as he looked down to where he had set his book on the table. He had broad shoulders and strong arms, without being too big where they shouldn't be. Ana thought he looked completely out of place in this dark, mystical room.'

She cleared her throat, looking away from him and back to where Genevieve was smiling at them too-widely.

"Can I ask what this 'much better' thing might be?" Ana asked.

"On the outskirts of town, not far from here, there are sacred ancient burial grounds belonging to our most powerful witch ancestors, which date back to the start of the seventeenth century. Some of their stone monuments still stand proudly; those date long before any witches were buried there, circa 3500B.C. Before their demise, witches throughout the subsequent centuries use these monuments to conduct some of their most sacred rituals and practices. Then some were hung and burned there after their suffering during the European witch trials.

"My son, Ezra, is an occult historian. He was always much more interested in the history of our ancestors' practices and the preservation of their knowledge rather than the practice itself, like I am. He came upon something most fascinating recently, didn't you dear?"

A sigh came from deep inside Ezra's chest. He nodded slowly and lifted his book once more, crossing his leg over his thigh and placing the book on his lap, opening it to the place where he had closed it before.

"I found some maps through my research on locations of witch burial grounds," Ezra explained, leafing through the pages. "We have found some artefacts at a few of these locations. Relics of magic and tradition, but nothing like what we found in the dig at the Raven Hill Monument. The artefact in question was thought to be a myth. We didn't know it was even supposed to be in the area, but here we are with something no folklore archaeologist ever thought would be located again."

He looked up from the pages to make eye contact with his mother, his brows turning down and his face contorting in an expression that settled somewhere between discomfort and hesitant irritation.

"My son doesn't think we should be getting the newspaper involved so soon," Genevieve said as she reached over the table to take her son's hand. "He is a professional at this kind of thing, like his father, and he doesn't like to count his chickens before they have hatched."

"It's more that I hold my reputation in high regard, and I would rather not sell a story before it has been authenticated and valued. We don't know what we have here, Mother. The world shouldn't know until we understand exactly what it is." Ezra said, frowning in what Ana guessed was a look of worry.

"Well, if I may say, it is a fascinating story. Perhaps we could come to an agreement that everyone is satisfied with?" Ana asked.

Hope fluttered in her chest. Maybe this story was what she needed to push her towards the world of real, worthwhile journalism. The idea of it excited her, but the very real possibility of Elianna Hearst denying her the chance to finally prove herself came down upon her in a blanket of cold sweat. This story could be taken away from her and given to someone with more experience, someone who normally took on cases like these. Someone who wouldn't need the exposure like she did.

"What if I promise you both that everything I record and write about in relation to this artefact will be strictly confidential until we can confirm its authenticity to your satisfaction? Then we can work on releasing your story into the world, unveiling it as the find of the century, with both your names and your store at the forefront of its find. I am just the storyteller; this is your show, I assure you." Ana said with a smile. She tried not to bounce in her seat, but the thought of having this story right at her fingertips was electrifying.

Genevieve smiled, squeezing her son's hand and shaking it as she nodded her head. "And then we can talk book deals, maybe even a documentary? That's what you have always dreamed of, right, Ezra? Your work being out there for the world to see?"

Ezra sighed again deeply, pulling his hand back from his mothers and pinching the bridge of his nose.

"Fine," he said, dropping his hand and looking Ana in the eye. It was the first time she had seen his eyes fully, and they burned through her with an intensity that took her by surprise. "But I want to approve everything you write. And we will investigate this together. You do not have any rights to investigate the artefact further without me present, am I clear?"

"Crystal," Ana said with a grin as she reached across the table to shake his hand, but he ignored it and set his book down instead. Her smile faltered, and she moved her hand to shake his mother's instead.

"Thank you for your time, Miss Davenport. It was a pleasure to meet you, and we are very excited to work with you at these most exhilarating times," Genevieve said as she stood from the table and walked around it. "Ezra is going to the dig site now, for an update from some of his co-workers on the item if you would like to join him?"

Ana nodded quickly as she closed her notepad and capped her pen. She hadn't even realised that she didn't scribble one note onto the lined paper as they were speaking. She tucked the book into her bag again and stood, pulling the strap over her shoulder and following Genevieve through the curtain and into the shop. The bright sunlight from the huge old windows made her wince, her eyes adjusting to the sudden brightness.

"Come. I have something I wish to give you whilst we wait for Ezra to leave." Genevieve added as she waved for Ana to follow her to one of the display tables. It was the table she had been looking at when she first arrived, the one filled with crystals of every colour and shape.

Genevieve reached forward, hovering her hand above each of the stones that lay there, moving from one to another as if gently appreciating them without touching them. She looked at each of them with such a motherly love that Ana couldn't quite understand.

She finally lowered her hand and lifted a black stone that hung from a rope chain. The stone was smooth and shiny, and the shade was the blackest she had ever seen.

"This is black obsidian. It is a volcanic glass stone, forged in the hottest lava in the deepest of volcanos. It is mysterious and beautiful, simple but powerful. It is the stone of protection and of truth. It will shield you from negative energies and help you on your journey for the discovery of the truth. Wear it with pride."

Genevieve passed the stone to Ana, and she held it in her palm, feeling how cold it was. She could almost feel it vibrating, but she shrugged it off and pulled the rope behind her head to tie it around her neck. Before she could say thank you, Ezra emerged from behind the curtain with a backpack on his shoulder and a set of keys in his hand. He walked to the door and opened it wide, looking over his shoulder to her with a quirk of his eyebrow.

He gave an unsure nod, and held his hand out in gesture for her to walk out of the door first, "Shall we?"

CHAPTER 2

"*I*t's my mother's car." Ezra said as an explanation to why a grown man would willingly be driving a busted-up, purple Volkswagen Beetle. "I crashed my car last week."

"Comforting." Ana said, giving a small smile as she looked at him out of the corner of her eye and opened the car door.

The inside of the car was stuffy and felt like an oven that had been left on high and forgotten about. It had been parked in direct sunlight in the carpark, and it was the hottest day of the year so far. The leather chair under her legs felt hot to the touch, and it took her a moment to get used to sitting there with the heat frying her skin. She watched Ezra enter the car and throw his backpack into the back seat before pulling his seatbelt on and starting the car with a loud grumble from the engine that did not sound healthy.

"Are you sure this thing is safe to drive?" Ana asked, quickly pulling her own seatbelt down over her shoulder and clicking it into place.

"Would you prefer to walk?" Ezra asked.

He didn't wait for an answer as he pulled out of the car park and onto the main road, then wound down his window and wiped the beads of sweat that had settled on his brow.

They were silent for a long while, and Ana leaned her elbow on the edge of the door and rested her head on her palm, watching the small roads and cobbled paths fade out and turn into country lanes and bright green fields. Ezra must have sensed the awkward silence also, because just before the silence got deafening, he reached forward and switched the radio on.

"You are listening to WWCJ Radio. The sun is bright, and the day is hot! The weather this week looks like it's going to stay warm, temperatures in the mid to high 30's and not a drop of rain in sight. Don't forget your sun protection and stay tuned to WWCJ radio for your perfect summer tunes to get you in the mood. Up next; it's the 80s music hour, starting us off is Cyndi Lauper, Time After Time. . ."

"I never pegged you for an 80s music kind of guy," Ana said, looking sideways at him as he drove.

Now she could see him in the sunlight, she could see the shape of his face. He had a strong jaw and a serious brow, piercing green eyes and a skin tone that was a little pale, but she could tell it would tan well if he stayed in the sun long enough.

"I'm not. It's the only station that can get any reception out here." Ezra replied as he drove. He didn't say anything else, or even glance at her, and Ana was getting a little irritated by the cold shoulder she was feeling from him.

"Listen, Ezra, I'm not sure what I have done to annoy you so much, but your mother called *us*, okay? I didn't chase after you guys for this story, and I'm not harassing anyone." Ana frowned, sitting upright and turning to look at him. "I know you don't like me, but you don't need to be so–"

"I never said I didn't like you." Ezra said, finally turning his head to look at her as he drove.

They stared at each other for a long moment, neither of them really knowing what to say. As she opened her mouth to reply, something white on the road caught her eye.

"Sheep!" Ana gasped.

Ezra snapped his eyes back to the road and slammed his foot down on the brake, his arm instinctively reaching out to shield Ana from lurching forward too far.

The old Volkswagen beetle squealed to a halt inches in front of the herd of sheep that were crossing the road with their farmer who was waving his arms angrily.

"Sorry!" Ezra called out the window, then took his arm back from where he was shielding her and let out a deep breath as he tapped the steering wheel with his fingers. "This is why I don't talk when I drive. I'm a terrible driver." he mumbled, waiting for the sheep to cross.

"I noticed." Ana panted. Her cheeks had gone red. She wanted to apologise to Ezra, but she wasn't exactly sure what for. Distracting him, maybe?

"For the record, I never said I don't like you." Ezra said as he glanced at her. "I just don't know you yet."

THEY REACHED the dig site faster than Ana had anticipated. She had barely calmed herself again from the incident with the sheep on the road that when they arrived, she was still resting her hand against her chest and staring at her knees. She only realised they had stopped when Ezra pulled the car into park and turned the engine off with a final splutter.

"We are here." he said, inhaling a small breath and pulling the keys out of the ignition. He seemed to be taking as much time as she was to get over their close encounter.

Collecting her bag and rolling her window back up again, Ana pushed the door open and scrambled to get to the safety of the tarmacked car park. Closing his door, Ezra waved for her to follow him up a rocky pathway that led over a small hill. He didn't even lock his car, not that anyone would want to steal the hunk of junk anyway.

The monument that stood at the top of the hill was larger than she expected. It was almost like a dome, with green foliage on the top, leaving the rest of the white stone exposed around the walls, which were completely circular, with a doorway at the front. It was perfectly kept, with the foliage at the top cut down neatly and the grass that surrounded it mowed in perfectly zigzagged lines. Surrounding the monument stood tall vertical stones that pierced the ground and had horizontal ones laid upon them. They almost looked like stone doorways or large tables. Each set was a different shape and size, but all were strong and looked like they had been there for longer than she could fathom.

Looking up at how far it was, Ana got the feeling that it was going to be quite the trek to get up there, and it must have shown on her face.

"I'm not sure you are wearing the best shoes for this," Ezra commented as he gave her a small sideways glance and the smallest hint of a smile curved at the edges of his mouth.

"My boots are more comfortable than they look." Ana smiled back.

Together they started up the path to the entryway at the bottom of the hill, where an area of willow trees and some small gravestones were sticking out of the ground at odd angles like loose, broken teeth. Observing the gravestones as they passed them, Ana got a heavy feeling in her chest that settled deep inside her. The air here seemed to be colder even in the sun.

"What is this place?" Ana asked, hugging herself to soothe the goosebumps on her skin.

A cloud fell over Ezra's face. He looked around at the stones with a solemn stare, then looked to his feet as he walked with his hands stuffed into the pockets of his jeans.

"Those are the witches graves. Anyone who was tried and executed as a witch could not be buried on consecrated ground. Some were just left to the elements to take care of their bodies, but some were brought here and buried at the base of the place of most significance to them." He said, looking away.

Words caught in Ana's throat as she looked over the grave-stones. She couldn't imagine what these people went through before they found peace at these graves. She wasn't sure she wanted to know, either.

Approaching the gate that led up the pathway to the monument, she noticed a brown figure standing beside it. It was a bronze statue of a young woman holding a baby. Tears were streaming down her cheeks and her face held an emotion so harrowing that Ana couldn't exactly place what it was.

"What's her story?" she asked, reaching forward to run her fingers over the plaque on the statue that read,

In memory of the souls lost to the witch burnings of 1588.

Ezra didn't look up from where he was opening the large iron gate. Whether it was because he had seen the statue so many times that he didn't need to look at it, or because he simply couldn't bring himself to, she didn't quite know.

"Her name was Mary Marion. She was the daughter of a local farmer whose fields were not too far from here," Ezra started, walking through the gate and waiting for her to follow before he closed it after her and continued up the path, looking over his shoulder as she came to his side and they started up the hill.

"Her whole family, consisting of her parents and her sisters, and her brothers, were all tried for witchcraft and heresy at the court-house over the span of a few weeks. They were all judged as guilty, pulled from their cells, and brought here, where the willow trees now stand, then they were all burned at the stake for their crimes. Mary was nine months pregnant when she was arrested and brought here. She was unwed, which was another strike against her in court. They tied her to the stake and burned her anyway and due to the stress of what was happening to her, she gave birth right there into the coals. The executioner pulled the baby from the coals, took it to the magistrate who was overseeing the burnings and asked him what he should do with the babe. He said that because the baby was born from a heretic, it was also a heretic by birth, and he ordered him to throw the child back onto the flames under its mother. So he did."

Breath was pulled from Ana's lungs, looking back at the bronze statue as she raised her hand to cover her mouth. She couldn't move, shock rooting her to the gravel path under her feet.

Ezra stopped walking and waited for her to come back from her thoughts, his hands in his pockets patiently. "There are a lot of those kinds of stories here. It's best to disconnect yourself so that you don't get pulled down by the sadness of it all. It is a heavy place down here, but up at the monument, it is much more magical, I promise. It holds much happier stories. Come. . ."

He opened his hand and waved her to come back to his side so that they would walk together, and Ana detected some sensitivity finally coming from him that she didn't expect. She nodded and walked to him where he guided her up the rest of the steep hill path. She didn't look back to the statue of Mary Marion again, finally understanding why Ezra had kept his head down this whole time. It was all just too painful to imagine what humans are truly capable of doing to one another.

As they crested the top of the hill, Ana had to stop and lean over, resting her hands on her hips and gasping in air that stung her lungs like flames and ice at the same time. She wasn't used to climbing rolling hills and over boulders, and it made her wonder how they kept the grass on the top of the monument so well-trimmed. She couldn't imagine a gardener lugging a lawnmower all the way up here when she couldn't even walk up to it without feeling like her lungs were going to collapse.

"You don't get out in nature much, do you?" Ezra asked with a sideways smirk.

He wasn't even out of breath, or sweating like she was, and he seemed to be finding her breathlessness amusing.

"Not exactly, no." Ana smiled through panting, giving a bashful shrug as she stood upright again. "I am from the city. The closest I get to nature is writing on paper made from trees."

"It shows." He chuckled, shaking his head. He had such a deep laugh, and it made her cheeks flush in a way she didn't expect them to.

The open door of the monument had a rope tied to two poles on either side, and a sign that hung in the middle in a dip that read, *Private. No Entry.*

"It's closed? We came all the way up here, and it's *closed*?" Ana asked, wiping her brow with the back of her hand and looking to Ezra expectantly.

"It's closed to the public, but that doesn't matter. The artefact was not found in there; it was found under one of the stones. Nina should still be there; she was supposed to be finishing up the examination of the site today." he explained.

He walked ahead again, and Ana stifled a groan as she followed him. She had a feeling she was going to be following him around quite a bit before she got the story she needed, and she wasn't sure her feet were going to keep up.

He led her around the side of the monument and to the south side, where there stood a tall set of vertical stones, with a horizontal one that laid on the top over them. Underneath the stones sat little yellow markers pointing to various things that she couldn't see, and some white rope that sealed off the whole area. Squatting in the dirt in the middle of the site was a red-haired woman with a small dusting brush in her hand. She seemed so focused on what she was doing that she didn't even notice when they walked right up to her.

"Nina," Ezra announced as he knelt beside the woman and surveyed the small dig site. He had such a concentrated look on his face, even though the hole seemed to be empty. "Did you find anything new?"

"Not since this morning" she replied, raising her head and nudging him playfully before she looked up to where Ana was standing. "Oh, this is the reporter, right?"

Ana tucked some hair behind her ear awkwardly and nodded. "That would be me. Ana Davenport," she said. "You don't mind if I take some photos for the paper, do you?"

"Go ahead, there is not much to see here. Everything of significance was taken to the research centre," Nina said as she stood and took a sip from a bottle of water that had been resting on a fold-out chair.

Taking her camera from her bag, Ana focused the lens and took photos of the site and of Ezra and Nina as they examined the area. "Can I ask what exactly was found here? This seems like quite the significant operation."

"You haven't even told her what we found?" Nina asked, looking to Ezra with wide eyes and nudging him again as he stood to join them.

"I didn't want to ruin the surprise." Ezra smirked, shrugging a little and stepping back from the hole. He folded his arms against his chest and flicked his eyes between them with a glint of something that Ana thought looked like excitement.

Nina scoffed and rolled her eyes before she looked back to Ana again and then moved to slump down on the chair. "We found an old witch box. It might not sound that interesting, but there have been tales in old manuscripts of such a box that was buried somewhere in this area. We could never find it because we couldn't get the planning permission to start randomly digging up a sacred protected site."

"So, you got the planning permission to start the dig and found it?" Ana asked, snapping another picture and then pulled the camera away from her eye so that she could look at it on the screen.

"Not exactly," Nina said, raising her brow and looking to Ezra as he held his hands up defensively and turned away from them to look around the hole again. "*Someone,* we do not know who" she started, subtly jutting her chin in Ezra's direction as his back was turned, "came in the middle of the night and dug this particular area. They left the top of the box exposed, with the rag it was wrapped in at its side, and when the gardener found it, he called me. And the police. The police have no idea who dug the hole, but I have my own suspicions".

"It doesn't matter who dug the damn hole, Nina, the only thing that matters, is that we found it. Finally." Ezra argued, his back still turned to them as he leaned over to look inside once again.

"Mmm-hmm" Nina hummed disapprovingly. "We still don't know what is inside the box, we couldn't open it. It seems to be locked, but we can't figure out how. I guess that bit is up to the both of you."

Nina leaned down beside the chair she was sitting in and lifted a canvas bag. It looked so small and light that if Ana didn't know any better, she would have assumed it was empty.

"I assume you are going to take her to the research centre to view the box?" Nina proposed, and when Ezra hummed in agreement, she extended her arm to hold the bag out to him. "Be a dear and take this with you? It's just a few fragments and pieces I found in the soil that we missed earlier. I am going to wrap up here. I have a vodka tonic and a sun lounger at home with my name on it, and I'd rather not be here all day."

Ezra took the bag and wrapped it up, placing it under his arm before he leaned forward to kiss her cheek. "Thank you. I will let you know if I figure anything out."

"You will. Happy hunting." Nina waved.

Ana said her goodbyes to Nina and quickly followed Ezra as he walked away from the site, half-walking and half-skipping to catch up with him.

"You were the vandal, weren't you? You dug that hole," Ana asked as she looked up at him.

"I will neither confirm nor deny any or all involvement in the digging of that hole." Ezra smirked, gazing at her sideways with a small shrug of his shoulders, "And it would be best if you didn't ask me that again."

"Oh? And why would *that* be?" Ana asked.

Ezra gave her a wide handsome smile and winked.

"Plausible deniability, Miss Davenport. Plausible deniability."

CHAPTER 3

$\mathcal{T}$he research lab was an hour's drive from the Raven Hill Monument, and Ana had spent the entire time with her hands bracing herself against the door and the dashboard in case another close call gave her a near-death experience. This time, the car journey had gone a lot more smoothly, and they pulled into an empty car park in front of a modern building. The sides of the building were made of glass and metal, and Ana could tell there was a lot of funding being pummelled into this building.

"Where are we exactly?" Ana asked as she looked out of the window after relaxing her arms from the dashboard.

"Welcome to The Daria Research Lab." Ezra said with a small smile as he opened his door and practically skipped out of the car. She could tell that he was excited about getting into the lab, and he didn't waste any time in reaching into the back seat to grab the canvas bag that Nina had given him.

Lifting her handbag, Ana closed the car door and approached his side, looking up at the white and glass building as the sun reflected off the windows.

"That's a serious-looking building. Is it solely for occult and witchy business?" Ana asked with a raised eyebrow. She thought it unrealistic to think that there was so much money in historic occultism.

"You don't have to look so judgemental; there is merit in what I do, you know. It's important." Ezra defended, pulling out his lanyard with his pass on it as they walked toward the building and looping it over his head. "But since you asked, no. It is a private research lab. I would never get the funding to own any of my own equipment, but my dad has contacts, so they let me in to use what resources I need as long as my dad keeps handing them a fat cheque every month."

He stopped at a keypad and scanner hanging above the metal handle on the large glass doors. He lifted his key card and swiped it against the scanner so that the red dots turned green.

"Fancy" Ana trilled with a smirk as the doors opened automatically and they walked inside.

The inside of the building was bright and clinical. All colours were gone except for some green artificial plants that adorned the corners of the lobby and the top of the reception desk. Ezra guided her into the reception area, walking to the desk and handing her a clipboard.

"I'm going to need you to sign in," he instructed, handing her a pen that had the logo of the lab on it.

She took it and signed her name, her date of birth, the date and time, her address, and her phone number, then set the clipboard back onto the reception desk.

"That's a lot of information for a sign in sheet. I'm surprised they didn't ask for my star sign," she mumbled, following him as he left the reception area.

"Don't need to. You are a Virgo." Ezra smirked as he walked ahead.

Ana raised her eyebrow as she followed him again and wondered how he would have known that considering he had been looking in the other direction when she wrote it down. Her train of thought was interrupted when they walked down the brightly lit corridors and into a large lab filled with buzzing machines and tall glass shelves. Each shelf was filled with jars of wet specimens, equipment used for dissecting and poking things, and microscopes and magnifiers. She felt like she couldn't move too quickly in case she knocked something over. Everything looked so breakable.

"My section is just over here." Ezra said as he walked to a large steel desk and set the canvas bag down. "I will get the box. You sit here. Don't move. No snooping." he pointed a playful finger at her and left the room through a door to her left.

Ana bit her lip as she sat down on the spinning chair and turned a little, observing the tabletop and the large mechanical magnifier. This place was pristine and expensive. It made her wonder what the hell his dad did that gave him the contacts to get Ezra into a place like this.

It didn't take long for Ezra to return. He had a white cardboard box in his hands with a cloth lying on top of it that he motioned for her to lift off.

"Lay it on the table and put on some gloves. We need to keep it as protected as we can. Besides, we don't know where your hands have been." Ezra said, though he had a hinting smile that suggested he was just playing with her.

Ana raised her brow at him again and shook her head as she followed his instructions, then reached for a pair of latex gloves from the box at the edge of the steel table. She pulled them on with a *snap* and wriggled her fingers, peering into the cardboard box when he opened the lid.

Reaching inside, Ezra lifted a bundle that looked like old brown rags and set it down carefully, peeling them back to reveal a brown, crumbling wooden box. It had symbols all over it that she didn't understand and had no discernible lock that she could see. As she stood closer to him to get a better look, she couldn't really understand what the big deal was. It didn't look special or display any valuable gold or jewels on it. In fact, if she had seen it without knowing it was a treasurable find, she would have thought it was nothing but trash. However, the look on Ezra's face was all it took for her to realise that it was much more than just a box. He was mesmerised and rested his eyes upon the box like it was made of solid gold. She reached down into her handbag and pulled her camera out from its case, lined up the frame, and took a few shots of him as he marvelled at it.

"Isn't she beautiful?" Ezra asked as he pulled his own gloves on and ran his fingers over the markings on the box.

"What are the symbols for?" Ana asked as she zoomed her lens to focus on the inscriptions. She figured talking about the inscriptions instead of divulging her actual thoughts was a much safer bet, and he didn't seem to notice the diversion as he slowly lifted the box and turned it over in his hands.

"They are witch mark carvings. They were placed there to protect the box. Most of them are sigils from whatever spell was cast over it before it was placed in that hole. Sigil magic is incredibly unique to the individual practitioner, so it's hard to tell exactly what they symbolise, but it looks to me like they are along the lines of a cloaking spell."

"I can see the lines where the lid meets the body, but there is no lock and no way of opening it. No glue was used to fuse it shut. I really don't want to take a saw to it to see what is inside, so we are waiting to put it through the x-ray tomorrow." He frowned, setting the box down again gently.

Ana set her camera aside and watched how his face had changed from wonderment to sadness at the idea of having to destroy the box to get to whatever was inside, and she hoped that the pay off would be worth the damage.

"What was inside the bag that Nina gave you?" Ana asked as she walked to his other side and lifted it. She opened it and reached inside, pouring out the contents onto the table and set the canvas bag aside.

What poured out of the bag also looked insignificant to Ana. All it contained were some small shapes of wood and some metal charms that didn't look much like anything anymore. She sighed and sat down on the other chair beside him and reached to lift the box, ignoring Ezra when he protested. Turning it over in her hands and scanning its edges, she noticed the box wasn't completely whole. Missing slots were at its base and lid, and she frowned in concentration as she held it up to the light to see it better.

"Be careful! Don't yank it around so much," Ezra snapped, reaching out to take it from her, but she turned her shoulder to block him.

"Would you shut up, please? I'm trying to think." Ana turned it upside down, ignoring how he rolled his eyes and put his head in his hands.

She had seen something like this before, but the memory was foggy in her mind when she tried to reach it.

"The missing slots, they look so familiar," She mumbled, turning back to him and setting it down before she glanced back at the pieces on the table that Nina had found. Then she gasped. "It's a puzzle . . ."

"What?" Ezra asked as he looked up from where he was holding his face in his hands.

"It's a puzzle. I used to do these kinds of box puzzles with my father. He was obsessed with them when I was young." Ana said as she reached to lift one of the wooden pieces from the table. "It can't be opened without the pieces. They are like keys, and they all have to be put in the slots in the correct order or it will never be opened."

She measured the piece against one of the slots and turned it over until she found one the same shape and size before she pushed it into it and moved onto the next one. There were six pieces, and when she placed the last one inside the final slot, they both heard an audible *click*.

"Holy shit." Ezra gasped, meeting Ana's gaze when she looked at him with a wide smile and passed the box back to him. "You are a genius."

She shrugged. "No, I just like puzzles."

Ezra placed the box back onto the table carefully and took a deep breath. He looked excited and nervous at the same time, and his hands were shaking as his fingers touched the edge of the lid.

"Are you all right?" Ana asked, stifling a laugh. "Do you want me to open it?"

"This is a big deal! Don't judge me." he said, then held his breath and slowly opened the lid.

The lid opened with a dull wooden creak, and Ana peered over his shoulder with her camera, snapping a picture. The sound made Ezra jump out of his skin; he glared at her with a frown.

"Sorry," she whispered, cringing and sitting back again.

Ezra opened the lid the rest of the way and reached inside to empty the contents. "It's a piece of parchment," he said, as he pulled an old piece of paper from the box and opened it gently under the light on the table.

"That's all? Just a piece of p-" Ana started.

"Shh!" he hissed.

He pulled the corners open gently, smoothing them out and peering over it like it was going to crumble any second. More etchings and markings that appeared similar to the ones on the box were scattered all over the page in faded brown ink. Darker brown writing also filled the page in a language she didn't understand. The document looked simple enough, but how Ezra was looking at it told her it was anything but simple.

"Well? What does the ink say?" Ana asked.

"It's not ink. The words are written in blood." Ezra muttered as he reached to lift his magnifying glass from the table beside him.

"Blood?" Ana blinked, repelling back from it and scrunching up her nose.

"It was a common practice to create a blood tie to an individual or to a blood family line, especially if the witch was inscribing the paper with a spell." he explained, then brought the magnifier above the paper. "It is in code. Witch code, obviously, which makes this a bitch to read. Every coven, or every family depending on how they ran their practices had its own specific code. There are similarities throughout the codes, but not everything is the same so I need to first identify the blood-line and then decode it once I know that. If I were to guess based on the location it was found, it probably belonged to someone from the Marion family."

"The same family as the statue of the woman and the baby?" Ana asked.

Ezra smiled. "Good memory. I won't know for sure until I get to the library, but it won't be open again until tomorrow." he said as he checked his watch.

"It is getting late, I guess," Ana pouted, lifting her bag to put her camera away again and looking up to his face. She couldn't help but feel a little disappointed that all that the box contained was some filthy old letter. This wasn't going to make the cut of a good story.

Her disappointment must have shown on her face because Ezra set the document down and turned to look at her.

"I know you want your story, and this doesn't seem like it is anything on the surface, but I have a really good feeling about this find. We will know more tomorrow, and if you are willing to wait and come with me, we can decode this together. I wouldn't even have it in my hand without your puzzle-solving skills, so I owe you. I will get you your story. I promise." He smiled handsomely, tilting his head and making her cheeks flush.

"Uh. . .well, yeah, I guess I can't just let you run off and have fun without me, can I?" Ana smiled, darting her eyes away from him as he continued to watch her, making her skin feel warm.

"No, you cannot." Ezra winked, then turned back to fold the paper carefully and put it into a clear plastic baggie. "I can take you back to town and introduce you to the B&B owner if you would like? You don't strike me as the kind of girl who would enjoy a 6:00 train journey from the city just to go to a library."

"You know me too well already." Ana nodded and stood from the table before throwing her gloves into one of the bins near the wall. "As long as you don't kill me with your driving on the way."

THE B&B in the town was quaint, which Ana had discovered from her recent apartment hunt in the city to be a nicer word for "small."

Ezra pressed the bell. The reception area was so small that Ana had to squeeze between Ezra and the wall to stand at the front desk. Being this close to him, she couldn't help but notice how good he smelled. He had scents of patchouli and sandalwood, and she was too busy breathing in his scent subtly to notice he had started talking to her.

"Davenport?" Ezra asked, bringing her head back into the room.

"Hm?" she asked, snapping her eyes from his shirt to his face.

"Do you have your ID?" He asked, opening his hand to her.

"Oh! Yes, sorry." Ana reached into her bag and pulled out her purse, sifting through it until she found her ID and passed it to him. "Don't look at my photo," she warned, narrowing her eyes.

"Well, now I have to look," Ezra chimed as he stretched his arm out of her reach to look at the photo. He laughed as she jumped to get it from him, wagging it above her. "Look at those cheeks, all young and rosy. How cute were you?"

"Shut up. I was a teenager when that was taken. Give it back," Ana said with a roll of her eyes.

"No, give it to me," said an older lady from behind the desk. Ana didn't even hear her walk in.

Ezra stifled a laugh before he cleared his throat and jutted his thumb in Ana's direction. "She needs a room for a few days. Do you have any space?"

"I do. I'll need her information and her ID," the woman said as she snatched it out of Ezra's hand, "and cash."

"I only have my card. I don't carry cash. . ." Ana frowned, looking between them.

"Fine. But you owe me," Ezra said, reaching into his pocket and counting some bills before handing them over to the woman.

She counted it, then nodded to herself slowly and wrote something down on her notepad before she reached behind her and grabbed a key, sliding it over the counter towards her. "Room three, right at the top."

"Thank you." Ana took the key and turned toward Ezra. "And thank you, too. I'll pay you back tomorrow."

"You will," Ezra said, then waved for her to follow him into the hall. "The stairs to your room are there." He pointed up a narrow staircase into a dark hallway. "I will pick you up here tomorrow morning, so don't be late. Get some sleep. It was nice working with you today, Miss Davenport."

"It was nice working with you, too." Ana blushed, biting her lip as he nodded and walked down the steps. "You can call me Ana, you know. . ."

Ezra paused at the bottom of the steps and pulled his car keys from his pocket before flashing her a smile and opening the door to his car. "I know."

CHAPTER 4

*B*exley Matthews was one of those friends who would drop everything that was in her hands to help someone she loved, even if what she was holding was breakable. She didn't care.

Her friends came above all else. Boys, her job, family. She would even leave her incredibly wealthy boyfriend of five years, who was waiting for her in their swanky city apartment to pack their suitcases for their yacht trip to the south of France, for her friends.

This was exactly the reason Bexley was knocking so loudly on Ana's door at the B&B at 8:00 on a Friday. She was there because she was a good friend.

She was there simply because Ana had asked her to be.

The door knocked again, bringing Ana back into the room from her sleep. She groaned and blinked away the sleep in her eyes, looking to the wooden beam ceiling in slight confusion. The room looked foreign, and it took her a moment to realise where she was, and who was knocking at the door. She had completely forgotten that she had called Bexley after Ezra left to tell her everything that had happened that day and to fill a bag of clothes and toiletries from

Ana's apartment. She hadn't expected to be staying in the town more than a few hours, never mind a few days.

Another bang rattled the door on its hinges, and Ana slowly sat up in her bed, rubbing her eyes with the heel of her hand. "Just a minute!"

She had slept in nothing but her underwear, so instead of greeting her at the door practically naked, she grabbed a towel that was hanging over the end of the bed and wrapped it around herself.

She barely managed to open the lock on the door when Bexley burst into the room, ushering Ana back to the bed so that she could set the large duffle bag of clothes on the floor and close the door after her.

"I have been knocking for ten straight minutes! What's wrong with you?" Bexley demanded, reaching to place a perfectly manicured hand onto Ana's forehead. "Are you sick?"

"I'm fine. I am just tired" Ana replied as she reached to lift the duffle bag and placed it onto the bed. She opened the zipper and sifted through the clothes, pulling out a pair of dark blue denim jeans and a black sweater with a white collar. "These aren't mine."

"No, they are not. Have you been inside your wardrobe lately? It's tragic, Ana," Bexley said as she surveyed the room, scrunching up her nose, "much like this room. What exactly are you doing here again?"

"I told you, I'm working on a story for *The City Herald*, and Elianna sent me here to–" she started, but Bexley held up her hand to silence her.

"I know all that. The story, *The Herald*, Elianna, blah blah blah. But what are you doing *here?*" Bexley asked, gesturing to the room. "It's not exactly the Ritz."

Ana sighed and rolled her eyes, pulling on the new pair of jeans Bexley had brought her and up over her hips and buttoning them. They fit surprisingly well.

"Well, I was originally coming for a puff piece on the local weirdos; you know Elianna likes to fill the back of the paper with those stupid stories so people who aren't into real journalism still buy the paper. But when I got here, it became something else. They told me they found an old witch box at a dig site, and it could be big news, you know? If we follow the trail, I could have a real story. I can show Elianna that I'm worth more than just writing stories about people doing strange things. It could put me on the map, Bex," Ana said with a smile as she lifted the black sweater with the white collar and pulled it over her head. She grabbed the makeup bag that contained her toothbrush and toothpaste and disappeared into the small bathroom.

"Sounds. . ." Bexley started, then shrugged and sat down on the edge of the bed, rummaging through the duffle bag to find the pair of boots she had packed for Ana, "Well, I don't know what it sounds like, but if you are excited about it, I guess that's all that matters. Does Elianna know you are going down this rabbit hole?"

"Not exactly," Ana murmured with a mouth full of toothpaste. She rinsed her mouth out with water and then fixed her face with make-up from the toiletry bag before re-entering the room. "Ezra said he didn't want anyone to know about it until we knew what we were dealing with, so I'm going to wait until we decode what we found before I give her my pitch."

"Oh? Who is Ezra?" Bexley asked, the name rolling off her tongue like she was mocking it.

"He's the guy who found t–"

Bexley gasped. "There is a guy?!" She opened her hands in excitement and wiggled them for Ana to sit beside her on the bed. "You didn't tell me there was a guy? Tell me everything!"

Sighing, Ana took the boots from Bexley and reached down to put them on her feet.

"There isn't much to tell, Bex. He is the son of the woman who owns the witch shop I was here to do the story on. He is an occult historian, whatever that means."

Bexley squealed, making Ana wince, and she laughed, taking Ana's hand and shaking it. "Is he handsome?"

A sound caught in Ana's throat, something between a groan and a hum, like she didn't know quite what to say. In truth, Ezra *was* very handsome, but she knew feeding into Bexley's questions would only cloud her mind. "I guess so, yes. But he is a source, Bex; this isn't some random romantic getaway. I'm working on a–"

"Story, I know, I know," Bexley said, raising her hands defensively. Her face softened with a pout at her and reached to tuck some of Ana's hair behind her ear.

"You know, it's been two years since Austin. I haven't seen you with a guy since him and you have been throwing yourself into every story Elianna has sent your way. It feels like you are still hiding away. It would be nice to see you step back into the light again."

Ana shrugged.

"I am in the light. I'm fine. Not everyone can have a perfect boyfriend, you know, and I am okay with that"

"Yeah, he is pretty perfect," Bexley sighed, then turned her wrist to look at the clock face of her glittering watch. "Which reminds me, I have a boat to catch in a few hours."

"Ah, yes, the amazing yacht trip with the amazing boyfriend to the south of France, which *may or may not* be a proposal in disguise, right?" Ana asked as she lifted her bag.

"Exactly. If this isn't a proposal, you *know* I'm going to be pissed," Bexley threatened as she looked to the window. The faint sound of a car door closing echoed from outside, and as the street in this sleepy town was usually so deserted, it was easy enough to hear.

Bexley walked to the window, peering down at the car that was outside. "Wait," she mumbled, pulling the white mesh curtain aside further. "Is *that* him?!"

"Who?" Ana asked, approaching the window, and seeing Ezra in front of his purple Volkswagen Beetle. "Yeah, that's Ezra, why?"

"You said he was handsome, but you didn't say he was *that* handsome, Ana!" Bexley teased with a gasp, turning to look at her and pinching her. "I knew there was a reason you were staying in this dusty B&B, and I sure as hell knew it wasn't for a stupid witch story! You almost had me fooled!"

Bexley reached quickly into her handbag and pulled out a bottle of perfume and sprayed it around Ana's neck, but in her excitement, most of it went into Ana's face, making her splutter and wince at the taste of chemicals.

"Would you please stop!" Ana laughed, shaking her head. "I am trying to be professional." Moments later, Ana heard footsteps climbing the stairs, followed by two firm knocks on the door.

"Professional-smeshamal," Bexley said as she waved her off. She walked to the door quickly and opened it wide before giving Ezra a large smile, "Hello there."

Ezra blinked as he came face to face with the tall raven-haired woman who filled the gap in the doorway. He tilted his head, then looked over his shoulder at the other room. "I must have the wrong room." He looked back again to her and then down at the two steaming take-out cups of coffee in his hands.

Ana scrambled to usher Bexley away from the door.

"No! It's the right room! I'm here." she announced with a small blush that tinted her cheeks. "This is–"

"Bexley Matthews"

Ezra jumbled the coffees in his hands so that he could take Bexley's outstretched hand, looking a little awkward. "Ezra Sullivan."

"Charmed, I'm sure." She smiled, taking her hand back slowly and looking him over not so subtly, then snapped her head to look at Ana, "Well, I guess this is my cue to leave. I will see *you*, when I get back from France, hopefully with a much heavier finger."

Bexley moved to Ana, kissing her on each of her cheeks and winking while her back was turned to Ezra. *"Don't fuck this up,"* she mouthed and walked through the door. "Ciao! I love you, kiddo."

With a flurry of dark hair and fair skin, Bexley was gone, leaving Ezra and Ana alone in the room in an awkward silence.

"I brought you coffee–"

"She's my best friend–"

They both spoke simultaneously, making Ana smile and shrug as Ezra bit his lip to silence himself.

"I had no clothes for my impromptu stay, so Bexley was kind enough to bring me some before she headed off on her trip. She's an amazing friend like that." Ana reached for the coffee he had in his hands. "Thank you for the coffee; I have a feeling I am going to need it."

"I figured as much. You reporters are all hooked on coffee; it must be something to do with the deadlines, huh?"

"Something like that," Ana said as she nudged her coffee cup with his, "What's your excuse?"

"I'm standing in your room at 8:00. What more of an excuse do I need?" Ezra smiled, then shrugged, walked back out of the room and started down the stairs.

Ana bit her lip and grabbed the door key from the nightstand. She then closed the door firmly and locked it, continuing down the stairs after him and out into the street.

Warm air hit Ana in the face as she walked to Ezra's car. Even though it was early morning, she could tell that by mid-afternoon the sun would be splitting the stones and there wouldn't be a cloud in sight. She pulled the car door open and got into the car. When Ezra entered and pushed the keys into the ignition, Ana noticed that he was wearing a fitted white shirt with the collar open, and his top button was undone. Matching his shirt with a pair of dark jeans, he looked a lot more dressed up today than the blue jeans and T-shirt he wore the day before.

"You cleaned up well," Ana commented as he pulled the car out and drove down the cobblestoned streets.

"Well, yesterday we were at a dig site, and today we are going to a prestigious library. Unlike you, I know how to dress for an occasion" Ezra smirked, looking sideways at her as he set his coffee cup in the holder between them.

"Watch the road," Ana said with a frown, looking down at her new clothes and pouting. "I will admit that my attire yesterday may not have been the best of choices."

"Best of choices? You went to a dig site in a pair of heeled boots." He laughed, shaking his head. "I mean as amusing as it was to watch you try to climb that hill, you looked like a deer on ice."

Ana blushed, bringing her coffee cup to her lips and shrugging slightly, "In my defence, you didn't tell me there was an actual nature walk to get there."

"How many ancient monuments have you been to that *weren't* in actual real-life nature?" Ezra asked as he indicated to signal to the cars behind him that he was turning onto a larger road.

"Well, up until yesterday, I had never been to one. Besides, I didn't come for a monument originally; I came for—" she started, but didn't finish the sentence. She had come to write a story on how crazy these people were. How unorthodox and strange they were. Guilt pulsed in her stomach, and she gulped it down, looking back to the road ahead.

"For the story on the shop, I know, but this will be much better, I promise. And from now on, you can wear your heels," Ezra said as he glanced at her. "Besides, they are cute. The boots, I mean."

"Shut up and drive." Ana smirked with a shake of her head, taking a large sip of her coffee to will the knot in her stomach to go away.

41

~

THE LIBRARY WAS HALFWAY between the old town and the city, meaning that Ana and Ezra needed to drive over an hour to get there. When they arrived and pulled into the car park, Ezra stopped the car and lifted his now empty coffee cup from its holder.

"We are here," he announced, reaching behind the seat for his brown satchel bag and pulling it onto his lap where he fastened the buckles and moved to get out of the car.

Ana blinked at the bag, then lifted her own and followed suit, closing the door, and hearing the clicker lock the doors.

"You own a man bag?" she asked, her brows raised. "I never had you down as a man bag kind of guy."

"How else am I supposed to carry around my papers for work?" Ezra argued as he waved for her to follow him up over the pathway that led into a group of trees.

"No, I get it, I just. . . You look very smart today; that's all." Ana replied as she jogged to catch up.

"There is a reason for that," he said, finding a bin at the edge of the trees and throwing his empty coffee cup into it. "The books we need to decode the parchment are in the old, restricted area of the library."

"Okay, so?" she asked, throwing her coffee cup in after his and walking through the trees. It was beautiful here in the denseness of the trees, and she couldn't imagine how a library would be anywhere near here.

"So, I might technically be banned from that area, and I might need to sneak my way in," he admitted, looking over his shoulder to her with a cheeky grin.

"Banned? From a library? What exactly does one need to do to be banned from a *library*?"

"It–" Ezra started before he stifled a breathy laugh and ran his hands through his hair to fix it from the wind. "Well, it has something to do with a very lascivious librarian in the rare books section, but I won't go into details."

"Okay, ew. Please don't. I don't need those details." Ana wrinkled her nose. "You are deplorable."

"She thought so too." Ezra smirked.

When they emerged out of the cluster of trees, Ana looked up at the huge old library building. Her eyes widened, and she stopped for a moment, to gape at the beauty of the building, the spires, and red, grey, and black brick walls.

"This is a library?!" She gasped, looking between him and the building.

"Spectacular, isn't it?" Ezra said as he nudged her on. "The architect was an amazing man. He crafted this building in 1849, and they named it after his achievement. It's called the Aldridge Library and consists of the main library, two wings dedicated to rare books, one restricted section, a café, conference rooms, a theatre, and a small museum area. Sir Aldridge drew inspiration for the building from the Tudor and Gothic characteristics of all his favourite old buildings. The majority of my education was drafted in those halls. I'm surprised you have never been here before."

Ana was still gaping at the building as they walked over the crisp lawns, having to remind herself to close her mouth. "It's stunning. I did most of my degree overseas, so I never really came to any of these places before."

She was beginning to understand how excited he got when he explained these things to her. There was something magical in the air in the places she had visited with him, and the feeling was infectious.

As they approached the door, Ezra stopped her, pulled her aside to the wall, cleared his throat, and removed something out of his pocket.

"When we go inside, I need you to remember something: My name is not Ezra. My name is Jake Dooley. Okay?"

"Jake Dooley? Who the hell is Jake Dooley?" Ana asked, frowning disapprovingly at him.

"He's a friend, and this is his," Ezra explained as he looped a new lanyard over his head and showed her the pass attached to it.

Ana reached to take the pass from his chest. It did indeed say Jake Dooley as the name. He was a professor who was 46 years old, with a photograph of Ezra badly glued over the top of whoever's face was under it.

"No one is ever going to believe that this is a legit pass, Ezra, nor are they going to buy that you are 46." Ana sighed, dropping the pass against his chest. "Does this friend of yours even know you have this pass?"

"Maybe." Ezra said cheekily, a curl of a smile pinching the corners of his mouth. "It doesn't matter; no one ever really reads these anyway. I will scan it and walk straight through. You are a guest, so you need to sign in. But we can't get into the restricted area without a pass, and I don't have one anymore. What do you expect us to do?"

"Keep it in your pants, maybe?" Ana mumbled. She sighed, then nodded slowly and rolled her eyes. She couldn't believe she was doing this. "Fine, let's go."

"Good. And remember, I'm Jake Dooley." Ezra said as he turned and walked in through the doors of the library.

The inside lobby of the library was huge, bigger than any library she had ever seen. It had massive swooping marble staircases, dark wooden floors and a large reception desk that looked older than anything else in this building combined. The whole room was warm and cosy, filled with the smell of old and new books, the sounds of footsteps on wood, and the thoughts of the academics who studied there.

"This is insane!" Ana gasped, looking around in awe at the high ceilings and the pillars gilded in gold.

"Shh, not so loud" Ezra whispered with a smile as he guided her through the wide lobby.

They passed a wide-open room with people filtering in and out through the giant archway that hooped from one end of the hallway to the other. Ana saw that every wall inside was covered in books that towered from the floor to the ceiling. It reminded her of an old fairy tale from one of her childhood bedtime stories. Realising she had slowed down to look inside the room, she looked ahead to where Ezra had walked ahead, and she had to take off in a jog to catch up, the sound of her heeled boots echoing off the marbled walls.

They came upon a long corridor that angled off the main hallway, and Ezra stopped to let her catch up.

"The restricted rare books wing is just down here" he said, waving for her to follow him.

The wing was long, with closed doors dotted around that led to reading rooms and lavatories. Right at the end of the hall stood another reception desk. An older man sat behind it, reading an old book that had frayed pages and a broken spine, and he looked up when they drew near. Her heart skipped a beat and her cheeks felt hot when his eyes connected with Ezra.

This was a bad idea.

"Yes?" the man asked when they stopped at the desk. He looked unimpressed and bored and examined Ezra with a suspicious eye.

"We need to access the restricted rare books section. My guest will sign herself in." Ezra said, not looking up at him.

He seemed calm, and a lot more collected than she had imagined he would be. Ana on the other hand, was quaking.

She gulped and nodded, reaching forward and taking the clipboard. Meanwhile, Ezra removed the pass from his neck and reached for the scanner to swipe it.

"I'll take that," the man asserted as he reached his hand out to take it.

Ezra paused, cleared his throat, and nodded with a charming smile before handing him the pass. Ana's stomach lurched. She felt like she might be sick at the idea of the man catching them out. It made her weak at the knees and her head feel light. Instead of looking up and giving the game away, she kept her eyes on the page and filled in her details to distract herself.

The man took the pass and pushed his glasses up his nose, looking down at it with a raised eyebrow. Eyeing the photo on the pass and then Ezra's face, he sighed and scanned it. When it beeped and the light shone green, he passed it back to him with a grunt.

"Happy reading, Professor Dooley," he mumbled, looking at the screen as his name was added to the list of patrons.

"Thank you. Miss Davenport, let's go." Ezra said, then quickly put the pass back around his neck and walked through the doors of the restricted room.

Ana thanked the old man and followed Ezra with some speed in her step. She could see another room from behind the doors, and although it was much smaller than the previous rooms she had seen, this room seemed darker and more cluttered. Upon entering, Ana saw rows upon rows of bookcases that filed out along the floor, so thinly spaced that she wasn't sure how they would fit between them to find the books they needed. There was no one else in the restricted room, which gave them the freedom to browse in peace without feeling like they were going to get caught.

"Okay, let's find this book." Ezra said as he walked through the middle of the bookshelves, pulling his phone from his pocket.

"You didn't bring the original?" Ana asked as she made it to his side and looked at the photo of the parchment on his screen.

"It's a piece of parchment dating back to 1588. I can't risk it getting lost or ripped; it's too fragile as it is. First, we need to find out whose bloodline wrote this. The sigil at the top, that is like a family crest, a symbol of their lineage. If we match that to a family, we can decode the letter from there."

He looked up from his phone to the bookcase he had stopped at and set his satchel bag on the floor. Then he ran his fingers along the old titles on the shelf. The books smelled old, like they had been stuck in an attic for too long. They were damaged, too, as if they had been passed down from generation to generation, and hidden away in dark places, lest they ended up in the wrong hands.

"Are these spell books?" Ana asked, her brow furrowing as she gazed over the spines.

"In a sense, yes. Each is a Book of Shadows belonging to a family," Ezra said as he located the book he was looking for and pulled it out from where it nested. Her face must have flinched because he gave a breathy laugh and shook his head.

"Don't look so horrified; it is not as dark as it sounds. They are simply the books of their covens' practices and beliefs, their family spells and traditions, their family tree, and their history. Each family book is unique, as each coven varies on what they believe and how they cast their spells, but the majority of it originates the same umbrella of magic. The shadow part simply means 'to be hidden,' or to keep hidden away from the prying eyes of those who would use it against them."

He opened the book to the first page, and the title read,

Witch families and their corresponding histories and practices.

"These are all the family crests or sigils, so we just need to match it to the one found on the document." Ezra said as he looked from his phone to the book and glanced down the page.

"Ah! I knew it! The Marion Family. They were mostly all burned at the mass witch burning in 1588, which is the date on the document. This means it was either written and buried before that happened, or some of them must have gotten away and buried it after. I would say the latter, possibly to preserve the contents of the secrets beyond their own family, for whichever ancestors would survive."

"This is amazing," Ana muttered as she reached into her bag quickly and lifted out her camera. Lining up the shot she took a picture of the book with the family sigils and then stood back to take another of him holding the book for her records.

Ezra closed the book and pushed it back into its place on the shelf, then looked down the lines of titles and lay his finger on another.

"The Marion coven Book of Shadows," he said with a grin, pulling it gently out of its slot and holding it as if it were made of glass.

The book was huge and looked heavy, and it had a hard cover that appeared to be made of thin wood. Leather was sewn over the spine to solidify it, and on the cover was a larger version of the sigil that matched the document. Small jewels were melted into the cover, glistening in the dim light of the room.

Ezra opened it to the back page and read the translations between his phone and the book, frowning in deep concentration. "This is going to take some time; we should take this to the table."

The sound of the door to the restricted room shoving open diverted their attention away from the book, making them snap their eyes to one another as they shared a look of panic.

"Ezra Sullivan! You know you are banned from this area of the library. You need to stop what you are doing and leave!" called out the voice of the old man who had taken the key-card moments before.

Ana gasped, and Ezra had to press her against the wall of books and cover her mouth with his hand to keep her silent. She panted against his hand and looked to him with panicked eyes as he listened for footsteps. He lowered his head against her to lean into her ear, keeping his breathing calm and collected.

"Ana, we need to take the book and run. We haven't had enough time to decode it. Are you with me?" Ezra asked.

Ana instinctively shook her head under his hand, trying to forget how close he was to her and how he had just used her first name for the first time. They were going to get caught for trespassing into a restricted area; how close he was to her should have been the last thing on her mind.

"If we don't take the book and run, we will never solve this, and you won't get your story. We need to run." Ezra stared into her eyes calmly and slowly took his hand from her mouth. "Okay?"

"Mr Sullivan! Come out here now! We are calling security!" the man yelled again.

Ana panted and nodded slowly, trying to gulp moisture into her mouth. "Okay," she whispered back.

Ezra pushed himself off her and reached down to grab his bag. He shoved the book inside and clasped the top of it whilst Ana grabbed her own bag and pulled the strap over her shoulder.

"Ready?" Ezra mouthed, waiting for her to nod before he took her hand in his and guided her down the back of the bookcases.

They rounded the side and up the aisle closest to the door, hearing footsteps echoing down the other aisle they had just been in. Walking quicker, Ezra looked around the end of the final bookcase, and when he saw a direct line to the door, he looked back over his shoulder at her.

"Now." he hissed.

They both ran, ignoring the shouts from the old man behind them, and bolted out the door. Ezra pulled Ana along, her heeled boots making it harder for her to run. They ran through the wing that led to the restricted area and out into the main lobby.

"Don't stop!" he called back to her. She could have sworn she saw a grin on his face, but the increasing sound of footsteps behind them directed her face toward the security guards that were after them.

Panting, Ana and Ezra emerged from the front doors of the Aldridge Library and onto its luscious green lawns. She ignored the shouting of the guards, the stares from local students picnicking on the grass, and how sore her feet were getting until they were once again among the shelter of the trees near the carpark.

Ezra dropped her hand and laughed, turning to look in the direction they had come from, running his hand through his hair with a pant.

"I think they stopped following us. They probably don't know we have the book, so we are alright for now."

Ana gaped at him, anger bubbling in her chest and tears springing to her eyes as she stifled a growl and shoved him.

"How dare you!" she exclaimed, gasping. She placed her hand on her chest to ease her racing heart. "You just stole a rare, expensive book from a seriously significant library! You are so reckless, Ezra!"

Ezra shrugged.

"It is fine! I used a fake key card, remember? They can't prove it was me."

"But they *can* prove it was me!" Ana frowned. "I had to sign in, remember? They have my name and address and my phone number! If I get into trouble at work over this, Ezra I'll–"

But she didn't need to finish her sentence. Ezra walked to her and took her by the arms to steady her, trying to calm her down.

"You will kill me or something, I know." Ezra smiled. He rubbed her arms and moved his head to look at her again when she tried to look away from him. "And if trouble comes your way, I will take full responsibility and return the book and repay them however I need to. I won't let you take the fall for it. I promise."

Ana gulped, the heat in her face subsiding. "Fine."

"Good," Ezra said, then let her go and motioned for her to follow him, "Come on. I don't know about you, but thievery makes me hungry."

CHAPTER 5

*A*na was still reeling in anger and nerves when they pulled up to the bar close to town. They had been driving for almost an hour, and they had not said a word to each other since they had gotten into the car. The sign outside the bar read, *The Horse and Cart Bar and Restaurant.* It was a charming building, with white walls, black wooden panelling, and timbers that scaled the outside walls up to the thatched roof.

"This place is nice and quiet, with good food and the best beer," Ezra said as he turned to look at her, giving her a weak smile.

"Well, you are driving, so you can't have any beer," Ana murmured.

She pushed open the car door abruptly and got out, pulled her bag over her shoulder, and closed it again with a *slam*, then walked ahead of him through the door of the restaurant.

The inside was surprisingly cosy. It had dim lighting and a large stone fireplace, a long wooden bar, and heavy tables dotted around the room, with little vases of fresh flowers sitting atop them. In fact, the whole place screamed country, tradition and old living.

"It's sweet, right?" Ezra commented as he came up behind her.

"Yeah. If you are into this kind of thing," Ana said, folding her arms. In all honesty, she *was* into this kind of thing, but she was still too angry to let him know that.

"Table for two?" a waitress asked as she approached them. She wore a yellow dress as a uniform and carried two menus attached to a slab of wood under one of her arms.

"Yes, please" Ezra said with a nod.

She guided them to a large table, opening her arm to suggest they take a seat, and placed the menus on it. There were not many people dining in the restaurant as of yet, so the tables surrounding them were also empty. Ana set her handbag on the table and took a seat in one of the chairs, Ezra doing the same opposite her as he looked up at the waitress.

"Can I get you both a drink?"

"I will have a coffee, please," Ezra said with a wide smile.

"And I will have a white wine. He's paying," Ana remarked, looking from the waitress to Ezra.

"I am?" Ezra smirked at her and leaned forward on the table with his elbows.

"You are, if you want to make up for your foolishness," she retorted, her jaw set and her eyes narrowing.

He laughed.

"Fair enough. White wine it is, finest you have."

The waitress left the table, and Ezra held Ana's gaze, tilting his head and lifting the menu.

"Are you going to hold this against me much longer?"

"Just a little longer." Ana said, lifting her own menu and studying the words. "You could have gotten us both in serious trouble. You still might, if they look up my information."

Ezra sighed. "Well, if you could get it out of your system now, that would be great. We have work to do."

Ana chewed her lip and looked over the menu. Perhaps she was being too hard on him. They didn't get caught, and if they hadn't stolen the book, the story would be dead.

"Fine. I'm done, but you don't get to do that again. Are we clear? You can mess with your own reputation, but you do not mess with mine. I have worked too hard to let someone else throw away all I've done to get here," Ana lowered her menu and offered him her hand. "Deal?"

Ezra smiled and nodded slowly, then reached forward to take her hand. He raised from his seat, brought her hand to his mouth, and kissed the back of it.

"Deal," he replied, then let her go and sat back down. "Now what are we going to have?"

Ana brought her hand back quickly and blushed. She cleared her throat and glanced down at the list of items.

The waitress returned to the table and set his coffee down beside the cutlery, then a tall glass of white wine beside Ana's, and looked down at them both with a wide smile, "Miss, what will you be having?"

Ana looked up from her menu and smiled softly at her. "I'll have the grilled chicken with a side salad please."

The waitress scribbled on her notepad, then looked to Ezra. "And you, sir?"

"The burger and fries, with those little crispy onions you have. Thank you." he said, passing the menu back to her.

"Now then," Ezra said after the waitress had left. He pushed his knife, fork, the vase of flowers, and the condiments aside so that he could place the book on the table, which landed with a deep *thud*. He took his phone from his pocket and opened it up to the photo he had taken of the document. After laying it flat, he opened the book to the back page and scanned the alphabet codes.

"Do you have a notepad?" he asked, looking up at her. "And a pen?"

Ana nodded, reaching into her bag and pulling out a sparkly

pink notepad and a gold pen before pushing them across the table to him. She took a sip of her wine with a small hum. It tasted amazing, especially after the day they had just had.

"Thanks" he mumbled and opened it.

They sat in silence as he looked over each symbol on his phone and matched it to the key in the back of the book, slowly building more and more words from the matched symbols. After a few moments, he had a sentence.

"The first part is simply a message of warning and protection," Ezra said as he continued to read through the symbols.

"Comforting." Ana replied, leaning over the table.

His hand moved fast, scribbling letters and words faster than she could read them.

Marion bond, Marion power, Marion blood,
Forged with iron and buried in mud,
Protect our line, our creed, our love,
So is below, as is above.

"That doesn't sound so ominous." Ana remarked as she sipped her wine.

"Well, it shouldn't. It's a simple protection incantation," Ezra said as he took a sip of his coffee with a happy moan.

Ana sat in silence for a long time, waiting for him to finish the rest of the page, and when he completed the translation, he sat back and took a deep breath, letting it out with a sigh.

"That was stressful," Ezra said, dramatically wiping his brow.

He closed the Marion Book of Shadows and placed it back into his bag on the floor before he took the notepad in his hand and tapped the gold pen on the edge of the page.

"But you finished it, didn't you?" Ana asked, already having finished her glass of wine. Her head felt like it was spinning. She had always been a bit of a lightweight.

"I did. It is a riddle. It gives us clues to find items of value. It doesn't say what they are, but there are three of them. I will have to consult some of my colleagues to figure out the riddle."

The waitress returned and set down a plate in front of each of them. Her stomach grumbled in hunger when the smell of the grilled chicken filled her nose, and her mouth watered. The waitress smiled at them both, then turned and walked away from the table, leaving them alone with their meals.

"This is exactly what I needed," Ezra approved as he lifted his burger and took a large bite with a moan.

"So, tell me what it says. Put me out of my misery," Ana said as she cut her chicken, taking small tentative bites in comparison to his large devouring ones.

"Well," he said after a gulp, then cleared his throat and held the notepad upright so he could read from it, "Tell me if you can figure any of this out."

Three treasures you must go and seek,
if you wish to find and keep,
the source of all our magic and power,
so you may shine in your brightest hour.
The first of us you will find,
forged in fire and perfectly aligned.
Hidden in the tallest tower,
in the most westerly place you can scour.
The second of us you will learn,
has been the reason of many a witch burned.
Taken from us and hung with twine,
you will find me with one of the Harrow bloodline.
The last of us you need to acquire,
is so beautiful and rarer than any other prior.
Red as blood and hard as stone,
you will find me below where the banshee moaned.

One final piece of parchment to aid,
can be found between the pages of hand and head.
Good luck and good fortune to you magic seeker,
free us all from our dark keeper.
With our freedom we will give you the power,
to shine and sparkle and grow and flower.
Blessed be.

THREE? There were three objects to find? This was going to take a lot longer than Ana had anticipated. She hoped that she had enough time to help him uncover them before her deadline, not to mention she still had to talk to Elianna and convince her to let her go down this rabbit hole.

"I don't have a clue what any of that means," Ana said, taking another bite from her fork and starting on her salad. "But I think the first thing we should figure out is what the 'final piece of parchment between pages of hand and head' is. Maybe it's something to help us locate the rest of them."

"That's a good guess. I am going to do some research tonight on the most westerly place and see if there are any towers there. That is the clearest of the clues in the document." Ezra said.

"Maybe I could help you with what you discover tomorrow…"

"No can do, Miss Davenport. We have a religious holiday tomorrow, so I have a rare day off," Ezra said, finishing his burger and wiping his face and hands with a napkin. "One that you are half invited to, actually, if you would like to attend with me?"

"Half-invited? How can someone be half-invited to an event?" Ana asked as she tilted her head in confusion.

"Well, tomorrow morning, my family and the coven affiliates have their Litha ceremony. It's a members-only thing, so you can't come to that, but you can come to the festivities afterwards. It's a lot of fun. It celebrates the summer solstice, or midsummer, when the sun is the highest in the sky it can be. After the ritual in the morning where they give thanks to the gods, we have this huge party with a bonfire, fable re-enactments, food and a hell of a lot of wine. My mother told me to invite you; she thought it would be good for you to understand some of our practices on one of the biggest holidays of our year." Ezra explained as he ripped out the pages he had used and handed the notepad back to her.

Ana frowned slightly. It sounded fun, though it made her heart sink when he told her he was only inviting her because his mother had asked him to.

Ezra noticed her frown and held his hands up defensively. "You don't have to go if it's too boring for you. I know you must get invited to a much higher calibre of parties in the city. It's cool, really," He folded the paper and pushed it into his pocket.

"No! No, it's not that. I would love to go. I can take pictures for my article," Ana said, renewing her smile.

"Good." Ezra grinned. "I wrote my number in your notepad. Send me a text in the morning and I will send you the details. Oh, and you need to wear white."

He stood from the table and lifted his satchel bag, pulling the strap over his shoulder and reaching for his wallet in his pocket.

"White?" She wasn't sure Bexley had packed her anything white. She quickly stood from the table to follow him, shoving the notepad and pen back into her bag and pushing her chair out.

"Yeah. Everyone wears white or yellow, but mostly white. You will stick out like a sore thumb if you don't." He paid the bill, then turned to leave through the door they had entered and out into the sunlight as he looked down at the receipt.

"Your wine cost more than our entire meal. I feel fleeced." He said jokingly, opening the door to his car.

Ana followed him, happier now her belly was full and that they were one step closer to solving the mystery of the items listed in the document. She smiled widely at him from over the top of the car.

"I promise I am worth it." She winked.

CHAPTER 6

*T*he internet was slow in the B&B. The building itself hadn't been updated in years, so Ana didn't have much hope for the Wi-Fi services, but she wasn't expecting it to be *this* bad. Checking the connection was still linked, she opened her web browser for the seventh time and sighed a breath of relief when the search engine finally loaded.

"About time," she mumbled, bringing her cup of steaming coffee to her lips and sipping it. It wasn't great coffee, but it was all the tea and coffee station in the room had.

Setting the cup back down again, she clicked on the search bar and typed *Litha*. Since she was invited to this event, she had best figure out what it was about before going, lest she be left like a fish out of water, or worse, offend someone. As much as she didn't believe in this kind of thing, she knew Ezra and his mother did, and she didn't want to hurt them when they had been so kind to her.

Scrolling down the links on the search engine, she clicked on one with the most in its biography and opened the page, scrolling down once more to begin reading.

Litha, also known as the summer solstice or midsummer,
is celebrated by pagans worldwide on June 21st.
On the longest day of the calendar year, it celebrates the sun in all
its glory.
The sun will begin to descend in the sky after this day and welcomes
earlier darker nights.
Predominately a fire festival, Litha is the time for being mindful of
what we have,
spending time with family with Litha corresponding traditions and
food,
and praising the sun god when he is most fertile.
Sunflowers and roses are featured heavily, as are honey cakes and
fruits,
although many pagans also celebrate with a wide array of hunted
meats.
The colours that signify Litha are white, gold, and red trimmings.
Use this time to be thankful for the bounty of summer before the
cold autumn and
winter nights set in. Eat and drink with family and revel in the
energy of the sun.
This is a time of harmony and peace.

The sun god. The bounty of summer. Energy of the sun.

All these things sounded so foreign to her, and although she was looking forward to witnessing the practices of people she didn't quite understand, she was hoping that the celebrations at the party would not blindside her so much that she would make a fool of herself or upset anyone. She just hoped she could keep a straight face.

"Whites, golds and red trimmings" She mumbled to herself, taking another sip of her coffee with a grimace.

She stood from her chair, walking to the bag that Bexley had brought her, and pulled out the clothes. Inside were some pairs of expensive jeans, black frilled shirts, tight T-shirts and some silk scarves. All the items still had their tags on them, meaning that Bexley had gone out of her way to purchase brand-new clothing. Lifting one of the tags in her hand, she flipped it over to look at the price, and her eyes widened.

"Damn it, Bex" she mumbled, dropping the label.

Unfortunately, nothing in the bag was white or gold. Running her hand through her hair and reaching for her handbag, she pulled it over her shoulder and walked to open her door. She locked it behind herself and made her way down the stairs to the lobby, where she pushed the bell on the desk. It was only 16:00, according to the clock on the wall behind the desk. If there was a clothes store in town, she could possibly make it.

"What do you want?" the woman croaked as she emerged from the back room, a cigarette in hand and a frown on her face.

"Sorry to disturb you, but I was wondering if you know of any clothes stores in town?"

"Do I look like the tourist information to you?" The woman said with a frown that creased the edges of her skin.

"Uh, well, no, but I figured since you live here, you would probably know if there were any nearby or not." Ana said, a little taken aback by her tone.

The woman sighed and tapped her cigarette on a glass ashtray on the counter and shrugged.

"Dolly's is down the road, not far. Go out the door and turn right. Big pink sign, you can't miss it."

"Thank you," Ana said, renewing her smile and turning to leave when the woman cleared her throat.

"You are going to that heathen festival tomorrow, aren't you? With that Sullivan boy?" she asked, making Ana turn around and gape at her.

"Uh, yes. His mother invited me. Why?" She asked.

The woman scoffed and shook her head as she took a drag of her cigarette and blew it out through pursed, wrinkled lips.

"It's a cult, you know. Lots of strange things happen up in that field at those parties. They think we are all stupid, but I've seen them. Dancing under the moonlight like some crazy fools, and that family you are floundering around with is right in the middle of it. They are at the devil's work, miss, and you would do well to stay away from the whole thing."

Ana sighed. Yes, she had figured it was a strange practice, but she would not judge people so long as they didn't harm anyone.

"That's all well and good, but they are nice people, and I didn't ask for your opinion. Thank you for the directions."

As Ana walked out the entrance of the B&B, the woman shouted, "Don't say I didn't warn you!" but Ana ignored her and turned right as the woman had instructed her to and walked down the cobblestoned footpath. It was so bright outside today, and the sticky heat in the air felt close against her face. There wasn't much wind, and the only shelter from the afternoon sun was the buildings she walked by. The unusually hot summer was taking its toll, and she was beginning to curse Bexley for only packing her jeans.

Dolly's Boutique was a beautiful little shop with a bright pink wooden door and window panels. The sign was hand-painted in black and pink above the door, and the smell of roses permeated the air around the potted plants that flanked each side of the building. Walking inside the shop, she was met by rows upon rows of clothing rails, filled with every kind of garment she could possibly need in a town like this. Floor-to-ceiling mirrors were positioned at the far end of the shop to make the store look bigger, and in the middle sat a counter with a till on top.

"Hello?" Ana called, walking along the rails and reaching her hand out to touch the fabrics.

"Oh! I am sorry. I was not expecting anyone else, so I was about to close," A man said as he walked out of a changing room and approached her side, clasping his hands together.

"What can I do for you?"

Ana smiled at him, eyeing the bright purple pantsuit he wore, with his black and white polka dot shirt and rope tie. "For starters, your suit is amazing, but also, I need something white."

"Oh, I know" He winked, then turned to look around the shop with a hum. "Wedding or cult?"

"Excuse me?" Ana asked, turning away from the fabrics to look at him fully.

"Well, if you are looking for white you are either a bride, or you are going to the solstice celebrations tomorrow," he said, a grin appearing on his face, "Which is it?"

"Solstice. I was invited, and I am afraid I don't have any clothes suitable. You are not a fan of the local pagans, I assume?" Ezra's family didn't seem to be well-liked so far.

"Au contraire, I plan on being there myself and well on my way to a hangover by mid-afternoon." He said, holding out his hand for her to shake.

Ana smiled widely and took his hand, shaking it with a small laugh. "Sorry, the 'cult' comment caught me off guard. It's not the first time I have heard that word mentioned in relation to all this."

"Yes, unfortunately, people in this town are deathly afraid of what they do not understand. I am not saying I *do* understand them, as I am not a member, but Genevieve invites me every year. We are the black sheep of business in this town. We need to stick together." He winked. "My name is Oscar, dear."

"I am Ana." she smiled, moving to look over the clothes again, then indicated towards the shop logo on the wall. "So, who is Dolly?"

"My dear mother. May she rest in peace," Oscar said, giving a small shrug and a sign before walking towards a rail on the opposite wall. "All our whites are over here. Come with me."

Ana tucked some hair behind her ear and quickly followed him over the shiny black floor to his side. The clothes on this side were a lot less glittery, which she was glad for, and she looked up to him as he flicked through the hangers.

"What is this festival actually like?"

"Don't worry, it's not as satanic as the old crones in the town would tell you it is. No sacrificial goats and pledges to the devil." He laughed, pulling out a dress and holding it against her before he shook his head and put it back on the rail.

"As long as you are respectful and open minded, you will have a lot of fun. Besides, the food and the wine are free, which is more than enough reason to go. Not much happens in this town, I am sure you have noticed."

He lifted a few more items and folded them over his arm, then turned back to look her over again as if to judge her size.

"You don't need anything glam for it. It's a festival in a field, and it's supposed to be even hotter tomorrow. Therefore, you will need something you can breathe in, but also look young and feminine because apparently fertility and abundance is a big thing there. Or so they tell me." He held another dress up against her.

"I think this is the one. A white, chiffon summer dress, not too pricey, nice flow to it so that when the wind catches it, the dress will ripple nicely. It has a straight neckline that ties behind your neck, so you will be supported without needing too many layers. It is also a high-low dress. Short at the front, long in the back. It is really pretty when it's on, you are going to love it!"

He took the dress to the counter and folded it up gently, then scanned the tag and placed it into a bright pink paper gift bag, "Do you need anything else?"

Ana blinked at how quickly he had spoken and put the dress in the bag. She hadn't even really seen what it looked like, but from how he was looking at her, she was confident he had gotten her size and shape right.

"I also may need shoes. I only have black boots with me." Ana said as she moved to the counter and pulled her purse from her bag.

"No, no. No shoes." Oscar said, shaking his head with his finger in the air. "You don't wear shoes to midsummer. You leave your shoes at the gate and frolic through the grass like the rest of us little lambs. It's something to do with being connected to the land. The grass is all cut down low, so you don't need to worry about your feet. Do yourself a favour though, and paint your nails."

Ana nodded as Oscar lifted a red nail polish from the stand beside the counter and popped it into the bag, then handed it to her along with the card machine that already had the total on the screen. She swiped her card, waiting to make sure the payment went through and then smiled at him.

"Thank you for your help. I am looking forward to seeing what the dress looks like." Ana laughed. "I will see you tomorrow."

"You will." Oscar waved.

As she walked out the door, Oscar came up behind her to turn the sign on the door to "Closed" and leaned into her ear.

"Oh, and don't go empty-handed. Bring sunflowers, or roses, or both. There is a florist across the street. Get some for your hair. They will look pretty in your shade of blonde."

"Thank you, again." Ana waved, blinking when he closed the door, and she was left standing on the cobbled street.

The florist was only a few doors down from Dolly's, and when she went inside, she quickly ordered a bouquet of sunflowers and roses, and a small bunch of hair flowers to be delivered to her room in the morning. When she found her way back to the B&B, the owner was luckily nowhere to be seen, and she quickly skipped back up the rickety stairs and opened the door to her room. She was pleased to find the room's air-conditioning was actually in working condition and had kept the room at a comfortable temperature while she had been gone.

Setting her bag from Dolly's and her handbag on the bed, she slumped down against the pillows and rubbed her temples. She knew that she had to call Elianna today to update her on the story, but the idea of it made her head hurt and her stomach cramp. She wasn't sure how she would react, and the anxiety of having to explain herself was a little more than she could handle. Ana had never disobeyed her before, nor had she strayed from a story so drastically. She just hoped she wouldn't lose her job over it.

Lifting her phone from her pocket and scrolling to find Elianna's name, Ana put the phone to her ear. The ringing buzzed for a few moments, and as she waited, she could feel her stomach tightening in more and more knots. Finally, Elianna's voice hummed in her ear, and Ana took a breath to steady herself.

"Ana, where the hell have you been?"

"Hi, Elianna. I'm sorry I have been a little on the silent side, but the story you sent me to cover has developed." Ana sat up on the bed and crossed her legs.

"Developed, how?"

"Well, when I got here, they said they could give me some stories for the paper, much like all the other ones they have done, or they could give us something of much more value. An exclusive, Elianna."

"And what exactly is this exclusive?"

"They found an old witch antique buried at a sacred site, and its contents have revealed that there are treasures to be found in certain locations. We are currently decoding the message, and hopefully, we will have found them by the deadline." Ana chewed her thumbnail.

A long pause hung in the air, then a sigh.

"I didn't ask you to go there to do an article for an archaeology magazine, Ana. I asked you to get something bizarre for the end-of-month issue. People read our paper for the absurd and for the strange. That's what I asked you for, Ana, and that is what I want."

"I know, Elianna, but this could be big! Don't you want to be the first to have access to this? At least let me come to you to throw you my pitch. The deadline isn't for over a week. I can chase this and if it comes to nothing, I can have the article you want on standby. Please, let me give you my pitch."

Another sigh filled the phone, and another long burst of buzzing silence passed between them before Elianna groaned.

"Fine. Be at my office Sunday afternoon. I will be here proofing for the headline stories for the next issue. Be prepared. I am not amused, Ana, not amused at all."

"Sunday? But it. . .well it's a Sunday?" Ana said, looking confused as she stared out the window from her place in her bed. On Sundays, Elianna needed total silence to go over the mock-up's before publication, meaning everyone did their work at home on the weekends. Ana had never worked on a Sunday.

"Do you think I don't know what day it is? I am aware. If you want your chance, Sunday is your only shot. If I do not see you in my office Sunday afternoon, I don't want to see you again at all, do you understand?"

Ana's cheeks went red. She gulped and croaked that she understood, and then the phone went dead, the tone radiating through her head like it was mocking her.

She had known before she even called Elianna that her reaction would be harsh, but she wasn't prepared for her to suggest that firing her would be the answer.

Pushing her bags onto the floor, Ana set her phone on the bedside table and lay down on top of the duvet, curling up on her side and closing her eyes. Her head felt cloudy and throbbed, and she felt the threat of tears behind her eyes. Instead of letting it linger, she rested, deciding that sleep was a much better way to manage her anxiety instead of spending the night fretting about Elianna.

She just hoped that she had enough of a story to convince her.

CHAPTER 7

*T*he morning came upon Ana in a gentle glow.

The sun shone through the window she had left open and onto her face, making her groan awake and stretch against the soft white cotton sheets. It had been warm the night before, making her sleep a restless one and her skin still sticky with sweat.

Sitting up in her bed, Ana looked over her simple room. The sunshine gave the space a beautiful golden glow, and the wind that blew through the open window rippled the lace curtains. For a day that celebrated the sun, she guessed from the heat of the room that it was already out in all its blinding beauty. What she didn't account for however, was how long she had slept in.

The clock on her bedside table read 10:35.

Ana gasped, lifting the digital clock and trying to shake it back a few hours, but the numbers stayed the same and she set it back down roughly. When she awoke from her nap after talking to Elianna the day before, she spent her night writing her pitch. She knew sitting up all night was going to make her tired, but she didn't think she would sleep right through the morning. She grabbed her phone that was lying on the floor, still plugged into the wall and charging. The phone had a full battery, at least.

Text: Ezra Sullivan

Text: Bexley Matthews

Calendar update: Elianna Hearst

Ana groaned and pressed her thumb against Ezra's name on the screen, his message opening with information for the party. He had sent the message at 7:47, most likely when he had been starting the religious rituals he had told her about the day before.

"I have a cab coming to pick you up at midday, be ready. Bring your camera if you want shots for your story. Wear white and don't be a party pooper. I'll be wasted by then so take this message as my sincerest of apologies while I'm still sober."

Drunk Ezra. She could barely cope with how reckless Ezra was sober, never mind drunk.

She exited his message and opened Bexley's, and a photograph popped up of her slender hand with a sparkling ring on her finger.

"He PROPOSED! Ahhhh! Isn't it DIVINE? He got on one knee on the shoreline! You are now talking to the future MRS DE LOUGHREY! We will be back in a few days and then I will come see you. We NEED to talk dresses. Ciao! Xx"

Bexley had a habit of texting in all capitals, and reading it made her head hurt. She was very happy obviously, and it made her heart warm that Bexley had gotten all she had dreamed of on her trip to the south of France. She deserved it, after everything she had done for Ana.

Looking back at the clock, Ana realised she had less than an hour and a half to get herself ready. She quickly ushered herself into the bathroom with her shower bag and reached over the bath/shower combi and turned the water on, feeling its temperature with a shiver. It was cold, but she was sure it would turn warm eventually. Even a B&B in such disarray as this one should have running hot water at least, right?

It didn't take her long to shower, and after making sure she had
shaved her legs and her underarms, she wrapped a towel around
herself and turned to the bedroom again in a plume of steam. The
room had a hairdryer already plugged into the wall, and lifting it,
she found that not only was it plugged in, but was also glued to the
socket.

"Who would want to steal a hairdryer?" she mumbled to herself,
then shrugged and brushed through her wet hair.

After drying and curling her hair with the curlers that were in
the bag Bexley had brought her, Ana clipped parts of her blonde
hair back behind her ears, letting the rest fall down her back and
then reached for the pink gift bag from Dolly's. Pulling out the
white chiffon dress, Ana held it up to her body against the towel,
looking over herself in the full-length mirror at how it fell. It was a
very pretty dress, and she saw from how it hung that Oscar had
gotten the size correct, which was surprising since he had only
gauged her size.

She dropped her towel and pulled the dress over her head,
letting it fall down her legs, then she fixed the bust, and tied the
strings at the back of her neck beneath her hair. It had a straight
neckline, so it didn't show much cleavage, which she was relieved
by. It was a little short at the front, with a longer back that fanned
out to her heels like a train. She turned, swaying this way and that
as she looked at the flowing dress in the mirror and imagined how it
would drift in the breeze.

Giving a small, excited giggle, Ana pulled on her boots over her
feet with her newly painted red nails and looked down at them with
a hum. She pouted, not sure how well her black leather boots would
look against the frilly dress, but it didn't matter. She finished her
makeup as the digital clock turned 12:00, and turned her head to the
open window when she heard a loud *honk*.

"Party time." She lifted her bag with her camera inside and
slipped her phone into it before grabbing her keys and running

down the stairs of the B&B. When she arrived in the lobby a bouquet of flowers was waiting for her at the reception desk.

"I think those are mine," Ana said to the woman behind the desk, reaching to lift them and the small bag of hair flowers she had ordered.

"Well, they aren't bloody mine. Do I look like a click and collect service to you?" she croaked. At least she wasn't spluttering smoke at her this time.

"No. Thank you. I will be back later; I will be checking out tomorrow."

She didn't wait for a reply as she bounced out of the building and into the hot sun, then walked to the open door to the back seat of the cab. She realised as she closed the door and set the flowers on the empty seat that she had no idea where she was going, and the confusion on her face must have been obvious because the driver laughed and drove anyway.

"Don' worry, flower, I know where you are goin'. There is only one stop for people in white costumes today. It's not far." He laughed.

"Thank you." Ana smiled.

She spent the time in the cab on the way to the party placing the dried hair flowers into the clips in her hair, fanning them out evenly. They were small and white, and as much as she thought praying to the sun was a little ridiculous, she did have a liking for the aesthetic.

The cab travelled along an old country road, passing paddocks with sheep and running horses and old white brick houses, until they finally came to a dirt road that was filled with cars lining the fences. In the distance, she saw an open gate and a crowd of people, but from here she couldn't spot anyone she knew.

"We are here. I can't get you any closer. The cars are too close, so you will have to walk to the field," the cab driver said, turning in his seat to look at her.

"Thank you, again. How much do I owe you?" she asked, reaching for her bag.

"The fare has been paid. Have a good day" he replied, turning back in his seat.

Ana blinked, then gave him a small smile and a nod before she lifted the flowers and exited the car. She closed the door and watched him reverse out of the dirt road.

As she walked toward the party, she saw more and more people dotted around the green field. Large white cotton tents were scattered across the field with a few wooden tables filled with silverware, plates and silver chalices. A food station with catering staff manned the area, the waiters wearing white shirts and black trousers. If she didn't know any better, Ana would have thought this was an extravagant garden party for one of the wealthy donors Elianna worked with.

People dressed in white and gold, with headdresses of flowers and crowns. Some wore masks made from feathers and in the shape of animal faces, contrasting against their elegant costumes and suits.

When she got to the gate, she looked down to the rows of neatly placed shoes and reached down to slip off her own, setting them in line with the others and entering the field. She searched the faces for someone she might know, not that she knew very many people here anyway.

"Miss Davenport! I was hoping you would show up, dear."

Ana turned to her right, and after a few people parted to let the owner of the voice through, Genevieve emerged with her arms open wide. She was wearing a white dress with long sleeves and a bright red scarf, with gold leaf make up that made her face shine in the sunlight.

"Genevieve! Happy Litha," Ana said nervously as she held the bouquet out to her, tilting her head a little awkwardly. "Did I say that right?"

"We say 'Blessed Litha', but you can say it whatever way you wish," Genevieve explained as she took the flowers. She leaned her face into them and smelled the scent of the sunflowers and the roses with an audible hum, and she pulled her into a warm hug.

"These are beautiful! Thank you, Ana. You got the memo, I see? Wearing white and bringing sunflowers. You have blessed the party with your presence."

"It's just a thank you for inviting me. You didn't have to, but it's appreciated." Ana smiled.

"I wasn't the one who invited you," Genevieve admitted as she smelled the flowers again and let her free from the hug. "Ezra did. He mentioned he would like to bring you, and I agreed. You should thank *him*." She winked.

Ana blinked and blushed deeply. She wasn't sure why Ezra had lied about who had invited her. He could have just asked her himself.

"Well," she spluttered, shrugging and rubbing her arms, "regardless, I'm happy to be here. It's a beautiful party. Where exactly *is* Ezra, may I ask?"

"Follow the trail of destruction, my dear; you will soon find him. The Battle will begin soon, so he will need to be ready for that. Perhaps you can straighten him out. Have a good day, Ana, and may the gods be with you." She leaned in to kiss Ana's cheek, then turned and walked back to her group.

Blushing deeply, Ana walked across the grass to the bar area, standing in line and looking over her shoulder at the people in attendance. Children were holding sticks with floating ribbons attached, screaming in playful happiness while their friends chased them, their little white dresses fanning out behind them. At the back near one of the tents, a group of women stood in a circle with their hands connected, their faces skyward and humming something she couldn't hear over the band that was playing nearby. The band consisted of flute players and stringed instruments that made her feel sleepy as she listened to them in the heat.

"Ma'am?" The bartender asked, shocking her back into her head. "What would you like?"

"Oh!" Ana jumped, stepping forward through the gap, "I will take a white wine."

She took the glass from the bartender and left the bar, walking along the edge of the fence and to one of the tall white tents that stood, the fabric shivering gently in the low breeze. She peeked inside the entrance as she passed. It was empty inside, but it was filled with carpets of every colour to cover the grass and had a table and chairs inside with a translucent crystal ball on the table.

"DAVENPORT! YOU MADE IT!"

Ezra's voice was recognisable in an instant, and Ana snapped her head away from peeking inside the tent to try and locate him. He was currently in a headlock by a shirtless man with a fox mask covering his face, and he pushed him off roughly, saying something to him she didn't hear, and made his way to her.

He was wearing an open white shirt that revealed his chest and a pair of white cotton trousers, and he looked like he was well on his way to being passed out by the early evening. He opened his arms to her when he reached her and brought her into a one-armed hug, looking down at her with a wide grin.

"You look. . .well, damn, Davenport, you look like a proper little country fairy," Ezra said as he looked at her. He let her go from the hug and reached for her hand that was free and took it, holding it out so that he could get a better look at her. "That's a fine dress."

"Thank you, I think." Ana smirked, swatting his hand away and taking a large gulp from her glass. "You have had quite a day already I see."

"It's the second biggest day of my year, and drinking is half the point," Ezra slurred, hooking his arm around her shoulder and looking back into the tent. "What were you doing snooping in the fortune tent? You know my mother could do that for you any time you wish" he said as he led her away.

"I wasn't snooping, just taking a look around" Ana defended as she walked with him, looking up to his face. The sun was behind his head, making his features darker and a halo of light surround him. He looked good.

"So, snooping, then." Ezra grinned.

He led her to a bench and sat in a slump, with his face towards the heat of the sun and seemed to be collecting himself as she sat beside him and sipped at her glass. The bench they were sitting on was one of many that looped around in a large circle. To the side of the circle sat a table that was covered in a gold cloth and had items on top that she couldn't make out. Whilst she was trying to figure out what the items were, Ezra had opened one of his eyes and was squinting at her with a grin.

"You look very pretty today, Davenport. Beautiful even," Ezra said, then straightened up and leaned in close to her. He was so close she could smell the scent of his patchouli and sandalwood cologne, and she blushed. She opened her mouth to say something to him, of what she wasn't sure yet, but he spoke first.

"I have to go to battle soon," he mumbled, then sat back from her.

"Your mother told me about a battle. What does that mean? It's not a *literal* battle, is it?" Ana asked as she downed the rest of her glass.

"In a manner of speaking, it is. I am the Holly King," Ezra grinned as he opened his arms to indicate to himself, then slumped again, "I have to fight the Oak King and win."

"You are not making any sense," Ana said with a raise of her brow.

"When does he ever make any sense?"

The masked fox man was back, and he sat on the grass in front of them, a new bottle of wine in his hands, which he reached forward and filled Ana's empty glass with.

"I always make sense." Ezra argued, shrugging and turning to look at Ana again, leaning in close once more. "This is Jasper. My best friend. Total ass, but he's a good kid."

"A good kid? I'm older than you." Jasper said, taking his mask off and setting it aside.

Jasper had dark skin that shone with a glittering gold of whatever oils he had used. He had a shaved head and a wide drunken smile, and his eyes flickered between them with a lazy gaze that threatened sleep.

"How long have you two been drinking?" Ana asked, shaking her head in disbelief. "And how soon does he have to fight? Because he is in no state to do anything right now."

"It's a rigged fight" Jasper laughed. "It's a re-enactment. Ezra plays the Holly King, who fights his brother, the Oak King."

"I don't follow," Ana replied as she took another sip of her wine, and Ezra closed his eyes, resting his head on her shoulder.

"Tell her the story." He yawned.

"Alright," Jasper said, then cleared his throat and set the bottle aside on the grass.

"A long, long time ago, our world was ruled by two brothers. One was called the Oak King, and he wore a crown of oak leaves and acorns, while wielding a magic staff. The other brother was called the Holly King, who wore a crown of holly leaves and antlers, and he used a mighty sword.

"Each of the brothers thought they knew how the world should be. The Oak King thought the world should be always warm and beautiful and sunlit until the end of days, but his brother did not feel the same way. The brother felt that the earth as they knew it should be colder and darker and should rest in its ways for the year. They fought about this over and over again, with no outcome of peace in sight.

"There was one person who saw some resemblance of a resolution though." Jasper smiled, looking to Ezra who finally sat up again to listen to the story, even though he had probably heard it so many times before.

"And who was this person?" Ana asked, already through her second glass of wine and feeling her head spin.

"A woman. A maiden, obviously." Ezra said with a shrug. "Men will fight and fight with no resolution. Women are the peace bringers. We would all be doomed without you."

"Who is telling this story?" Jasper cut in, laughing when Ezra held his hands up defensively before continuing.

"Both the Holly King and the Oak King were madly in love with the maiden, and she loved them both deeply in return. She brought a solution to the table; they should each rule over one half of the year, split it down the middle. The brothers would not be persuaded.

"One hot day, when the sun was the highest in the sky of the whole year, the Holly King had had enough of the heat and the unwavering sun in all his glory, and he snapped and drew his sword against his brother. The Oak King fought bravely, but he was too sleepy from his lazing in the sun that day that the Holly King dealt a fatal blow with his enchanted sword, and the Oak King fell.

"The second his brother's bleeding body hit the hot earth, the Holly King sunk to his knees and held his brother in his arms, cradling his head against his chest and crying into his hair. His heart was full of regret because even though he had gotten his wish, his brother was its victim, and he mourned.

The maiden covered the Oak King in blankets of gold and swept him away, leaving the Holly King to rule over the earth in the way he had envisioned.

"The days grew shorter throughout the year, and the moon stayed in the ink blue sky longer each night. The days became colder, and snow started to fall near the end of the year, freezing the earth as the Holly King had wished it so, but all he could think about was his brother, his heart becoming more and more frozen like the earth under his feet. When the land was bare the animals slumbered, and the sun was in the lowest point in the sky on the winter solstice, the maiden returned with news for the Holly King.

"His brother had not perished in the fight. The maiden had nursed him back to health and he was back to fight his brother once more to take control of the earth and bring it back to the sun. Out of the snow and the ice, the Oak King emerged with his mighty staff, and with tears of joy in the Holly Kings' eyes, he didn't see the blow coming, and he fell. It was not a mortal wound, but he relented, and the Oak King took his brother's hand and pulled him to his feet. He told him it was his turn to rule, to bring the earth to warmer days so that food could grow and the animals could awaken again.

The Holly King agreed, and he hugged his brother. His brothers warm skin melted his frozen heart and he left on his sleigh pulled by stags, leaving gifts to all of those who weathered his lands, with a promise that he and his brother would exchange the crown once more when the sun was again at its highest.

The days grew longer and warmer, and the moon rode the horizon low in the sky once more. Green returned to the earth, the animals awoke from their slumber, and the plants began to grow, until the summer solstice when the brothers met again, and the cycle started once more. Each year the cycle continues, giving us the seasons in all their wonder, with their rulers watching over the earth's children with parental wisdom."

Ezra clapped loudly, putting his fingers in his mouth and whistling his approval of the story, and Jasper drunkenly took to his feet to bow and laughed when he fell back down again.

"You are a wonderful storyteller, Jasper." Ana smiled as she reached her glass forward for him to refill.

"It is not often we have an outsider to tell it to, but I think I dusted off the story well" Jasper said, shrugging as he filled her glass.

"How long have you been the Holly King in the re-enactment?" Ana asked, sipping at the wine with a hum and looking to Ezra as he leaned back on the bench.

"I have had one summer battle and two winter battles. This year we have a new Oak King. The previous one died for real this year. My mother's brother." Ezra frowned.

"I'm sorry. Who has he been replaced by?" Ana questioned, looking between Jasper and Ezra as they shared an uneasy glance.

"My father," Ezra said with a grimace.

Jasper groaned and lay back on the grass, basking in the sun. "You need to forgive him already."

"I do?" Ezra challenged, his eyes narrowing with contempt.

"He isn't a bad guy, Ezra. He's miles better than my dad. You shouldn't be so hard on him," Jasper said as he shielded his eyes and tried to look at him through the sunrays.

"Don't tell me how to feel; it's insulting. I can inwardly hate him, so long as he keeps his distance and I keep a look of pleasantries on my face. Then, we can coexist I guess."

Ana thought it wasn't the time nor the place to ask him why he hated his father so much, so she let it go, lest she ruin his good mood. "Well regardless, you need to get yourself ready if you don't want to fall over and ruin the battle." She reached to fix his shirt.

Ezra wasn't listening to her. His eyes were focused on the people at the edge of the circle as they filled the seats all around the lawns, leaving the middle free for the battle to take place. His mother was standing by the table of items now, and she was observing everyone, waiting patiently for everyone to take their seats.

"Speaking of the Oak King. . ." Jasper said as he sat up quickly and grabbed his fox mask, placing it back on his face and sitting down beside Ezra.

He then gave Ezra a shake, and began to help him take off his shirt.

"You don't have to be so nervous."

"I'm not nervous." Ezra said as he stood from his seat and passed his white shirt to Ana. "Hold this for me?"

Ana blinked as she looked from the shirt and then up to his face. She wasn't expecting him to be suddenly shirtless and asking her a question. Although he was obviously going through something internal that he was struggling with, all she could think about was his chest.

"Uh, sorry, yes, of course" she said, taking it and folding it on her lap.

Ezra nodded and shook out his shoulders, then walked the short way to the table beside his mother, who took his hand and kissed his cheek. She mouthed something quietly to him that made him nod in return.

A man emerged from behind the crowd and walked into the circle with an extended arm in the air and a wide smile. She could tell he was Ezra's father, as they looked so alike. He had peppered, greying hair that hung loosely around his ears and a well-kept beard that hugged his strong jawline. He also wore a white shirt with a heavy dark animal fur cloak. The crowd clapped and cheered when he walked to the table and looked between his son and Genevieve with a wide, warm smile that Ezra didn't return.

"Son" the man said, looking him over and tilting his head. "You look well. How is business?"

"None of yours." Ezra's jaw pulsed, and he took a small breath, then turned from him to the table of items.

Genevieve cleared her throat and eyed her son into silence before turning to the crowd. The band that was playing stopped when she held her hand up, and everyone fell quiet.

"Ladies and gentlemen! Our children, our family, our friends! Welcome to The Battle! It's the day to be thankful for all the abundance our gods and goddesses have given us, and to give our offerings of appreciation and love for the shorter days and longer nights that are still to come. The sun is now at its highest peak it will be," she said, indicating the bright solar disk in the sky. "He will be no higher than this for the rest of the year, and as tradition dictates, it is at this exact time our godly brothers fought to bring us the balance of the seasons. Sit back, and bear witness to our two kings!"

The crowd erupted in cheers as Genevieve lifted the crown of Oak leaves and acorns. Ezra's father smiled and knelt on the grass in front of her with his head bowed, and she firmly placed the crown on his head, then handed him a huge heavy wooden staff that had a shiny yellow crystal on its top.

"Alexander Sullivan, you have been blessed by the Oak King! Please rise!" Genevieve shouted.

He stood and raised his staff in the air, the crowd crying out for him as he walked away from the table and took his place in the middle of the grass circle.

Ezra watched his father take his place, then nodded to his mother when she indicated for him to kneel at her feet. He did so and bowed his head, and Ana could see his mother gently stroke his head in comfort before she lifted the crown of antlers and holly leaves. She held it above his head and smiled, then positioned it on his head, tucking his hair behind his ears. She then lowered the heavy silver sword from the table into his hands.

"Ezra Sullivan, you have been blessed by the Holly King! Please rise!" she shouted.

Ana saw a small smile curl at the edge of his mouth as he stood, and when he did, he thrust his sword in the air, the crowd clapping and cheering for the rise of their king. He walked away from his mother after kissing her cheek and then took his place in front of his father.

"Kings! Bring us our balance! Bring us our seasons!" Genevieve smiled proudly. "Fight!"

Ezra and Alexander tapped their weapons against each other to show that they had accepted their challenge, then took a few steps away from each other and turned.

"Surely this isn't fair if it is a rigged fight for the winner in Ezra's favour?" Ana asked Jasper. "And his dad has a stick; how can he have a fair fight if Ezra has a sword?"

"It may be rigged, but this is real," Jasper whispered. "They will both come out of this at least with a little blood. Why did you think he gave you his shirt?"

Ana shrugged and drank her wine as she watched the two men square their bodies towards each other. There was a sudden cry as Alexander launched forward and swung his staff around the back of his head to bring it down on Ezra. He was clearly not expecting his father to come at him so hard, and at the last second, he shielded the blow with his sword, but the force of it sent him reeling back onto the grass.

Rolling out of the way and back onto his feet, Ezra set his sights on his father, turned his sword in his hand, and righted his crown with the other before he swung quickly, steel meshing with wood in a frenzy that Ana could barely keep track of.

Alexander swung hard again, his fur cloak fanning out behind him as his staff whipped around to slam Ezra in his ribs, sending him sideways. He brought his hand to his side to hold where it hurt, but Ana noticed there was no pain on his face. Either he was too drunk to feel it, or he had the best poker face she had ever seen.

"I thought he was supposed to be winning?" Ana suggested.

"He will. That doesn't mean Alexander will make it easy for him, though." Jasper replied as they leaned forward.

Ezra was faster now with anger under his heels, and he swung his sword swiftly, waiting for his father to raise the staff above his head so he could change direction, slicing the sword over his side of his fathers' stomach as he passed him.

Alexander's shirt ripped open, and he bled. Ana saw him wince as he righted himself. Ezra was smiling now, obviously having numbed his pain with seeing his father bleed.

In retaliation and using his son's moment of ego to his advantage, Alexander shoved his staff forward to collide with Ezra's chest, twisting the sharp crystal edge of it to cut him before he pulled it to his side, his chest dripping red.

Now they were even.

Ezra inhaled an audible breath, seeming to prepare himself as he faced his father. Alexander gave him a nod to tell him it was okay, and he pushed his staff out roughly, giving Ezra the perfect chance to grab it with his free hand. With the sword in the other, Ezra pushed the sword with force through his father's stomach. It went clean through, and Ana thought it must have been some kind of trick until the blood came and a scream caught in her throat.

"Shh, don't speak!" Jasper hissed, putting a hand over her mouth as she breathed into his palm to quieten herself.

Ezra helped his father to lie on the grass, throwing his staff to the side and kneeling beside him as he held the sword firmly in his belly. He stared at him, then reached forward and took the crown from his head before standing once more to thrust it in the air.

The crowd erupted in applause, cheering loudly for the victory of their king, whilst Ana sat in horror, her face losing its colour and her head feeling light.

"We need to call an ambulance." Ana sniffled as she stood quickly.

Ezra moved back to his father and pulled the bloody blade from his stomach, holding it in the air again with the crown before he turned to look down at Alexander, who was squirming. He looked in pain, but as quickly as the emotion flashed upon his face, it was gone, and he slowly stood, wiping his hand over the blood on his stomach. The wound was gone.

Alexander gave a small laugh, clapped his son on the shoulder with his bloody hand and then bowed to him. "You ruined my shirt."

"Think ahead next time. I took mine off for a reason," Ezra said as he walked back to his mother and handed over his weapon.

He kissed her cheek and lifted a crown of flowers, waving at everyone as they cheered for him. He jogged quickly back to Ana and knelt before her with a handsome smile from under his crown of antlers and holly and held the flower crown out to her in his hands.

"Will you be my maiden?" Ezra asked breathlessly.

Ana was still shaking, looking from where Alexander was celebrating with his group, to where the crowd was watching her, then back down to Ezra's smiling face. "W-what?"

"I need a maiden to dance with to complete the ritual. Please don't make me dance with my Aunt Nelly again. She steps on your toes," Ezra said as he stood and moved to place the crown on her head of blonde hair, fixing it around her face. "Everyone is watching, please say yes."

"Y-yes" Ana sniffled, wiping her cheeks.

Ezra took her hand, walked with her to the centre of the grass circle, and brought her into his arms as the music started up again and others joined them in The Battle circle.

"I don't understand, Ezra. He was bleeding. That was a real blade; I saw it go straight through him. Y-you were bleeding too! What the hell just happened?" Ana asked as he took her hand and placed it against his chest, looking down at her.

"It's an illusion, Ana. My father is fine. I am fine," Ezra said as he tried to calm her nerves. Her hands were shaking in his, and he squeezed them tighter to calm her down.

"You should get your wound seen to" she mumbled, finally beginning to slow her racing heart as she looked up at his face and how happy he seemed again. "You are still bleeding."

"I'm not bleeding" Ezra swayed with her to the music and

removed his hand that held hers to swipe some of the red substance on his chest. He brought it to his mouth and sucked it away with a wide playful grin, then spun her quickly and brought her back to him. She grimaced.

Laughing, he leaned down to give her a comforting nuzzle. "It is just strawberry sauce, Ana."

Ana breathed deeply and closed her eyes as she rested her crown of flowers against his chest. "I need a drink."

CHAPTER 8

*T*he sun was beginning to descend in the sky by the time the dinner celebrations were finished. They had venison and summer veg with the food piled high on their plate, and fruits and cakes dripping in honey for dessert. When the waiters came to take their silver plates from the table, Ana was left with a feeling of satisfaction deep inside her belly. As shaken as she was after The Battle, seeing how Alexander was laughing and joking with no apparent pain had made her let the whole event go, even if none of it made any sense to her.

"That was absolutely fantastic," Ezra said as he leaned back in his chair between Ana and his mother.

"It really was delicious. Thank you, Genevieve." Ana smiled widely.

"It would have been a little better if my son opted to take his crown *off* and put a shirt *on*, but alas." Genevieve smirked.

Ezra opened his arms and shrugged happily. He was no longer drinking from a chalice anymore, deciding that a whole bottle was going to fit his needs much better. His crown was askew on his head, and he reached to fix it before he leaned to tap the flower crown that was still nestled on Ana's head.

"If she gets to keep hers on, I get to keep mine. Besides, I'm the fucking Holly King!" Ezra shouted happily, a chorus of cheers erupting from another table.

"And this Holly King has one more ritual to attend to," Jasper said as he rose from his seat and pressed his hands on Ezra's shoulders. "Come, King, I will help you walk."

Ezra rolled his eyes and leaned in to look at Ana drunkenly.

"I will be back. Don't go anywhere," he said, then poked her nose and stood from the table.

Jasper wrapped Ezra's arm around his shoulder and helped him cross the field and into one of the tall white tents, leaving Ana alone with his parents. She was watching his back disappear through the entrance of the tent when Genevieve placed her hand on Ana's and stood from the table.

"I have something to attend to as well. Will you be alright alone, Ana?" she asked kindly.

"She is not alone. I'm sure we can find something to talk about in your absence." Alexander said.

Genevieve waited for Ana to nod, then left the table with a slight look between them.

A long pause hung in the air after Genevieve left until Alexander turned in his seat to look at her with a wide smile.

"She is not my biggest fan." He shrugged.

"Neither is Ezra, or so it may seem," Ana suggested as she sipped the water in her chalice. She had already had too much wine that day, and her head gave a dull throb in reminder to stay hydrated.

"No, he is not. I try my best, but sometimes there is no right way through the eyes of your children." Alexander said, looking past her to the white tent where Ezra had disappeared into, then looked back at her face, "My ex-wife tells me you are a reporter.

Usually, the reporters work with Genevieve, not Ezra. What is your angle?"

"My angle?" Ana asked a little defensively, sitting straighter in her chair and letting a frown furrow her brow.

"Yes, your angle. Your story. There must be some reason you are running after my son hand and foot. Genevieve said you have been spending quite a lot of time together."

"Genevieve tells you quite a bit considering she is your *ex-wife*." Ana pouted.

"Touché." Alexander laughed. He had a warm laugh that was inviting and calm, like Genevieve's. "The suspense is killing me, Miss Davenport."

Ana relented, not wanting to be rude. "Ezra found a witch box at the monument. I have been tagging along to see where it leads for a story for *The City Herald*. It may just be the break I need," Ana said. She leaned forward on the table and reached for one of the strawberries that were in a large gold bowl. For some reason, as nice as Alexander was, she felt like she was betraying Ezra by even talking to him.

"He *found* it?" Alexander asked, his eyes widening. He stroked his beard, then chuckled to himself and shook his head. "He found the witch box on the Raven Hill?"

"Why is that so surprising? Ezra is a smart man." Ana shrugged as she threw the top of her strawberry away.

"That he is, but that damn box has been his white whale, so to speak. He has been obsessing over its location for *years*. I can't believe he actually found it. He doesn't tell me these things anymore. We used to be close. We used to figure these kinds of mysteries out together. A kind of father-and-son team, if you will. I guess he has me replaced." Alexander said, his smile faltering.

Sadness came upon Alexander's face for a moment, but when he saw Ana looking at him, he renewed his smile and shrugged. "May I ask what was inside? Call it professional curiosity."

Ana cleared her throat from the taste of strawberry and reached for a napkin to wipe her hands. "We found an old document with clues to the locations of old, so called 'magical items.' Three in total."

Alexander's eyes flashed with what looked like excitement, and he clasped his hands together with a laugh. "What bloodline was the witch box linked to?"

"The Marion Coven. You know a hell of a lot about all this stuff. What exactly is it you do?" Ana asked as she narrowed her eyes at him.

"I wrote the book on this 'stuff' as you call it, Miss Davenport. Quite literally. I am the head professor of all things occult. I teach at the university. Mostly folklore and history, occult archaeology, that kind of thing. Everything Ezra knows, I taught him. Like I said, we were close once. He would never allow it if he knew, but if he gets stuck in his quest, you can always come to me for advice. I will help him in any way I can, but you may need to convince him. It's just an offer. I'm always just a phone call away, Ana."

Their conversation was interrupted by a sudden flash of light, and Ana drew her eyes away from Alexander to find its source.

Ezra had emerged from the tent and had just let a flaming arrow off into the huge bonfire at the back of the field to set it alight. People were cheering again, and Ezra passed his bow off to someone else and started walking back to the table with Jasper on his heel. He was stumbling drunkenly, and when he made it to the table, he almost crashed into it with a force that knocked him into his chair.

"Davenport! We lit a bonfire!" Ezra grinned, then noticed that his father was sitting beside her and frowned. "What were you two talking about?"

"You." Alexander smiled. He got up from the table and gave a bow to Ana before he nodded to his son and left the table.

"What did he say?" Ezra slurred, watching his father until he disappeared into the crowd of people.

"Not a lot." The last thing drunk Ezra needed was to get angry over something *she* caused. "He just wanted to know how you have been. What happened over there?"

"Well," Jasper began as he approached the table, "he singed his hair, for starters." He shoved his friend. "I need to stay here with my family, but you should really get him home to bed before he ends up killing himself." He laughed.

"How am I supposed to get him home? I don't have a car, and I have been drinking," Ana asked.

"He lives in the house at the end of the dirt road. It's a five-minute walk. Please, I don't think his liver can take much more," Jasper pleaded as he helped Ezra to his feet.

"I am right here, you know," Ezra said as he shoved his friend off and staggered, his crown crooked on his head. "And I can walk by myself. I don't need help up."

Jasper sighed and looked at Ana again with a sorry frown. "I'd take him myself but I have things to attend to before we start to do the clean-up. Make sure he is safe."

"I will." Ana sighed.

Jasper departed, and Ana was left to chase after Ezra as he stumbled towards the gate. The sky was changing rapidly now, the bright blues that once held strong now turning to dark purple and navy. As they were leaving, the rest of the party was just beginning to light candles on the tables and torches in the field, and she took a moment to admire the beauty of it before she found her boots and pulled them on quickly.

Jogging, she finally caught up to Ezra. She held onto his side and let him lean on her as he wrapped his arm around her shoulder and looked to the stars that were slowly piercing the sky.

"You don't have to walk me home, you know; I have been in worse states than this," Ezra mumbled.

"I wouldn't feel right leaving you to walk alone down a dark road. You will end up in a ditch, and I won't have a story," Ana said as she watched the dirt road ahead of them to make sure they wouldn't stumble.

"Ah, your precious story. You are so focused on your goal, yet I didn't see you take one picture today for your article."

Ana shrugged as she tightened her grip on him. "Well, why would I?" Guilt pulsed somewhere in her stomach again and pressed up against her throat, but she gulped it back down. "The party had nothing to do with the box or the items; there is no need to put your holiday on show like that."

Ezra stopped walking then and looked down at her, smiling drunkenly. "I appreciate that. What did you think? Of the celebrations, I mean?"

Ana pulled him along again and smiled, looking back over her shoulder at the lights in the field as they grew smaller and smaller. "It was beautiful. I still have no idea how you did that 'illusion' with your father though. I expect an answer when you are sober."

Ezra laughed and shook his head. They were nearing his house now, and they could see the bulbs in the garden lighting the little path.

"If you attend the winter solstice, I may tell you my secret after I get my head bashed in, hm?"

"Sure, whatever" Ana teased as she pulled him through the little gateway. "Is this your house?"

The house in front of her was a beautiful country cottage with a thatched roof and white stone walls. The garden was well-kept, and from what she could see in the darkness, it had little gnomes all over the lawn and plant pots filled with blooming flowers.

"HA! No. This is not my house," Ezra said as he pulled his keys from his white cotton trousers and stumbled across the paving stones. "This is my mother's house. My house is in the back."

"You live with your mother?" Ana asked, raising her brow and following him around the side of the house.

"Not quite. I have my own bungalow. I'm a momma's boy, what can I say? Don't judge me." He fumbled to find the right key. With his attention drawn away from his feet, he walked straight into a plant pot, sending it across the stones.

"Jesus Christ." Ana sighed, watching him right himself and carry on down the path to a small bungalow.

The building was also nicely kept, but in the moonlight, she could tell that it was a much newer build in comparison to his mother's house.

"I can't find the key." Ezra groaned as he leaned against the door.

Ana took his set of keys from him and searched for the right one for the lock. She tried one, and it stuck, so she pulled it out and tried the next one, trying to ignore the feeling of his eyes watching her. "What are you looking at?"

"You." He smiled, leaning against the door with his shoulder. "You are beautiful with your little crown on." He said, reaching to rub a petal from her crown between his fingers.

"You are drunk," Ana said, trying the next key, which also stuck.

"Doesn't make it any less true," Ezra said, folding his arms against his bare chest and waiting on her.

Ana opened her mouth to say something but stopped when she tried the next key and the door opened, which made Ezra fall into the hallway. She laughed as he picked himself up off the floor and walked into his living room.

The room already had the wall lights on, and she saw an open-plan kitchen with a cooker and a coffee machine, an old ceramic sink, and a pile of washing in front of his machine. The living room was humble and simple, with a small stove against the wall and a sofa on each side of the room. A doorway stood at the back, most likely leading to his bedroom, and a small dining table that was stacked high with books was positioned near the window.

"Home sweet home" Ezra announced as she approached his side to steady him and guide him to one of the sofas where he slumped down, bringing her with him. "Thank you for coming today."

"About that," Ana said as she reached to take off his crown for him, but he stopped her, taking her hand instead. "You said your mother invited me, but when I thanked her for that, she said she didn't. She said *you* invited me. Why lie?"

Ezra gave a breathy laugh and shrugged. "Damn." He grinned. "Would you have come if I was the one to invite you?"

Ana tilted her head and tried to think of something to say. She wanted to stay as professional as she could, but the more she got to know him, the more difficult he made it.

"Yes."

"Good," Ezra said, nodding. His brow furrowed in concentration, as if he were trying to get his brain to work through the fog of alcohol. "I am going to kiss you now."

Before Ana could react, Ezra had her in his arms and his hand held her chin out to him so that he could softly kiss her. It was gentler than she was expecting him to be, and she was surprised that he kissed her with a warm tenderness, even through his drunken fog. As he deepened it, and her shoulders relaxed against him, her mind brought her back into the room and forced her to finally break it. She smiled as she leaned against him and placed her finger on his lips when he leaned in again.

"You need to sleep," she whispered.

"I really do," Ezra said against her finger. He took her hand from his face and kissed the back of it before he took off his crown and laid it on the floor. He flopped back on the sofa with a groan, and she could tell that his world was spinning from how he was trying to keep his foot on the floor.

"Ezra, where are your blankets?" Ana asked as she stood and

leaned over him to fix his hair away from his face. He simply groaned, and she rolled her eyes and turned to the door at the back of the room that led to his bedroom.

Inside was surprisingly neat, with a perfectly made bed and neatly folded laundry. She grabbed some extra blankets from his closet and returned to the sofa, tucking one of them around him gently to avoid waking him, but the movement made him stir and he reached out for her hand.

"Thank you," he mumbled, "for being my maiden today." Then he let her go and rolled onto his side.

Ana smiled down at him warmly, tilting her head at him and how quickly he was back to sleep. She couldn't just leave him here while he was so drunk, in case he vomited in his sleep or hurt himself, and it wasn't like she could call a cab from here. She didn't even know where she was.

Biting her lip, she lifted the extra blanket and opted for the other sofa so that she could keep an eye on him. She fluffed the pillows, trying to make the sofa as comfy as possible, but it was old and appeared much lumpier than his. She took her crown off and lay down anyway, reaching to switch off his lamp and pulling the blanket up to her shoulders as she lay on her back and willed herself to sleep.

CHAPTER 9

Something was pushing down on her chest, making it nearly impossible for her to gasp for air. It clutched at her chest, and she found when her hands gripped at her dress, hands were there already. The hands had sharp edges and felt ice cold to the touch.

"Where is it?!"

Ana snapped open her eyes when she heard the voice in her head. She saw nothing. A big black hole, blacker than any shade she had ever seen.

"Where is it?!"

A scream caught in her throat as sharp hands grabbed onto her dress and shook her into the sofa, pressing her down so hard her chest felt like it might just cave in. A blanket of cold sweat came over her, and suddenly there was a shifting in the blackness. A pair of red eyes pushed through the darkness.

A scream finally made its way out of her throat and into the air around her. She closed her eyes and turned her face away from the darkness that seemed to want to consume her.

Light suddenly filled the room; it spread through her eyelids in yellows and reds, and she found herself being shaken.

"Ana! Ana, wake up!" Ezra's voice called over her screaming.

Ana gasped, finally opening her eyes and looking up into his face as he held her shoulders. She was shaking, her skin cold to the touch and her hair sticking to her face.

"You were screaming," Ezra said, his face full of concern.

"I was awake. I mean, I think I was awake, but there was something on top of me. I c-couldn't move," she stuttered.

Ezra helped her sit up, and he tucked some of her hair behind her ears. "What did you see?"

Ana sniffled and placed a hand on her chest where she had felt the sharp cold hands. She rubbed her skin gently to stop the tingling. Her heart rate slowed, and after a few deep breaths she began to see through the panic. Maybe she had dreamt it.

"Nothing. It doesn't matter. I am sorry for waking you." Ana said as she looked up at him when he let her go.

"Are you sure? You are very pale." Ezra stood and walked to the open plan kitchen. He filled two glasses of water and retrieved a small tub of aspirin, then returned quickly.

"Thank you," Ana said as he passed her the glass and gulped it. "What time is it?"

"4:00," he mumbled, popping two of the pills. He downed them with water and then moved to sit beside her again. "And I have a hangover from hell."

"I am sure you do." Ana laughed, finishing off her glass of water quickly. "I'm sorry for waking you so early. You can go back to sleep."

Ezra shrugged as he pulled his phone from his pocket. His brow furrowed as he scrolled, then pressed a button and put his phone to his ear.

"What is it?" Ana whispered.

Ezra held his finger up to signal for her to be quiet while he listened. His face grew darker and more worried, and finally, he took the phone away from his ear and turned to look at her.

"That was Nina. I have six missed calls and two voicemails. She said she needs to see me immediately." He said, worry evident on his face.

"What time did she send them?" Ana asked, setting her glass on the table in front of them.

"3:04," Ezra muttered. He pulled up the last one from Nina on the screen. "She said to meet her at the monument. It's urgent, apparently. I need to go."

He stood quickly and disappeared into his room, returning dressed in a black T-shirt and jeans.

Ana frowned in confusion. Why would Nina want to meet him at the monument this late at night? She blushed and bit her lip, cocking her head at him when he pulled on his jacket.

"Should I come? Or is this a little rendezvous that requires only yourself?" Ana asked with a quirk of her brow.

"Huh?" Ezra was pulling on his shoes and hardly listening to her. "What? No. She is like a sister to me."

"All right, then I will come along. It could be about the box, right? Do you have a coat I can wear?" she asked as she stood. She was still wearing her dress from the party, and as warm as it was here during the day, the nights were ice cold.

He nodded and handed her a coat from behind the sofa before he opened his front door and walked out.

"Wait on me! I need to get my shoes on!" Ana called after him as she scrambled to pull on her black boots and his coat. It was big on her and hung down to her knees when she zipped it closed, but at the very least it would keep her warm.

She ran out of the bungalow and closed the door, following the path to where the car was parked. Ezra was already inside and had the engine running. She got into the passenger seat and closed the door after herself, frowning at him when he pulled out of the driveway quickly.

"Slow down, Ezra! I think you are still drunk. You shouldn't be driving. I can drive us if you show me the way."

"I am not drunk. I am fine," Ezra said as he sped down the dirt lane and onto the road. His eyes were focused on the road, and his hands were gripping the steering wheel so tightly that his knuckles were white.

"Ezra, what's wrong with you? What is going on?" Ana demanded, the car jumping when it drove over a pothole. The car squeaked and moaned at the jolt, and her heart raced faster again. "Ezra! Talk to me!"

"I don't know! Okay? I don't know. Why would Nina be calling and texting me at 3:00, Ana? Hm? I have a really bad feeling about this and I'm worried. Just let me worry."

He didn't even look at her, which she supposed she was glad about considering his terrible driving skills, and he should be looking at the road anyway.

"Okay, all right, yeesh," Ana snapped as she sat properly in her chair and held the handle above the door.

They drove through the dark in silence for a long time before they turned onto the road that led to the base of the monument.

Finally, Ezra turned to look at her, his eyes intense as he watched her. "What did you see at my house? What woke you from your sleep?"

"It was a nightmare. Ezra you are starting to freak me out. I'm sure whatever Nina wa-"

"You said you were awake. I shook you, and you said you were awake. What did you see?" he asked again.

"Nothing. It was a nightmare! Would you just chill out?"

He dropped the conversation and didn't waste any time getting out of the car when it stopped. Opening the trunk, he lifted two flashlights and passed one to her. Without speaking, they both walked the path that led to the monument.

The monument looked so different at night. The moon was bright, casting a glow on the gravestones and the trees that lined the bottom of it.

Ana tried not to look at the gravestones as she passed. The chill that she felt here when she had seen them the first time still lingered in her bones, and it seemed to get even colder as she neared the statue of Mary Marion.

Passing through the gate, Ana saw little lights on the top of the hill where the monument was, and she rushed to Ezra's side.

"Look, there are lights. She must be up there," she said, trying to comfort him, but he was still silent.

They climbed the hill together, and Ana was thankful for her better footwear as she climbed, though her breathing was still coming as rapidly as it had done the first time. She was falling behind, as Ezra was taking the trail in long strides to scale it faster, and she found herself scrambling to keep up.

Finally, they crested the hill, and Ezra took to a jog around the side of the monument to where the little lights were and stopped dead in his tracks. His flashlight shook in his hand, making its beam unsteady, and his free hand flew to grip the hair on his head. He seemed unable to move.

"What? What is it?" Ana panted as she finally caught up.

She trailed her eyes from Ezra and along the beam of his flashlight to where the erected stones stood, the same ones the witch box was buried under.

Sitting hunched on her knees with her hands tied behind her back and linked to the rock sat Nina. She was naked, her skin blue, and her head was tilted forward so that her damp red hair hung over her face. Lit torches were sticking out of the ground around the stone she was tied to, and something white linked them in a circle all around her. Little inflamed ringed cuts covered her whole body, leaking red down her thighs and collecting under her feet.

Ezra dropped his flashlight into the grass and sunk to his knees, the breath leaving his body in plumes of cold air and Ana rushed forward. She gasped, her lungs seeming to seize, and she began to hyperventilate at the sight of her.

"N-Nina?" She gasped, stumbling towards the edge of the circle.

Nina didn't move.

Ana gulped and stumbled to the edge of the white circle, reaching out a shaky hand to find a pulse.

"Don't! Don't touch her," Ezra called, finally pushing himself back on his feet and rushing forward to pull her arm away from Nina. "You can't touch her."

"W-we need to check if she's still alive, Ezra." Ana hiccupped. She couldn't see through the stream of tears that were clouding her eyes.

"She isn't," Ezra said with a shake of his body as he took her face in his hands to force her to look at him. "Don't look at her. Look at me."

Ana couldn't stop looking at her, checking for any signs she was breathing or any signs that she was alive, but all she could see were the hundreds of cuts all over her skin.

"Ana, goddamn it, look at me!" Ezra shouted at her, finally bringing her eyes to his. "Okay, good. Now, breathe."

Ana took a steadying breath through her nose and out through her mouth, her shoulders shaking.

"Good. I need you to go back to the car and call the police. Can you do that for me?" Horror was written all over his face, but she could tell he was fighting it hard to try and keep her from breaking down.

"B-but what if whoever did this is still here? What about you?"

"I will be right behind you. I need to break that circle, but I promise I will be quick." He pulled her from where she was rooted to the ground and towards the path again. "Don't look back. Keep walking until you get to the car, and don't open the door for anyone but me."

Ana nodded as she gripped his hands at the edge of the path and willed her feet to move on their own. Before she had too long to think about it, she let him go and started to walk down the grassy hill. More and more tears dripped down her cheeks, and her pace switched to a jog, then a run, and before she knew it, she was sprinting to the car. Scrambling inside, Ana closed the door and locked it, then reached into her bag and searched for her phone. Her hands were trembling so much she could barely hold it, and she had to cradle it with both hands to keep it from bouncing out of her palm. Wiping her tears on Ezra's coat so that she could see the screen, Ana dialled the number and brought the phone to her ear.

"P-police! Police, we n-need the p-police!"

THE LOCAL POLICE station was just as cold as the outside had been. Ana had been sitting in the lobby for the past hour alone, having finished her interview with the detective first. She had been hysterical when the police arrived at the monument. Ezra had been damn near catatonic, and it had taken them the whole journey to the station to calm herself enough to explain exactly how they had gotten to the monument and why. They had insisted that they be interviewed separately, to make sure they had nothing to hide and that their stories were the same without any time to construct a fake one, she supposed. She had watched enough cop shows to know that much at least.

The station was quiet, a by-product of it being 7:00 and she couldn't help but notice that the few policemen who *were* there were all staring at her. She looked down at her knees where her hands were gripping them. She wasn't shaking as much anymore, but the cold had settled in her skin so deeply she feared she would never feel warm again.

Finally, the door to the interview room opened and Ezra walked out, the tall detective following him as he closed his notebook and shoved it into his pocket.

"I think I have everything I need from you both for now, but I will be calling you in a few days once you have recovered. Don't leave town." He said and passed them his cards with the number to the police station and his own personal line.

Ana sniffled as she stood unsteadily, taking the card and picking at the edges of it with her fingers. "I have to leave today. I don't actually live here, I live in the city. I have a meeting with my boss that I need to show up for, but I will be reachable by the number I gave you."

"Alright. Go home, get some sleep if you can. I will be in touch."

Ana turned quickly and walked straight for the door. She couldn't wait to get out of the station and away from the staring eyes. Ezra followed her, catching up quickly. They didn't speak to each other until they were back inside his mothers' purple Beetle that was parked outside the station doors. It was only after they got inside and she looked at his face that she noticed how red his eyes were and how pale his skin had gotten.

"Are you okay?" She reached across the car to take his hand as he stared at the steering wheel.

Ezra didn't say anything. He just slowly shook his head and squeezed her hand back tightly.

After a few moments of deafening silence, Ezra cleared his throat and let her hand go, starting the car and taking the road back home.

"You are leaving?" he finally asked.

"Yes," Ana said as she sat back in her chair and pulled his

coat around her face to force some heat into her skin. "I am sorry, I must have forgotten to tell you. I have a meeting about our story."

Ezra gulped, and she could see his jaw clench as he grit his teeth, most likely to stop himself from crying again. She didn't mention it.

"Ezra. . ." she trailed off, looking up at his face. "What were those cuts on Nina's body?"

Ezra closed his eyes at her question, having to force himself to open them again so that he could watch the road. "Please, Ana. I can't think about it anymore."

"Please. Tell me. I need to understand what happened. I need to know why she was like that. Was it some kind of ritual?"

Ezra took a deep steadying breath and bit his lip hard, taking a moment to compose himself. He quickly wiped his cheek and cleared his throat, sitting up straighter in his seat.

"During the witch trials between 1560 and 1630, the witch hunters and priests who conducted the trials were not only finding and burning accused witches. Once they captured those who confessed, they would torture them until they gave them the names of their coven. Most of the time, the women were not witches; they had only confessed so that they could avoid the stake. Therefore, when they began to torture them, they said any names that would come to their mind just to end their suffering. The cuts you saw on Nina's body were one of the torture methods they used to get the women to tell them what they knew. I think whoever did this to her was trying to get information from her. The only connection she had to anything of an occult nature was me. I think someone was looking for the box. Her body was tied up *right* where we found it. She wouldn't have known where I had hidden it to free herself. I am the reason she is dead."

Ana watched him with wide eyes, and she shook her head vigorously, reaching out to clench his shoulder. "No. This was not your fault. You couldn't have known this was going to happen to her. How could you have stopped it?"

"I could have done as she asked me and left her site undamaged. I could have stopped looking for the box when I was denied permission to dig, I could've. . .I could have been sober and answered my phone when she called me. I could have saved her. . ." Ezra said through gritted teeth, having to drive with one hand so he could lean on the door with his elbow and hold his head in his hand, watching the road.

Ana sighed sadly and took her hand away from his shoulder to roll down her window. She knew nothing she could say was going to ease his guilt, no matter how hard she tried. "I'm so sorry, Ezra."

Ezra gulped and shrugged, wiping his cheek dry with his thumb. "Nothing can be done about it now; she's dead anyway. But whoever is looking for that box and the manuscript inside will still be looking for it, and I can't be responsible for any more pain."

"What's that supposed to mean?" Ana asked as she watched his face, trying to catch his eye but he wouldn't look at her.

"It means that this is over," Ezra said, rubbing his temple. His hangover was clearly kicking his ass, and his grief was weighing him down. "It means I am going to destroy the box and its contents, and we are going to forget any of this happened. I know you want your story, and I will ask my mother to give you something else, but I'm sorry, Ana. I can't have anyone come for you, or me, or my mother. I can't let that happen." He was finally looking at her, his eyes full of pain and fatigue. "You were leaving anyway, right?"

"I was coming back on Monday. . ." Ana said, watching him with wide eyes and tears threatening them again.

"Well, now you don't have to." Ezra said as he pulled up outside the B&B and parked the car.

Ana clenched her teeth and set her jaw. Whilst she was angry and upset, she refused to show him that. It was just a story, right?

She grabbed her bag from the car floor and got out, slamming the door closed and making for the entrance of the B&B.

"Ana!" he called through the window.

She turned around, her arms folded and her face pale.

"My jacket. . ." he mumbled.

He had a sorry look on his face, like he was torn in some way, but that just made her feel angrier. Taking his jacket off roughly, she rolled it up in a ball and threw it at him through his window, hitting him in the face with it. Walking inside, she slammed the heavy black door of the B&B closed.

CHAPTER 10

*A*na knew her city well. It was familiar territory, filled with the places she knew and loved and could walk easily without directions. It was the place she had grown up, the place she had stared out her classroom window, dreaming she would be a part of it all. The place where all her greatest memories had melted into every street corner, every brick, and every sidewalk she walked on. What she wasn't banking on when she returned to the city again though, was how much she missed the smells and rolling hills of the countryside. She missed how the sun caught on the leaves, and how the breeze always smelled fresh instead of the warm stale draft the city offered instead.

She stood opposite the shiny silver skyscraper that housed *The City Herald* offices, waiting on the lights of the crossway to turn green so she could pass safely. When she got to the B&B after the police station, she had raced to pack her bags and caught the two-hour train journey to be back in the city in time to go home, change and take the subway to the centre where she stood now. Her body felt tired, and her eyes still felt the sting of tears behind them. But she kept them at bay, trying not to mess her makeup for the millionth time.

The lights finally turned green, and she walked with the rest of the pedestrians across the white lines to the other side before heading inside the building. The offices were on the seventh floor, which normally she would try to walk to get her exercise, but today she was just too tired, and opted to lazily press the button of the elevator. It pinged open instantly, and she stepped inside, pressing the button to the floor she wanted and leaning back against the mirrored walls. Ana hung her head and sipped her coffee gently. It was lukewarm now and almost completely full. She must have forgotten she had bought it.

When the doors opened, Ana was met with the familiar *City Herald* logo that adorned the wall at the back of the reception desk. The desk was empty, as was the usual corridor that on weekdays were full of people running up and down the halls to meet deadlines. On Sundays however, the place was usually barren of all activity, unless something major happened in the world. Everyone except Elianna Hearst, that was.

Ana walked through the white marbled halls and up the small staircase that led to Elianna's office. The glass doors were open, and inside she could see Elianna at her long desk, papers fanning out all over it. She was going through them, most likely proof reading and using the printouts to place everything in her mind. Usually this would all be done on the computer, but Elianna had taught her that unless you can see it right in front of you, you never got to see the entire picture.

Much like everything in life, she guessed.

Elianna looked up when she neared the door, looking over the rim of her lilac cat-eye glasses and waved her inside.

"You look like you have been pulled through a hedge backwards" Elianna commented as she sat back in her chair and lifted her teacup to her lips. "Did you even brush your hair this morning?"

Ana reached behind her to brush out her high ponytail with her fingers. "I didn't have time."

Elianna tutted, then motioned for Ana to take a seat at her desk opposite her.

"Thank you, for giving me this meeting. I really appreciate it," Ana said as she slumped down into the chair. Her legs were numb and her feet were sore, so she was thankful for the gentle reprieve from standing that the chair gave her.

"We shouldn't have needed this meeting, Ana. You had very clear instructions, and you agreed to them. You have never gone so far off your task. What is going on with you?"

Ana's throat tightened and she shook her head. "Nothing. Not anymore. I am sorry for straying. The story I was going to bring you is dead now anyway. The source is unwilling to go any further with me."

"And what of the original story, with the original source? You didn't screw that up, too, did you?" Elianna was watching her with such intensity that Ana had to look at her coffee cup to break the contact.

"No. I have been assured that Genevieve Sullivan will still give me a story. I was going to head back up there tomorrow to get it straight from her," Ana said as she looked back up to Elianna to judge her reaction.

"Good," she then looked back down at her paperwork and began to sort them again.

Ana gulped and took a breath to steady her nerves, then cleared her throat to get her attention again, making Elianna sigh and sit back again, taking her glasses off.

"What?" she demanded, looking unimpressed as she stared her down. "Well, spit it out, girl."

"I have leave to take, right? I was hoping that perhaps once I finished the interview that I could have the rest of the month off. I need some time t-"

"Ana, I don't care," Elianna said with a wave of her hand. "So long as your story is uploaded onto the server by the thirtieth, I don't care what you do. Just be back in the office on the first. It's fashion month and it will be all hands on deck, so whatever *this* is," she waved her hand again to motion all around Ana's dishevelled appearance, "fix it by then."

Heat rose in Ana's cheeks and she felt a knot of shame twist in her stomach, but she nodded anyway and stood, pushing her chair back to the table and turning to walk toward the doors.

"Oh, Ana. . ." Elianna said as she watched her turn, "don't let this happen again."

HER APARTMENT WAS SMALL. Basically, every apartment in the city was, but what little space she did have, was neat and tidy, with white walls and green plants hanging off every shelf. They were artificial, obviously, because she was never home often enough to keep them alive, but she liked how they kept the room looking clean and fresh.

When she arrived home from her meeting with Elianna, she immediately changed into her favourite grey lounge hoodie and was now sitting on her couch in front of her television dipping Oreos into a tub of peanut butter. She switched on her normal viewing of crime scene documentaries, but after what happened with Nina, she found she couldn't stomach it and switched it to a daytime talk show that was boring her to tears.

Suddenly, her phone rang, vibrating beside her on the blanket that she was wrapped up in. Bexley's name and picture popped up on the screen. She lifted it and realised it was a video call, and she sighed, thinking about denying it. She knew Bexley would just keep calling though, so instead, she pressed the accept button and propped her phone out so she could see her face.

"Hey, baby!" Bexley's voice sang.

She was wearing sunglasses and was lying on a sun lounger in a red bikini with perfectly tanned skin.

"Hey," Ana mumbled with a mouthful of Oreos, munching it down dryly. "How's the south of France? Let me see the ring!"

Bexley's face frowned, and she moved to take her sunglasses off and squinted her eyes, obviously trying to see Ana better.

"What's wrong?"

"What do you mean, 'What's wrong?'" Ana asked as she dipped another Oreo into the tub and shrugged.

"You are wearing your pathetic 'feel sorry for me' hoodie, and you are eating cookies and peanut butter. Something is wrong. What happened?"

She was moving now, getting off the sun lounger and moving into the apartment she was staying in. It looked fancy, from what Ana could see, but then again, everything about Bexley was fancy.

Ana sighed and sat up straighter, pouting a little and trying not to cry. "The story I told you about is dead. Ezra stopped it and now Elianna is mad at me and I have to go back and do the original one and I don't want to have to go back there." She sniffled.

"That little toerag. Send me his number; I'll fix it. Why did he end the story?"

"His co-worker was murdered." She left out that it was they who had found her, and that it was maybe their fault. That kind of conversation was better explained in person.

"Oh. Well, that's a better excuse than I was expecting. Still, I'm sorry. You know, I can cut my trip short and come home today if you need me?"

"No. I will be fine. I'm just upset, but I will be all right. I thought that story was going to push me a little higher, ya know?" She frowned, biting into another Oreo.

"Ana! Get some perspective! A woman just died. There are

bigger things going on in the world than one story. There will be more stories."

Ana just pouted. She knew she was right, but deep down she knew that as much as she wanted that story, it wasn't all that she was upset about. She nodded, giving a deep sigh and laying back on the sofa with a groan.

"Now I want you to get up, have a goddamn shower because I can smell you from here, and give yourself a shake before I come home and do it for you. Okay? Bigger picture Ana, bigger picture." Bexley had gone back outside again and was laying down, slipping her sunglasses back on and sipping at whatever blue concoction was in her glass.

"Yes, Mom." Ana said with a roll of her eyes, but she was smiling softly again. Bexley had that kind of effect on people. "I will call you later when I am feeling more up to it."

"Yes, please do, because right now you are a total killjoy. I love you. Ciao!"

The phone went black again and Ana sat up, looking down at the tub of peanut butter and her pack of Oreos with a grimace. Bexley was right, she needed to get her shit together. She closed the lid and took them back to her cupboard, shoving them inside before she pulled her grey hoodie off over her head and threw it into the laundry basket.

Maybe she didn't need that story after all.

Maybe she was aiming too high, too fast.

Maybe she had to earn her dues.

Maybe.

She walked into her little bathroom and turned the tap on to fill her bath with warm water, and as she was waiting for it to fill, she stripped her clothes off and stared at herself in the mirror. Genevieve's black obsidian gemstone still hung from the rope chain on her neck and glistened in the light of the bathroom. She reached to hold it, turning it over in her hands and sighing at the memory.

Maybe the story would work out alright in the end.
Maybe.

CHAPTER 11

*S*tanding outside *Strange Curiosities and Wonders* was the last place Ana wanted to be at 10:00 on a Monday. Unfortunately for her, it was exactly where she was, coffee cup in hand and her handbag in the other. The building looked exactly the same as it had when she was last here, but the feeling in her stomach had changed since then. Whilst there was excitement and hope in her belly when she had left with Ezra through that same door to drive to the monument, now only a sense of depressing heaviness remained. She pushed it down and set her jaw, then moved forward and opened the door to the little shop. The door creaked, and the bell rang above it to signal her arrival.

The shop was quiet inside, and Ana felt exposed as she stood waiting for someone to emerge from behind the curtain, hoping to God it wasn't Ezra that rounded it. It wasn't. When Genevieve's face peeked out from behind the fabric, Ana couldn't help but smile at the warm inviting look she gave her.

"Ana, I wasn't expecting you today," she said as she walked out to her and took her hands, holding them gently. "Ezra told me what happened with you both and how you found Nina. The police were here just an hour ago talking to us again. How are you coping?"

Ana shrugged a little and gave her a weak but professional smile. "It's a tragic loss for you all. I'm a little traumatised from the night, I won't lie, but I didn't really know her. It's her family, and you whom I feel for. It must be hitting you all hard. Ezra said they were close."

"They were. We all were." Genevieve sighed. She let go of her hand and walked back to the curtain, opening it wide. "Come inside and sit with me. I assume you came to talk?"

Ana nodded and followed her silently, walking through the curtain and into the candle lit room. She sat down in the same seat she had sat on the first time she was here and pulled out her notepad and a tape recorder, setting it on top of the table neatly and waiting for Genevieve to join her.

"Ezra is upstairs if you want him to join us," Genevieve suggested as she rounded the table, placing a hand on her shoulder and smiling down at her.

"If It's all right with you, I would really rather he didn't," Ana said as she focused on setting her things in the correct place. "We didn't part on the best of terms."

"He told me," Genevieve said as she tapped her shoulder with her finger. "That is between the both of you, but before you decide to completely end the partnership, you should come and see what I found. Follow me."

She walked away from the table and through a door to Ana's left, leaving her looking torn as to whether she should follow.

"You should leave, you know."

Ana snapped her head to the curtain that led back into the shop, her eyes falling on the old woman she had met when she had first come here. She was leaning heavily on her cane and was looking at her with a deep frown, disdain written all over her face. "Um, yeah. I plan to once I get the story from Genevieve."

The old lady tutted and walked across the wooden floor towards her, her wrinkled bony finger extended and jabbing the air in front of her. "You are not welcome here. Leave! Before it is too late," she croaked, then walked around Ana and made her way to the staircase that led to the upper levels of the store.

Ana blinked at her as she disappeared up the stairs, her cane barely making a sound and her long curling grey hair hardly swaying behind her. She shivered, hearing Genevieve call for her from the doorway she had entered moments before, "Y-yeah, I am coming!" She gulped, then made her way through the doorway.

Surprisingly, it led to a staircase that moved downward into a basement, and she could see the back of Genevieve's body disappear into the room at the bottom. She followed her down the staircase, taking the steps one at a time and holding onto the wall.

Through the doorway was a large room that was the same size as the shop and the back rooms of the upper floor combined. Bookcases lined the walls, cluttered with trinkets and books. Candles hung from the stone walls, and large paintings of people she didn't recognise were held in gold frames, their eyes following her and making her feel watched. In the middle of the room on the floor, there was a large circle painted in white with a star in the centre, and the memory of Nina flashed before her eyes. She flinched, turning to find Genevieve with wide eyes.

"What is this place?" Ana asked. The air down here was close and warm, and it made her feel on edge.

"It is my private temple. I come here for my private rituals and spell casting when I need to. Don't worry, you are safe down here. Nothing negative can enter here, I promise." Genevieve was standing beside a solid wooden bookstand and was beckoning her over with her hands.

Ana gulped and approached her side, looking down at the bookstand where the Marion Book of Shadows lay open.

"It is still here? I thought Ezra would have sent it back by now," Ana mumbled as she studied it.

"He was going to, but as much as he wants to, I think he wants to solve its contents more. The box is here as well. This room is enchanted and protected, so no one can enter if I haven't decreed it so." Genevieve said, a smile still on her face.

Enchanted. Protected. Those words repeated themselves again. How could a room be completely protected with enchanted magic? Magic didn't exist. She understood the tradition of the old ways, and it could be beautiful, but she wasn't going to be pulled down into the idea that it was *real*.

"Ezra showed me the translation of the document, and I have been trying to help him solve it," Genevieve said as she pointed to the piece of paper with the translation, and highlighted was the sentence that read, *One final piece of parchment to aid, can be found between the pages of hand and head.*

Ana frowned softly. She felt like she shouldn't even be looking at these things again. The story was over, Ezra had said so himself. Being here and so close to it again made her want it.

"I don't know why you are showing this to me, Genevieve. I am not here for this anymore, remember? Ezra pulled the plug. I just want to get the original story over with so that I can go home. Please." Ana frowned as she looked up at Genevieve again with a pleading look on her face.

"I know, I know, just indulge me, hm?" She smiled. "I kept reading that sentence over and over again. It suggested that there was another piece that could be found to help you both if we could only find it. But where would the pages between hand and head be?"

"I have no idea." Ana said, finally relenting with a deep sigh, bringing her hand to her forehead to rub it. Her head was beginning to throb.

"Well, this is a Book of Shadows. A book of a coven's practices that can be passed down from generation to generation to teach those yet to come. It literally is a magical guidebook with diagrams, explanations, potions, healing magic, and my favourite, divination." Genevieve said with a grin. "So naturally, I went to the palmistry section, to the pages about the magic of the palm and the heart and head lines."

"The pages between hand and head!" Ana said with a small gasp, her eyes widening, "Between the literal pages of the palmistry section?"

She grinned and nodded, flicking the pages until she came to a section with a drawn hand. The hand had lines and symbols drawn on it, explaining the methods behind the divination practice. The back of the page was about the head line. Ana reached forward and took the page between her fingers, turning it over. The corners of the page were frayed, and she could see how that page was thicker than the others.

"So, where is the parchment?" Ana asked.

Genevieve smiled and reached for a candle, "Hold the page up."

Ana did so, and as Genevieve held the candlelight closer to the page, she could begin to see through it, the yellow flickering flame making the page slightly translucent. Right in the middle was a dark square, as if something were stopping the light from getting through, and she gasped, looking up to Genevieve's face.

"The parchment is glued between the pages!" Ana exclaimed.

Genevieve laughed and set the candle aside to take Ana's hand, "We decided to wait on you before we removed it."

"We?" Ana asked.

The sound of someone clearing their throat came from the door behind them, and Ana turned to see Ezra standing there, leaning against the door frame with his arms folded against his chest and watching them.

She frowned instantly and stood up straighter, looking between them both and being glad it was dark in the room so that they couldn't see her pink cheeks.

"You don't need to wait for me for anything, Genevieve. This is not my story anymore," Ana said as she made to leave, but she stopped her, a look on her face that begged her to stay put.

"I am going to go and make some tea. If you really want to wash your hands from this, I will meet you upstairs for your story," she said, then leaned to kiss her cheek and walked to the door where she patted her son's shoulder and walked up the stairs, leaving them both in the room. Silence filled the atmosphere in the private temple, and Ana looked down at her feet.

"Ana" Ezra started, stepping towards her, but Ana took a step back.

"I don't want to hear it," Ana said as she shook her head again and began to walk around him.

Ezra blocked the doorway with a sigh as he dropped his arms, taking a step towards her as she took more steps back until her back hit the bookstand that the Book of Shadows was sitting on, and it wobbled. She didn't want to be close to him. He was charming when she was close to him, and she was too mad at him to let him be charming.

He sighed and reached to take her hand, but she pulled away from him and folded her arms against her chest, looking up at him with her brow furrowed.

"Ana," he repeated, tilting his head at her and moving away from her to the book, running his hand down the page. "At least let me apologise."

Ana turned her back to him, her eyes finding the flickering candles on the walls and the paintings, trying to look anywhere but his face.

"What for, exactly? The part where you just dropped the story, so I had to grovel back to my editor and get my ass handed to me, without even talking to me about it first? Or the part where you just discarded me like a piece of trash and left me to put the pieces of that night together all by myself, in that B&B, alone?"

Ezra winced as he flicked the pages and turned to look at her. He opened his mouth to say something, but she cut him off.

"Where did you go after you just left me on the side of the road, freezing, Ezra? Did you come here? To see your mom? I don't know, maybe have someone *comfort* you? That would have been nice." She finally looked at him over her shoulder. "You don't get to kiss me and be sweet and charming and then just throw me away like that when it suits you. I am not your plaything, Ezra."

"No. You are not, and I am sorry." he said as he looked up from the page to her. His features were dark in the dim light, and he looked like he hadn't slept since she last saw him.

"One of my closest friends was murdered, Ana. I am sorry if I was harsh with you. I am sorry it felt like I was throwing you away, but that wasn't my intention. I just wanted you to be safe. Nina was clearly murdered by someone looking for the box *I* found, the box *we* decoded the contents of. I was trying to keep whoever did this to Nina away from you. I can't have your blood on my hands. I thought ending the story was the best way to keep you safe."

Ana frowned at him as she turned her body back to face him.

"I do not need someone to save me. I'm a big girl. You are not my knight in shining tin foil, Ezra. I don't need to be babied, and I don't need you wasting my time."

"I would never waste your time. I buckled. My head was not in a good place, and I'm sorry. If it's any consolation, I want to keep investigating this with you. My mother drummed some sense into me and helped me find the next clue inside the pages. If I asked you to come aboard again, would you?" he asked, giving her a weak smile at the corners of his mouth. "Please?"

Ana chewed her lip and slowly shook her head, looking down at her feet. "No. I can't. I'm sorry."

Ezra had clearly not expected that answer, and his smile fell, a look of confusion replacing it.

"What? Why? How many more times do you want me to apologise? Because I can keep going all day if I have to."

"It wouldn't matter. It's out of my hands now. I was supposed to give my pitch for the story to the editor yesterday, but you pulled the plug so I didn't. That was my only chance. She wants the original story about the life of witches in the countryside and your practices, and if I don't give it to her, I am fired. I can't help you." Ana shrugged. "Even if I wanted to, I can't."

Ezra sighed. She could see the gears in his brain beginning to turn as he thought. He hummed to himself and moved to lift a pair of tweezers and a knife, turning them over in his hands.

"All right." he mumbled, reaching for the page of the book and examining its edge. He peeled the two pages apart very slowly. "So, you can write the story with my mom. That doesn't mean you can't investigate this with me."

"Did you not just hear what I said? Elianna will not let me investigate this with you."

"I heard what you said. You can write your story with my mom and still investigate this with me anyway. It doesn't have to be a story for the paper. It could be your own thing, your own story that you can publish yourself." He mumbled through concentrating. "Get this story done and show it to your editor. If she likes it, which she will, she will most likely put it in the paper over something she's seen a thousand times. Many papers have worked with my mother about our practices. It's nothing new."

Ana didn't have the heart to tell him that Elianna didn't actually want to know about their practices or their religion. She wanted a freak show, and she wanted Ana to deliver that to her.

"You don't know Elianna," she said as she rubbed her head. "Although, I do have some leave coming up. She said as long as I

have my story in by the end of the month, I can have some time off.
. ."

"Okay, so what's the problem?" Ezra finally pulled the papers apart.

Ana shrugged. "Maybe I just don't want to work with you again. Maybe I don't like you anymore."

Ezra stopped pulling when they were far enough apart, and he plucked the piece of parchment out from between the pages with the tweezers with a small breathy laugh. "Oh, you like me."

"What could possibly make you think that I like you?" Ana said as she leaned in closer to get a better look at the parchment. He stared at her with a stupid grin on his face.

"Because you kissed me back." He smirked.

Ana blushed deeply and looked up at him, her throat growing tight as she shook her head.

"Just open the damn parchment."

Ezra laughed and turned his head back to the paper between the tweezers and laid it down on the book. It was folded twice, and it took him a moment to open it so that it wouldn't crumble in his hands. Smoothing it out, he ran his finger above the words on the page.

"It's a map." Ezra grinned, almost bouncing on the balls of his feet. "Look, it indicates where the objects are located. This is going to cut our investigation time in half!"

Ana smiled softly at how excited he was getting, and how the tired look and dark features he had on his face had started to lift.

"I hate to burst your very excited bubble, Ezra, but this parchment is from 1588. Don't you think that the places it is indicating to may have changed since then?" Ana asked as she looked over the map.

"You can doubt me all you want, but I am not letting you ruin this." Ezra held the parchment up against the light. "Besides, it's just a guide.

It doesn't point directly to the objects, but to the general area where they were hidden. It is at least a start, Ana." He turned to look at her and smiled charmingly, setting the parchment down. "So? Are you in?"

Ana chewed her lip and looked him over. This investigation was tempting. Ezra was tempting. She had the rest of the month off anyway, she supposed, and what Elianna didn't know couldn't hurt her.

"I don't know. That depends. Are you going to ditch me on the side of the road again?" she asked, peering into his eyes.

"No. Never again."

"And what about this killer who is out to find the box?" A sense of dread filled her stomach.

"That is a little more concerning. From what I saw where Nina was taken from us, this person knows their shit. They are powerful and determined, and I don't think they are going to stop if they went to these lengths already. They are going to keep coming, so we need to be prepared." Ezra frowned.

"But why go after Nina? Why not come to us when we were the ones who had it?" Ana asked.

"Don't roll your eyes, but. . ." Ezra started as he stood straighter and looked around the room, "whoever this person is, they are using magic. I know you don't believe in it, but to me it is real, and my guess is they went for the person who couldn't protect themselves. Nina was vulnerable. She had no knowledge of how to protect herself against these kinds of things."

"Neither do I." Ana said, trying her best to keep her thoughts to herself, "They could have come after me."

"Ah, but they did. The nightmare you had, it wasn't a nightmare. I saw it all over your face. Someone was projecting upon you to get the box's location. They just couldn't show themselves because I was there."

Ana sighed and looked to her feet. She admitted that it did feel very real, but she wasn't about to jump to conclusions that someone was able to leave their body to haunt her for information. That was ridiculous. Rather than offend him, she simply shrugged and accepted his version.

"And you think your mother and the box will be safe here while we hunt these objects down?"

"My mother is stronger than me. As long as she keeps her wits about her and the box and the map stay in here, they will be safe. No one can enter this room without my mother's magical permission." Ezra shrugged. "So…are we solving this, or not?"

Ana bit her lip again and sighed, looking from his face to the parchment and then back to his face again.

"Fine" she mumbled. "Where are we going?"

CHAPTER 12

They had been driving for three hours straight. Ana had pushed her seat back so that she could lie down. She had her shoes off, her feet resting on the dashboard whilst she held the printed picture she had taken of the map they had found. The map had the generic shape of the coastline to the west drawn in shaky brown lines, and the rest of the page was filled with the towns that surrounded it, filing all the way to the other side where Ezra's town was.

"So, going through the research you gave me that you worked on, the most westerly place is the coast of Blackrock. That is where the map has been circled. More specifically, it's literally at the water's edge." Ana said as she exhaled a breath and blew a bubble with the pink bubble gum that was in her mouth. It popped, and she chewed it again, flicking the papers on her lap.

"Yes, I noticed that, but where is the tallest tower?" Ezra asked as he sipped at his energy drink. He was wearing sunglasses that covered his eyes, and the window was rolled down, making his hair blow in the wind.

Ana watched him with a smile, laying her head back against the headrest. She lifted her phone from her lap and searched the town of Blackrock. From the search results, she could see that the town was right on the edge of the coast. It was a quaint little town, used mostly as a tourist stop and a place for surfers and camping folk to spend the warm days wandering.

"There is a tourist information centre beside the beach in the middle of town. If you head for the beach, it should be signposted. Whatever the tallest tower was back in 1588, we will find it by looking at their records first."

"And this is exactly why I needed you with me, Davenport. You are quite the little detective." Ezra smirked as he drove.

Ana spent the last half hour of the journey looking out the window and admiring the scenery. It really was beautiful in this area of the country. She had never had the time to stray too far from the city, and as she watched the rolling hills flatten out to fields and then to cliff edges and water, she regretted having not taken the time to appreciate it before. Everything was so much calmer out here, where the wind seemed to blow differently, and the smells seemed so much more flavourful. The colours were brighter, the sounds were calmer, and she was beginning to feel a kind of kinship with the countryside that she had never felt for the city. It felt like coming home.

Just as she was falling asleep, Ezra pulled the car onto a smaller road, and suddenly the scenery was replaced by golden sands and crashing blue waves.

"Wow. . ." Ana sat up in her seat, taking her feet down from the dashboard to sit up straight and look out the window. "This is beautiful! Who needs the south of France when you have this on your doorstep?"

"Sometimes, when we live somewhere long enough, we forget to admire what gemstones are right under our nose, forgotten about for dreams of bigger and wilder places," Ezra said as he waited for a car to pass so that he could pull into the car park at the edge of the beach.

He parked the car, turned the engine off and then looked at her with a small smile.

Ana lifted her papers from her lap and folded them neatly again, putting them into her handbag and getting out of the car. It was another stunningly hot day, but thankfully, it was much later in the afternoon and the sun was descending in the sky, making the temperatures easier to handle. Ezra followed her after closing and locking his door. He came to her side and walked with her across the car park to a walkway that led towards the beach town.

It was a small town, tiny in fact. The main shopping area had a long ascending hill that led all the way up to a lighthouse. Rows of beautifully built shops lined the rising hill road. Vintage clothing stores, French cafes, surfer shops, and antique bookstores all had their doors open with people filing in and out. As they walked, Ana could smell the aroma of buttery pastries coming from the bakery, and her stomach grumbled at the thought of what delights were inside. They hadn't eaten a proper meal that day and had opted instead for car snacks to save time.

Up ahead, a brown sign labelled "Tourist Information" pointed down a little alleyway near an old-style jewellery store. Together they walked down the little cobbled street, and when they got to the door, Ezra opened it wide for her and she thanked him.

Ana saw display boards of information, which showcased their exhibitions on the local wildlife and how to find the best spots for bird watching, the local history on people of importance, local fables and legends, and the top ten places for walkers and ramblers to check out. What she didn't find on those display boards, however, was anything to do with towers.

Along the walls were long tables filled with every type of pamphlet imaginable. Places to stay, the top ten parks for kids, how to stay safe in the sun, the local menus for every restaurant and the numbers for tour guides.

But again, nothing to do with towers.

"Can I help you both?" asked a man from behind the reception desk as he smiled at them and tapped his pen on the edge of his clipboard. He looked relaxed, with a large black bushy beard and fluffy eyebrows that pushed against the rim of his glasses.

Ana turned to look at him from where she was gazing at the pamphlets and walked to him quickly, leaning against the counter and smiling.

"Hello! I am Ana Davenport with *The City Herald.* We have come to do some research on the town of Blackrock and the buildings that would have been here around the mid-to-late 1500s. More specifically, we are looking for any towers that would have been built back then and still exist today."

"It sounds to me like you need a local historian," the man said as he reached onto the counter, where he lifted a card from one of the holders that sat there and held one out to her. "Luckily for you, that would be me. I am Edward Bolton, head of the Blackrock Historical Society."

"Lucky, indeed." Ezra said as he leaned on the counter beside Ana and looked down at the man in the chair with a smile. "Can you help?"

"Well, back around those times, there were two towers here in Blackrock. One is no longer here but the other is, though barely. They were built at the very end of the medieval period in 1500," Edward said with a small sigh as he opened a page on his computer, clicking his mouse over the screen.

"And which one was the tallest?" Ana asked.

"The one that is barely standing. It is a round tower, with a point at the top. It stands at 130 feet tall with a circumference of sixty feet. It was originally used as a bell tower, and the people of those days also used it as a lookout point." He glanced over at the screen and clicked print. The printer moaned and groaned as it woke from its sleep and began working.

"And is it possible to go there to take a look?" Ana asked, then tilted her head and gave him a smile. "So I can take pictures for the paper, I mean."

"You could, but I wouldn't recommend it right now," he said as he pushed his wheeled computer chair over to the printer and collected the paper he printed. "It's right at the top of the lookout cliff on the coast, and the trek is a rocky one. You could get up there in time, but by the time you head back, it will be too dark to come back down safely. I would suggest starting your trail tomorrow morning to be on the safe side." He folded the paper and passed it to Ezra, giving them both a smile.

"Thank you for the advice. Could you give us directions on where to find the tower?" Ezra questioned as he folded the page further and put it in his pocket.

"They are already printed on the page; it's not hard to find." He said as he looked between them both. "So, for the article in your paper, my name again is Edward Bolton. That's E-D-W-A-"

"I got it." Ana smiled as she waved his card in her hand. "I will make sure to thank you for your help."

She turned from the desk and gave Ezra a small shrug as they walked out of the building and back into the street. The sun was a lot lower in the sky now, but not completely gone, and she observed the shopping areas.

"We will need to find somewhere to stay the night if we can't go to the tower now," she said with a frown. She didn't bring any clothes with her again, not having expected to even be talking to Ezra, never mind travelling with him.

"Don't worry about that. I had a feeling we would be stranded out here tonight, so I brought provisions," Ezra said as they passed the shops that were closing their shutters.

"Provisions?" Ana looked up at him sceptically.

"You will like it, I promise." Ezra winked.

An hour later, Ana was standing on the beach, the sun now low on the horizon and the sky turning from blue into a beautiful pallet of pinks and golds. Ezra had erected a tent on the beach and was struggling to light a flame over a fire he had made from driftwood and dried seaweed. He frowned in concentration as he struck the metal fire starter in his hand with the striker, but the little sparks that came from it would not settle on the kindling long enough to ignite.

"Damn it," Ezra said as he struck it again.

Ana laughed, her hands on her hips as she watched him struggle, and she moved to kneel opposite him on the other side of the pile of wood. "Can't you just use all that fancy *magic* you have?" She asked sarcastically, looking down at the sparks as they died with a grin.

"I don't practice, remember?" Ezra said as he sighed and sat back on his haunches in the sand. He held the starter out to her. "Why don't you do something useful and try to help, rather than mock me, hm?"

"All right, all right, I'm sorry." Ana smiled as she stifled a laugh and took the starter. She leaned down low and struck the metal, watching the sparks fly onto the kindling. It took her a few tries, but when a few settled she quickly tucked her ponytail back and began to blow on the kindling, watching it as it smoked and finally light.

"Show off," Ezra said as he slumped back to sit on the blanket he had laid outside the tent. "How did you learn to do that?"

"My dad. He liked to take me camping when I was a kid." Ana sat beside him on the blanket.

"I thought you didn't get out in nature?" Ezra asked.

"I don't. Not anymore. My dad died when I was ten," Ana leaned back on her hands and watched the sun set. She always loved how the colours of the sky changed when the sun went down.

"I'm sorry." He cleared his throat and pulled the large picnic basket closer to him.

He opened it and pulled out some tin foiled covered plates and passed one to her, then laid out some extra boxes of fruits and snacks before he finally lifted two glasses and a bottle of wine.

"What is it with you and wine?" Ana asked as she took her glass from him with a shake of her head. "I'm fine with my water."

"No, you are having a drink with me, and we are going to talk about something other than this investigation for once. I want to know more about what makes Miss Ana Davenport tick." Ezra opened the bottle and filled her glass.

He filled his own, then took a large sip of it and set it aside on one of the trays that came with the picnic basket before opening the foil on his plate. Inside was an array of sandwiches, cold meats, and pasta that his mother had packed them, and he lifted one of his sandwiches and took a bite with a hungry moan.

"All right," Ana said as she opened her own after setting her glass aside with his and took one of her sandwiches in her hand. "But if you get to ask questions, I get to ask some, too. A question for a question. Deal?"

"Deal." Ezra smiled, "But you drink after you answer. I'll go first. What happened to your dad?"

"Wow, straight in with the emotional trauma! Thank you for that," Ana said. She took a bite from her sandwich and collected her thoughts before she swallowed and shrugged. "We were cycling around where we used to live. It was a busy street, and we really shouldn't have been out in the dark. My mom always warned us that it was dangerous, but we thought we were invincible. I thought *he* was invincible. He wasn't. A car came out of nowhere, I guess they didn't see us, but they crashed straight into him and ran him over. They drove off, didn't even stop. Luckily, there were apartments nearby and I was able to knock on the doors until someone answered and called for help. He died on the way to the hospital."

Ezra had stopped eating his sandwich and was watching her

with a frown on his face like he regretted asking the question. "I'm sorry. That's tragic." He waited a beat, then gave her a soft smile in comfort. "You forgot to drink."

"Oh. Well, I need it now, so thanks." Ana smirked, taking a gulp of her wine, and clearing her throat. "Okay, so my turn. On the topic of fathers, why do you hate yours so much? He seems like a nice guy."

Ezra sighed as he lifted some cold meats and took a bite out of it. "I don't like this game anymore."

"Tough. I answered." She said and nudged him.

"Fair enough. My dad and I were close for a long time. Side-kicks. Best friends. That's why I followed in his footsteps. I wanted to make him proud by going into the field of occult history and folklore and the archaeology of witchcraft. He was my idol." He said as he took another bite and swallowed hungrily.

"So, what happened?"

"We were working on a project. I hadn't finished my degree yet. I was ambitious and wanted to get my hands dirty straight away and so I started looking into finding the lost ferryman coins of the northern pagan colonies. I had done four years of research. My dad helped me here and there, but it was my first big investigation and I wanted to make him proud. Anyway, long story short, I found one of the lost coins. I knew it was going to be *huge*. It would be the find of my career and I hadn't even started it yet. I was so excited that I showed my dad all of my research and my coin, and I was in the process of writing my findings to be published so that I could take it to the museum after I had collected all the data from the lab.

"So, the day before I was supposed to hand it in, I went out with Jasper and a few other of our friends and drank until I couldn't see. I slept in the next day, and when I woke up and opened the museum website to find their number to tell them I was going to be late for the meeting, there was a news post on their main page.

'Local occult and folklore historian Alexander Sullivan finds

rare coin, thought lost to time.'

"I was furious. He said it was because I didn't have my degree yet. If I didn't have my qualifications, they could just take the coin away from me and not take me seriously. But if he took it in under his name, the find would stay in the family. It was bullshit, obviously. He's an entitled, thieving piece of shit, and I wanted nothing more to do with him. He knows I hate him for it, but I smile through it to keep the peace. My mom doesn't like us fighting, and I need the monthly cheques to keep me above board at the Daria Research Lab."

He leaned forward and knocked his glass against hers as he took a large swig and looked out over the ocean. His jaw was twitching like he was biting down anger, but his face was blank.

"Oh. Okay, that sucks. I can understand why you would be so mad at him. That's quite the betrayal." Ana frowned. His dad had seemed so nice when she met him at the Litha celebrations, and as sincere as he had seemed when he offered them his help, she was glad she hadn't told Ezra about his father's offer. She had a feeling he wouldn't take it well.

"Yeah, well, it is what it is. My turn." Ezra grinned as he turned his head to look sideways at her. "Who was the last person you dated, and why are you single? What happened?"

"Okay, I'm not playing this game anymore. I am not talking to you about my dating life." Ana laughed as she finished off her sandwich and shook her head.

He grinned and nodded his head, pointing his finger at her. "Yes, you are. Those are the rules. The question has been asked, Davenport, come on."

Ana groaned and closed her eyes as she rubbed her forehead. "This is embarrassing."

"Just answer the damn question." he said with a roll of his eyes.

"I was in my last year of university. His name was Austin. I thought it was serious; he clearly didn't see it that way. We were dating for about two years, and then one day I tried to send him a message online and he had blocked me. Turns out, his fiancé had no idea I existed, and I only found out about her when I searched his name and found his other profile and his picture of them at their engagement party." Ana cringed. "In my defence he never told me he was engaged."

"Damn, Davenport. That sucks." He laughed. "Did you love him?"

"That's two questions," Ana said after she took her drink and gulped it down. "But yes, I did."

"Double suck." Ezra said, with a small shrug. He leaned forward and popped one of the grapes in his mouth and then passed her the bowl.

"My turn. What happened between you and *your* last girl-friend?" she asked with a wiggle of her eyebrow.

"I wouldn't know. I've never had one." Ezra shrugged.

Ana's eyes widened, and her mouth dropped in a look of mocking shock. "What! That's not fair. You can't lie in this game!"

"I'm not lying!" Ezra insisted with a laugh. "I mean, don't get me wrong, I've had many conquests, many women I've been intimate with, but I was never a relationship kind of guy. It always seemed pointless to me."

"Well, that's a very sad and jaded way to look at things."

"I don't know if you have noticed, Ana, but I come from a very strange family with very strange practices. Once anyone finds that out, it's usually curtains for me. That, and I have been always too busy with my work and trying to carve out some form of career for myself. It wouldn't be fair to ask someone to be happy with coming second best to that, she wouldn't understand." Ezra shrugged as he reached to refill their glasses.

"So, you just have meaningless one-night stands with women in the rare books sections of libraries?" Ana asked with a raise of her brow.

"Pretty much."

Dusk was hanging over the beach now, and after all the driving they had done that day, Ana found herself growing tired as she looked over the fire and how it flickered. The sunset glow had given way to a new inky black and stars were piercing through, littering the sky in little lights. It was beautiful, how bright they looked in comparison to the light polluted skies of the city.

"Well, I don't know about you, but I am exhausted. I think I am going to sleep," Ana said as she downed her last glass of wine and passed it to him, "Thank you for the wine, and the food. And the game."

"You are very welcome, Miss Davenport. I left you one of my shirts and a pair of my shorts inside if you want to sleep in them. I am going to stay out here for a bit longer to finish the wine and think a little. I will try to not wake you." Ezra said as he took her glass and set it aside.

She paused for a moment and then leaned to kiss his cheek and ruffle his hair. "Don't drink so much you give yourself a hangover. We have work to do tomorrow."

Ezra looked at her when she kissed his cheek. She couldn't tell if it was the flickering of the fire, or the wine, but he had a dumb smile on his face and his cheeks were flushed. "Good night."

Ana stood from the blanket and ducked inside the tent, where she undressed quickly and knelt beside her sleeping bag. On it he had laid a powder blue T-shirt that had the name of the university he had attended in white on the front and a pair of black shorts beside them. She smiled softly and pulled them on quickly, then zipped herself in the sleeping bag.

She could see Ezra's shadow cast against the outside of the tent from the light of the fire, and she found herself watching him and how he breathed and ran his hand through his hair as he drank his wine and looked at the stars. Finally, sleep took hold of her, and she closed her eyes to the sound of the waves that crashed on the beach.

CHAPTER 13

"*H*ey... wake up."

Ana groaned from where she was hugging a pillow that was stuffed inside her sleeping bag. She was being shaken awake as Ezra whispered to her.

"Ana, wake up. We need to pack up and leave if we are going to get to the tower and drive all the way home before dark," he said from where he was resting on his elbow beside her in his own sleeping bag.

Ana rolled onto her back and looked up at him. He was sitting up with no shirt on, and the only thing that was covering his legs was a sleeping bag that was tucked low around his hips.

"Are you *naked?*" Ana hissed as she sat up sharply and looked him up and down.

Ezra laughed and shook his head before he unzipped his sleeping bag and rose to his knees, revealing his black boxers. "No. I mean, not unless you want me to be. . ."

Ana groaned and lay back down, looking up at the fabric ceiling. "What time is it?"

"Dawn," Ezra said as he pulled on his jeans.

The tent was too small to stand up in, so he had to lie back on his sleeping bag to pull them up to his hips. Ana watched him silently, blushing at how they hugged his hips, and when he finished, he turned his head to her, catching her looking at him.

"What?" he asked, sitting back up to pull his black T-shirt over his head.

"Nothing. I'm just waiting on you *leaving* so I can get dressed." Ana retorted, looking away and back at the ceiling with a blush.

"All right, don't get your panties in a twist. I'm done." He held his hands up defensively and ducked down low to get out of the tent's doorway.

Ana took a small breath and centred herself before she quickly sat up on her knees and changed from his blue university T-shirt and boxers and into her own clothes. She folded them neatly, then zipped up their sleeping bags and headed out of the tent. Ezra was already packing up the picnic basket, and when he was done, they took the tent down and walked together towards the car, awkwardly trying to juggle everything so that they only had to make one trip. Shoving everything back into the trunk of the car, Ezra jumped into the drivers' seat and started the engine.

There was no one around the beach this morning. The sun was just coming up, leaving the sky in a misty morning blue, and there were a few clouds hanging low in the sky. It was cold still, and Ana hugged her sweater closer to her body as she got into the passenger side seat and instantly reached to turn the heating system on in the car. She brought her hands to her mouth and blew on them, rubbing them to warm them up and then pulled the piece of paper from her pocket and opened the folds.

"The directions the guy gave us yesterday say that we have to go to the main road of the main street in town and drive up the incline of the big hill we saw that leads to the lighthouse. A mile over the top of that hill is a country park. If we park there, there is apparently a walking trail that leads deep into the countryside and over the ridge of the cliffside. It says here that you literally can't miss it once you are past the cliffs." Ana said as she folded it again and lay it on her lap, rubbing her hands again to bring heat into them.

"All right, boss," Ezra said as he pulled out of the carpark and drove towards the town.

They drove past the shops they had seen the day before and came to the bottom of the incline that led up the mountainside towards where the lighthouse was. He stopped the car at the bottom of the hill and set it into park with a deep frown on his face, then he moved to open his door and get out.

"Ezra," Ana hissed, "you are supposed to drive *up* the hill, not park at it."

"I know this hilled road," he mumbled as he closed his door and walked towards where the smooth road ended and the cobblestoned hill road began.

Ana sighed deeply and rubbed her head in irritation as she got out of the car and walked after him. "You know you can't just park in the middle of the road Ezra!"

"It's 5:30. No one is going to care, Ana. Just give me a second," Ezra said as he walked up the first part of the hill.

On the side of the road were remnants of an old brick building, only one wall having survived the test of time. A large metal plaque was screwed onto the wall, with inscriptions and a carving of a woman being forced into a wooden barrel.

"What is this?" Ana asked as she came to his side as he read over the plaque.

"Holy shit, I *studied* this. I didn't realise there was a Barrel Hill here. I knew it looked familiar." Ezra said as he frowned. He looked from the plaque and then up the cobbled hill, a dark expression falling over his face.

"What is a Barrel Hill?" she asked him, following his eyes up the hill like it would give her the answer.

"During the European witch trials, the witch hunters and magistrates were becoming more and more blood thirsty. They tried to come up with extra, more inventive ways they could execute people condemned for witchcraft." He placed a hand on the carving of the woman being shoved into the barrel by men with torches.

"I'm not going to like this story, am I?" Ana hugged herself, half out of comfort and half to keep some warmth in her body.

"Well, all over the country, in towns that had steep roads like this one, they started to use them as Barrel Hills. The hunters and the magistrate would commission the blacksmiths and the woodworkers to combine their efforts and make a barrel big enough for a human. Inside the barrel, rows of long spikes lined the entirety of it. They apparently drew their inspiration from the old iron maiden torture device. They forced the women inside and nailed the lid shut. There was enough space inside for her not to be pierced when it was standing upright, but then the people outside it would tip it over and roll it all the way down the hill to ensure she was pierced right through. The men were so terrified of witches that they chased it to the bottom and set it on fire where it stopped rolling so the evil could be burned away and never set free again."

Ana shivered, tears pricking her eyes. She looked to the bottom of the hill where the cobblestones stopped and silently wondered how many women succumbed to that fate. Frowning at the road, she turned back to look at the plaque and read it over. It had lists of names of known women who had suffered from it and then just above the engraved drawing were the words: *Exodus 22:18*.

Ezra was already walking back to the car when she finished reading, and she had to run to catch up, getting into the car and closing the door after her.

"What is Exodus 22:18?" Ana asked.

Ezra winced and started the car again before driving up the Barrel Hill.

"Thou shalt not suffer a witch to live."

THE DRIVE to the country park didn't take long, but the hike was taking its toll on Ana's feet. Not being used to walking so much, Ana felt her heels beginning to blister, and her knees ached. Ezra, on the other hand, hiked like he was walking on air. He never slowed down, or moaned about it like she did, and he was barely sweating or out of breath.

"How are you not even out of breath?" Ana asked as he stumbled over another rock and had to steady herself.

"This isn't even a hard hike, Ana." Ezra smirked as he turned to look at her, his hands holding the straps of his backpack as he waited on her.

"Can we at least stop for a moment? I am dying." She panted. Her throat was hoarse from trying to gulp down breaths, and her calves felt like they were on fire. "Give me your water."

Ezra sighed as he pulled his backpack from his shoulder and opened it. He took out a bottle of water and walked back to her, watching as she scrambled to open it and gulp down half the bottle.

"We are close," Ezra said as he looked around. "The round tower should be just over this last hill. You can do it."

Ana groaned and gulped more of the water, then closed the lid and started to walk again. They had been walking for three hours straight, and it was nearing 9:00. The sun was up now, making the sky brighter and the temperature rise, and she was losing the energy to keep going.

"You are taking me for the biggest breakfast you can afford when we are done with this," she said, her stomach grumbling.

"Sure, just keep walking." He took her hand and pulled her along to make her walk again.

When they finally crested over the hill they paused, observing the land in front of them.

"Wow, there she is." Ezra smiled as he shielded his eyes from the sun to look across the rocks to where the tower stood.

It wasn't far, and they walked the distance quickly, approaching the front of the circular tower and having to crane their neck to look up to its pointed top. It was tall but thin, and it was so old that bricks had fallen from it, leaving holes in its walls and rotten wooden beams hanging from the gaps. There was an archway as a door, which was eight feet above the ground, surprisingly with no steps up to it to get inside.

"Why is the door all the way up there? How are people supposed to get inside?" Ana asked as she took the reprieve from walking to catch her breath. Sweat lined the back of her shirt at her neck, and she fanned herself with her hand.

"Well, one of two reasons. One, if they used their ladder, all they had to do was lift it up here, and they were safe from animals or attackers. And two," He said as he took a few steps back away from the tower, looking up at the top, "these towers are tall and thin. If you put a door at the bottom near the floor, it would dramatically weaken the tower's structural integrity. Putting the door seven to ten feet from the ground makes the tower more stable."

Ana watched him take more steps back and look at the tower's distance from his feet. He seemed to be sizing the door up, and she narrowed her eyes at him.

"What are you *doing?*" she asked.

"Getting inside that tower." Ezra mumbled.

He took off in a run towards the tower, and when he got to the wall, he jumped, scaling the wall and climbing up onto the ledge through the door. He grinned when he got inside, and he turned to look at the view from above.

"Okay, your turn," Ezra said as he waved for her to join him.

Ana blinked at him with wide eyes, looking back to where he had run from and then up the wall to where he now stood, "There is no way I am making that, Ezra."

"Just take it at a run and reach for my hands. I will pull you up," Ezra said as he took his backpack off and set it behind him, then lay down on the floor of the tower and held his hands over the edge. "Come on."

Ana tried to jump up and reach for his hands, but she was too short and he was far too high up. "You are too high! I can't reach!"

"Take a few steps back and run up the wall, Ana! Come on, it's not hard. Let's go!" he encouraged with a smile as he looked down at her, his hair falling in front of his face.

Ana groaned and relented, taking a few steps back and then ran to the wall, trying to run up it and grab his hand but she slipped and fell again, resting her head against the bricks. "I can't do it."

"That was a pathetic attempt, Davenport. You didn't even try. Do you want to find this thing or not?" Ezra waved for her to stand back, "Try again."

Ana took a deep, determined breath and set her jaw as she walked back, then took a further few steps back than he had taken. She shook herself and focused on Ezra's hands. All she had to do was reach for his hands, then he could pull her up.

She nodded, as if to convince herself it wasn't as high as it actually was, then took off in another run. She was faster, and she found that when she jumped this time, she knew where to place her feet. Ana pushed herself up on the brick and grabbed onto Ezra's hands. He then gripped them tightly and pulled her up and over the threshold with a pant.

He laughed as they rolled on the floor, keeping one of her hands in his and patting the back of it. "You are heavier than you look."

"Shut up!" Ana laughed as she hit his chest with her hand and scrambled back to her feet, looking over the inside of the tower.

Looking up, Ana could see that the bricks on the pointed top were caved in on the right side, and the bell that once hung at the top near the little window was now lying on the floor at their feet in the centre of the tower. The beams that had held it were broken and old leaves and fragments of the wood littered the floor. A wooden spiral staircase rolled up the walls, circling around and around up to the very top. There were missing steps, and the ones that were still there looked unstable.

"What exactly are we looking for?" Ana asked as she brushed off the dust and dried mud off her knees and looked around the tower.

"The parchment said it is 'forged in fire and perfectly aligned,' so I would say whatever it is, it is made from metal. Aligned would mean balanced and well-made." Ezra said from where he was laying on the floor of the tower.

"Maybe it's the bell? That's made from metal," Ana said as she crouched next to the bell.

She saw nothing that showed any indication it was something of value. She tipped her head upside down to look inside the bell as it lay on its side. Inside was the metal ringer, and she reached in and unhooked it. Pulling it out, she examined it in her hand. It was surprisingly intact, save for some rust and some chips.

"Could it be this?" Ana asked, leaning over to hand it to him where he lay.

He sat up and took it in his hands, shaking it to see if anything rattled or fell out, but it was solid. "No, I don't feel anything inside."

He handed it back to her and then lay back on the floor, looking up at the ceiling and along the wooden staircase that spiralled all the way to the point. At the very top was a flat stone square that looked out of place and a lighter grey than the rest of the bricks. He narrowed his eyes and took to his feet, then reached for his back-pack to pull out his flashlight. He clicked it on and shone it to the top of the tower, illuminating the lighter square, and he gasped.

"A stone safe is up there." He said, moving towards the stairs and testing a wooden step with his foot.

"A stone what?" Ana asked, following the beam of his flashlight and finally seeing the square he was focused on.

"It's like a thin piece of clay they put over the top of a hole and painted as close as they could to the surrounding area. It was used to conceal valuables. All you need to do is break the clay and you should be able to get your belongings back. It hasn't been broken yet," Ezra said as he bit his lip and took another step. "I need to get up there."

He kept walking up the steps, holding onto the wall, but when he reached the sixth step, the wood caved under his weight and he crashed down, having to jump off onto the floor at the last second, "Damn it."

Ana put her hand to her forehead as she paced. "So, what do we do now? It's too unstable."

"For me, yes, but for you. . ." Ezra said as he handed the flashlight to her. "You are a lot lighter and smaller than me, so it should hold your weight."

"Should? I'm not going to walk up there and end up killing myself on a *should*, Ezra. No way!" Ana stepped back from his extended hand and flashlight.

"Well fine, we can just pack up and go home then, because I can't make it up there." Ezra shrugged as he moved to the doorway. "If we can't get up there, we can't get whatever the object is behind that encasing."

Ana crossed her arms over her chest and surveyed the height of the tower, and the flimsy wooden staircase. "I am scared of heights, Ezra. I can't go up there."

"Just try. I will be here to catch you if you fall." He said as he smiled at her.

"You will catch me? From thirty feet in the air?" Ana asked, looking horrified.

"Well, we are already seven feet up, so technically it's only twenty-three feet." He looked at her with a raised brow, "You can trust me. I would never let you get hurt."

"That doesn't make me feel any better," Ana said as she took the flashlight from him, a feeling of dread filling her stomach.

She moved to the first step and walked up the first few slowly, holding onto the wall. Her heart was hammering against her chest, making her feel lightheaded the further up she went. The wooden stairs were holding, but they groaned and moaned under her feet in protest as she got higher and higher. Halfway up, the wall stopped and gave way to a gap in the bricks where they had fallen, leaving a large hole and a space between the wooden steps. She could feel the wind blowing through the gap, making her feel unsteady as her hair whipped in front of her face, and she began to panic. Her vision blurred and she had to close her eyes, holding onto the wall as her legs shook as she tried to stay perfectly still.

"I can't go any further, Ezra. The steps are missing! The wall is gone!" Ana called out, her voice catching in her throat.

"That's okay! Just keep calm and step up to the next one carefully!"

Ana nodded and reached a shaky hand to hold onto the top edge of the hole in the wall and pushed her leg forward so that she could push off the step and jump onto the next one.

It cracked, and she yelped, having to take the rest of them two at a time until she reached the ledge at the top. She slumped to sit down on the concrete ledge and gasped for breath, holding her hand over her heart, and looking down at Ezra, who whistled.

"Yes! I knew you could do it! Now what do you see?!" he called.

Ana was smiling widely, a sense of adrenaline filling her body and making her feel brave, and tingly all over. She looked to the square of grey clay and ran her fingers over the markings she recognised that were etched into it.

"Those thingys are written all over it!" Ana called down to him.

"What thingys?" Ezra called, walking sideways to try and get a better look.

"Those symbol thingys on the parchment!"

"Sigils? That's it! You found it! Smash it open with your flashlight!"

Ana steadied herself on the ledge and took the end of the flashlight in her hands, then began hitting it against the clay plaque. She had to hammer it a few times, but finally it smashed and caved in, the clay falling onto the ledge and revealing a hole. Something was inside, so she set the flashlight beside her to reach in. It was fabric, and when she grabbed it, she could feel something hard under it. Pulling it out of the hole she placed it on her lap, her hand shaking as she grinned.

"I got it!" She shouted.

"What is it?" Ezra bounced on his feet, trying to get a better view of her.

After Ana freed the cloth and the string that tied it, she found a long decorative dagger inside. It was beautiful, with carved filigree on the gold handle and up the silver blade. There was a hole in the hilt, which made it look like it was missing something, but other than that, it was perfect.

"Oh wow. . ." She whispered and reached to lift it by its handle.

The second her hand touched the hilt, a sharp pain entered Ana's head. Her hand tightened around the dagger, and her body became light and weak, her vision blurring and black beginning to filter through the edges of her vision. Then everything went dark, and she found herself falling from the ledge. There was a flash of light from somewhere below her, then blackness, then nothing.

Nothing but a voice.

"Find us. Find the source of the power. Find the missing pieces and you can set us free! Beware the watchers. You have awakened the ones who watch and the ones who hunt now you have given

freedom to the first. Find the others before they do, before they find you. Before you join us."

As the voice repeated itself over and over, it faded and she felt her body again. She was lying on something hard, and she was being held by someone who was rubbing her face.

"Ana? Ana, wake up!" Ezra called to her.

He seemed so far away until she finally fluttered open her eyes. Her body still felt tingly all over and her ears were ringing, but when her eyes refocused, she could see that she was on the floor of the tower, looking up at the ceiling she had fallen from. Ezra was holding her in his arms as she lay with her head against his chest, looking at her with a face full of concern.

"What did you say?" Ana asked dryly.

"I told you to wake up. What happened up there?" Ezra asked, tucking her hair behind her ear as he kept hold of her until the feeling came back to her limbs.

"No, before that, something about the watchers. Who are the watchers?" she asked, slowly moving to sit up.

"I didn't say anything about watchers," Ezra said, watching her in confusion.

"Wait. . ." Ana using his shoulder to push herself up onto her feet. "Did you catch me?"

Ezra stood and brushed off his knees, not meeting her eyes as he busied himself with picking up the smashed flashlight. "I told you I wouldn't let you fall."

"From all the way up there?" Ana asked with a raised eyebrow. He didn't have a scratch on him, nor any dust or dirt like he would have if he had caught her and fell under her weight.

Ezra shrugged, then moved to where the old rag and the dagger lay on the ground and reached for it.

"Don't touch it!" she said, taking his arm to pull him back. "I think it might be like. . . radioactive or something."

"Radioactive?" Ezra asked with an unamused look on his face.

146

He lifted it by the hilt and turned it over in his hands, examining it. "See? It's just an athame."

Ana bit her lip and watched him as he seemed to be unaffected by the dagger. He was looking over it and holding it with such tenderness. She was sure that it was the dagger that made her black out; she just didn't know how it didn't affect him either.

"What's an athame?" She let the thought go and approached him to take a closer look at it.

"An athame is a witch's tool. It's used to hold and direct energy so that the witch can manipulate the power they possess through it. It magnifies intention and the strength of your power during spell work." Ezra said as he looked over it closely, marvelling at it. "It has the Marion sigils all over it. Do you know how valuable this is? Not only the financial value but also the historical and the occult value. This is. . . I'm amazed!"

"I don't think it's safe to have," Ana said as she frowned at the dagger. She didn't know how to explain the voice she heard, or if Ezra had said it and he was just messing with her, but she was spooked. "If someone really is looking for the things that were written on the parchment, and we have one, then we need to hide it, and quick. I have a really bad feeling about this."

Ezra nodded. He wrapped it up in the cloth it came in, carefully put it into his backpack, then turned to look at her. "Then it's time to go. We can take a closer look at it when we get back to the shop."

He pulled the backpack over his shoulder and made for the door, jumping out the entrance and leaving Ana to stare up at the ceiling where she had fallen from. She shivered at how high it was and tried to feel for any pain in her body, but there was none, as if she hadn't fallen at all.

"Curiouser and curiouser. . ." she mumbled, then walked to the entrance and jumped out of the door.

CHAPTER 14

"I thought we were going to your mother's shop?" Ana asked as Ezra parked his car outside Genevieve's house.

"We were, but by the time I managed to drag you across that trail and into the car, it was closed, not to mention the three-hour drive home," he said, pulling the keys out of the ignition. "It's already past 7:00, and I am starving. Besides, my mother is the *best* cook."

He got out of the car with his backpack on his shoulder and Ana followed him, walking in the setting sun, down the little stone path that led to his mother's country house with the thatched roof. Walking through the door they were met with the smell of dinner as it permeated through the halls. It smelled like pasta and cheese, and freshly baked breads.

"Mom!" Ezra called as he placed his keys on the table inside the hallway and made his way to the kitchen, smiling widely when he saw her cooking at the stove.

Genevieve was humming along to music as she cooked and sipped her tea. The kitchen was rustic, with an old large oven and an island in the middle, already set with plates and cutlery.

"You're home!" She smiled widely, opening her arms to him when he dropped his backpack and swooped in for a hug. She hugged him back, then pinched his cheek and reached for the spoon that was still in the pot, lifting it out and hovering it in front of his face. "Taste."

Ezra leaned in and tasted the sauce, closing his eyes and nodding his approval, "Wonderful. I can't wait; we are starved."

Ana smiled as she hovered at the door to the kitchen, giving Genevieve a wave when she saw her, "I don't have to stay if it is too much trouble, I can go to the B&B. . ."

"Pish-posh." Genevieve said with a wave of her hand and turned the stove off before she walked to her and reached for her hand. "You are staying with me. I can't have my two little adventurers going hungry. Take a seat, dear."

Ana sat on a chair at the island, leaning on the table as she watched Ezra and his mother together. She could tell that they were awfully close, and that he doted on his mother in a way that she wished her mother would with her.

"So, tell me, how did your little camping trip go? Did you find what you needed?" Genevieve asked.

"As a matter of fact, we did." Ezra grinned. He sat down beside Ana, reaching for the pitcher of lemonade and filling their glasses. He took a large sip of his drink and then grabbed a slice of warm bread from the basket.

Her mouth watered as she reached for one of her own, spreading a little butter on it and then bringing it to her nose to smell it. It smelled divine, but before she could take a bite, Genevieve was talking to them again.

"And? Well? Spit it out, kiddo! What was it? I have been waiting all day!" she said, leaning on the countertop opposite them and watching them both expectantly.

Ana and Ezra shared a look, though hers seemed more unsure in contrast to his gleeful one.

"We found a dagger," Ana said, taking a bite from her buttery bread.

"Not just any dagger, Mom. It's the Marion coven athame. I didn't get a good look at it while we were there, but it's real and it's perfectly preserved. There is something missing on the hilt, but it is beautiful." Ezra said in excitement as he finished his bread.

"Well, where is it?" his mother asked, her mouth hanging open in awe.

"It's in my backpack, I can show you after dinner. Is it ready?" he asked, already standing and lifting the plates.

"It is. Will you plate it for us, dear?" Genevieve asked. Ezra was already at the stove and was plating the food high on the plates in his hands as his mother continued, "And you? What do you make of all this?"

Ana considered the question and took a sip of her lemonade to bide her some time to contemplate her answer. "I won't lie to you, Genevieve, this is all a little strange for me. I see him get so excited about these things that I don't understand the significance of, and a lot of strange experiences have been happening that I can't explain. I don't like things I can't explain. . ."

"No shit." Ezra laughed from the stove as he brought them the plates and set them down in front of Ana and his mother before he shuffled to get his own.

Ana looked down at the tall plate of carbonara and felt her mouth water again. Her stomach grumbled, and when Ezra joined them at the table with his own plate and started eating, she took it as her cue to start wolfing it down herself.

"What kind of strange experiences?" Genevieve asked.

"Well," Ana said, covering her mouth as she swallowed, "when I touched the dagger-"

"*Athame,*" Ezra corrected.

"Athame, whatever," she said with a roll of her eyes. "I touched it so I could see what it was, because it was wrapped up in a cloth, and something happened. I blacked out, but it was strange because I wasn't passed out completely; I was somewhere else inside my head. I had the feeling that someone else was there watching me. They said we needed to find the rest of the items before the watchers did. I thought it was Ezra playing with me, but he said he didn't say anything, right?" Ana laughed.

Ana looked up from her food and noticed that they had both stopped eating and were watching her. They weren't laughing with her.

"What?" Ana said, her smile falling.

"You didn't tell me that," Ezra said with a frown. "Why didn't you tell me?"

"I was embarrassed. I had just blacked out and found myself on the ground, with you holding me from my fall, I thought I was imagining it. I mean, I *was* imagining it. It's strange where your mind can go when you are blacking out and all the chemicals rush to your brain." Ana gave Ezra a weak smile.

"I'm sure that's all it was, darling," Genevieve said, giving her a smile as she started to eat again, "What was this fall you speak of? Did you get hurt?"

"Actually, it's kind of funny. I had to climb up to the top of the tower to get the athame, and it was thirty feet high! So, when I blacked out and fell, I thought I would wake up hurt, but Ezra caught me. I'm not sure how he did it, but both of us are fine, thankfully. It could have gone very wrong." She shrugged as she sipped her lemonade.

Genevieve was watching Ezra, and he wouldn't meet her eyes as he focused on eating. Ana could see a redness prick his cheeks until he finally looked up at his mother.

"Well, it's lucky he is a good catch, hm?" Genevieve said.

Something unsaid passed between them, and Ana felt like she had said too much, but what, she wasn't sure. She gave a small bashful shrug and ate her food, moaning at how good it tasted.

They ate in silence, listening to the soft jazz music that played on the radio and enjoying their meal. As she looked up at them from behind her fork, she could tell that something wasn't right. Genevieve seemed unhappy with Ezra, and he was trying not to look his mother in the eye like a scolded child.

When their plates of food were finished, Ezra took them to the sink where he left them inside and returned to lift his rucksack, putting it onto the table and finally looking to his mother a little sheepishly.

"Let's get a look at this athame then," Genevieve said, her warm smile returning as she rested her elbows on the table in anticipation.

Ezra reached inside his rucksack and pulled out the rolled-up rag, placing it on the table and pushing it closer to his mother. He sat down beside Ana again and bit his lip, his foot bouncing on the floor as he waited for her to open it. They hadn't had much time to look at it back at the tower, so seeing it again now would be like seeing it for the first time.

Genevieve pulled the fabric towards her. She opened it gently and laid it out flat on the table of the island.

"Oh my. . ." She lifted the dagger in her hands and held it gently. It was a little dull, but nothing a little bit of polish wouldn't fix. The handle was expertly carved, with beautiful leaf filigree in gold trailing up the handle. "This is stunning. The blade itself looks completely intact with no chips or marks, so it is definitely an athame. They were not used for defence or for any kind of slicing, so the blade should be unmarked. This is a very rare find, Ezra."

Ezra nodded eagerly and reached forward, pointing a finger to where the markings on the blade were. "These are the same as the sigils on the parchment that we found inside the box, which links it straight to the Marion family coven. This is most certainly the first of the objects they wrote about. We would never have found it if it wasn't for that map."

"You are right, there seems to be a piece missing." Genevieve acknowledged as she turned it over in her hands and ran her finger down the hilt and to the large semicircle hole. "I am not sure if it is on purpose or if it simply was damaged, but it is incomplete."

"Do you feel anything from it?" Ezra asked.

Ana raised her brow. She knew he must have meant if she felt magical things, but it was still strange for her to hear. By no doubt, these people she had grown to know were nice, but their belief in the existence of real magic still made her want to groan. She didn't, though, and instead leaned in closer for a better look.

"Nothing that is of any significance. There should be a lot of power in this athame, so I am surprised it feels so empty," Genevieve said as she set it back down on the rag carefully and looked at Ana. "What happened when you touched it?"

Ana shrugged again and rested her chin in her hands, "I don't know. I guess the stress from the climb up and being so scared of the height of it, and then the relief of finding it was too much for my head to take. I just blacked out."

"Can you remind me of the voice you heard?"

"It was just a blacked-out induced dream, Genevieve." Ana frowned, sitting up straighter.

"Even still, indulge me. . ."

Ana sighed and closed her eyes as she tried to remember what the dream had said.

"It said something about finding the source of the power, and the missing pieces so that something could be set free. Then, something about being aware of the watchers and that they are awakened now, and to find the rest before they do." She said, opening her eyes and reaching for her drink so she could sip it, "At least, that's what I think it said."

Genevieve hummed to herself, a worried look stretching across her face. "I think we should consult the cards about this, Ezra. I do not like the sound of this."

"Cards?" Ana inquired as she looked between them both.

"Tarot cards." Ezra said.

"Will you come with me?" Genevieve said to Ana as she stood from the table and walked to a door near the back of the kitchen.

Ana instantly bit the inside of her cheek to stop herself from sighing. She didn't want to offend Genevieve, but she also couldn't pretend like she thought any of this was real. Weighing everything up in her mind, she figured keeping Genevieve at ease would be the kindest thing to do.

"Sure." She stood from the table and watched as Genevieve disappeared into the room through the doorway.

"Ana," Ezra said as he reached to take her arm. "Be open-minded. Be kind. This stuff means a lot to my mother, and if she thinks this will help, I trust her."

Ana nodded slowly and gave him a forced smile. "I'm open minded. I would never hurt your mom's feelings." She took her arm back, then walked around the island in the kitchen and through the door Genevieve had walked through.

The door led to a large glass conservatory filled with plants. Pots adorned the ledges of the windows, and hung from the ceiling and down the walls. It was a greenhouse of sorts, and Ana could sense a different kind of feeling that this room gave her radiating through her skin. It was humid but calming and so aromatic that she wanted to breathe it in as deeply as she could. If she believed in real magic, she guessed this was what it would feel like. Tingly and warm and hopeful. But she didn't believe in magic, and she was reminded of that when she looked closer at the small tables that were around the room.

On the tables were crystal balls, gemstones with strange mark-ings carved into them, standing black mirrors, and a bowl smoking with incense. Genevieve sat at the table in the middle and lay a purple cloth over her knees, then smiled up at her and opened her arm to indicate for Ana to sit down opposite her.

As she sat at the little table, Ana looked over the top of it. It had a black and gold velvet cloth laid on top and to the left of Genevieve's hand was a deck of cards. They were face down, and Genevieve shuffled them between her fingers in a flourish without even looking at them.

"Have you ever had this done before?" Genevieve asked.

"No, I can't say that I have." Ana said as she watched her.

"Because you don't believe in this kind of thing." Before Ana could open her mouth and defend herself, she smiled and waved her off. "Don't worry about it, it doesn't matter, not for this."

Genevieve put the cards together after shuffling them and began to knock them with her knuckles. Ana's face must have expressed confusion as to why because she laughed and knocked them harder.

"The knocking is to cleanse the cards from any previous energies that may still be lingering. Vibration cleanses energy; therefore, no one else's energy can interfere with the message yours is trying to tell." She then shuffled the cards back into a deck and reached them out to her. "I need you to shuffle these."

Ana blinked at the cards, then nodded and reached for them. There were a lot of cards, and they were longer and bigger than traditional playing cards so she found them hard to shuffle. Her fingers fumbled, and some of the cards fell, making her pick them back up again awkwardly. Shuffling them once more, she handed them back to Genevieve and folded her hands on her lap beneath the table.

"All right. Let's find out what we need to know about this situation, shall we?" Genevieve said with a comforting smile.

Genevieve cleared her throat and closed her eyes, breathing deeply and feeling the deck of cards between her hands. She took a moment, taking her time connecting with them until finally she laid them on the table. After opening her eyes, she took one card from the top and turned it over.

The card had a picture of a young man and woman. They each held a cup in their hands and were extending them out to each other.

Above them, a winged staff floated, and on top of that, a lion's head roared.

She turned over the next card and laid it down beside the first. It showed a stonemason working on a column in a cathedral with tools in his hands in front of two architects holding a plan for the design.

"Ah, this is what I expected," Genevieve said as she smiled warmly, looking up at Ana from under the badger stripe on her fringe. She pointed to the card with the couple and the cups. "This is the two of cups. It symbolises love, partnership, and attraction. The lion represents a fiery sexual attraction between two people, but that's not all that this card means."

Ana's cheeks instantly turned crimson, and kept her eyes focused on the card so that she didn't have to look up into Genevieve's eyes.

Genevieve chuckled and shook her head. "The two of cups placed upright like this means the start of a relationship. That could mean love, yes, but in this situation, it most likely means the business relationship that you and Ezra share. It means there will be a deep mutual connection as you create a new partnership that is equally beneficial and balanced on both sides. You both need to be equally invested for this relationship to move forward. You will share the same wavelengths and the same vision on how to proceed with everything that will be put in your path. A perfect team playing to your individual strengths for the good of the whole. It is unconditional support and love, always wanting the best for each other. It's a beautiful card."

She smiled at her and pointed to the card with the stonemason.

"This is the three of pentacles. It means teamwork and learning. Each of these people, the stonemason and the architects could not make this magnificent building without first working together. It shows that even though they are skilled in different things and that they have different beliefs, they can work in harmony with the same goal in mind and overcome anything; that is what you and Ezra must do.

"Those are not surprising; I could see that you both work well with each other. He likes you, you know," she said, her finger teasingly tapping on the corner of the two of cups before she turned to the deck again. "Now, we shall figure out the intentions of this person who is after the items you seek. The person who killed Nina."

Genevieve took a breath and turned over two more cards. The first showed five men fighting each other with long sticks, and the second was a knight in shining armour, riding a white horse with his sword thrusted high in the air.

She sighed and laced her fingers under her chin, leaning on them as she gazed over the cards in deep thought.

"This is the five of wands. It suggests that this person will bring you conflict at every angle, will cause great disagreement, and is fiercely competitive in his ways. He will fight you tooth and nail to get to these items. And this one," She said, pointing to the knight, "is the knight of swords. He is a man on a mission who will stop at nothing to get what he wants, no matter the cost. He is driven, callous, harsh and highly motivated. No matter the obstacle in front of him, he will strike it down. That will include yourself and Ezra. You need to be careful and protect yourselves against him; he is an immensely powerful person. He will not hesitate to hurt you if he does not get what he wants."

"Can you tell who it is?" Ana asked as she leaned in closer, studying the knight on the horse and the focused look on his face.

"That's not how it works, dear. I wish it was." She frowned, then rubbed her temples. The last drawing of cards will be for the outcome of this journey that you and Ezra are on. We need to know if we have a fighting chance."

She took a deep breath and hovered her hands over the cards, then drew the next three in quick succession.

The first showed a man lying face down on the ground, presumably dead, with swords upright piercing his back. The second was a tower on the edge of a rocky mountain, lightning in the sky as two people leapt from the windows. The third revealed a skeleton dressed in black armour riding a white horse with a staff flying a black flag in his hands.

Genevieve tutted and rubbed her temples harder, tilting her head at the cards, then pointing to the picture of the dead man with the swords in his back.

"This is the ten of swords. It means a painful but inevitable ending. There will be loss and betrayal and crisis. One or both of you will be the victim of a betrayal, perhaps even to each other. It will hurt deeply and leave a lasting wound that will be hard to shake." She said, then pointed to the next.

"This is the tower. It means awakening, upheaval, and sudden change. It suggests that just when you think you know what is going on, the rug will be pulled from under you, and you will be brought down in chaos. Things will never be the same again, what you knew will be over and you will have to live in a new world that is foreign to you. You will need to rebuild and refocus and think again. This is not a good outcome, Ana, but this suggests you can overcome whatever this is if you are willing to do the work that needs to be done."

Genevieve looked up at her and frowned deeply, then looked to the last card, the one with the black knight skeleton.

"This is death, the card of transformation, of endings, and of transition. The ending of this quest you are on with my son will be hard and painful and extremely dangerous, but whatever happens, it will come with extreme change to everything you hold dear. You can overcome it if you try to move with the change. If you don't, you will only make things harder on yourself."

"That's ominous." Ana frowned, sitting back in her seat. She didn't believe that anyone could read her future in a deck of cards, but that didn't mean what Genevieve had seen didn't make her nervous.

"It is. This will be a dangerous time for you, and I will admit, I am worried for you both. If this person looking for these items catches up with you, if he is the reason for the betrayal and the abrupt change, then you need to ask yourself if these items are worth the risk of your life. Is it?"

Ana bit her lip and looked down at the cards again, then up into her face. "I don't know."

"Then you need to think deeply about this before you continue. I know you want to excel in your career, but it is not worth your life and it's not worth my son's life."

"No, it's not," Ana said with a deep sigh. "Why did you want to read my cards and not Ezra's? Maybe he could give you a clearer reading than mine can."

Genevieve smiled, but the smile didn't quite reach her eyes. "I can't read Ezra. He blocks everyone out each time someone tries to." She stood up. "Besides, your cards were very clear indeed. Come, it is getting late. I will have Ezra show you to your room for the night, and then I need to speak with my son about all this privately if you don't mind."

"Of course," Ana said with a smile.

She stood from the table and followed her out of the room, looking back over her shoulder at the table and the cards. She didn't understand how a simple pack of cards could tell the future at all, but someone *was* looking for those items and someone *did* kill Nina. However, she had reason to be careful, whether the cards said so or not.

Ezra was still sitting at the island in the middle of the kitchen, looking over the athame in deep concentration as he made notes.

"How did it go?" he asked, looking up from his notepad and setting it down with a tired smile.

"As well as can be expected. Show Ana to Abby's room, then

come back here before you go home. I need to talk with you," Genevieve said, her voice suggesting that she still wasn't happy with him.

Ezra pulled his lips into a thin line and nodded to his mother. "Okay. Look after the athame while I am gone." He waved for Ana to follow him, and they walked out through the hall together to the wooden stairs that led to the second floor. "What did your cards say?"

"Something about betrayal and change and death." Ana sighed as she followed him up the stairs.

"Oh yeah? What else?" he questioned, looking over his shoulder at her with a small grin.

"You need more than death and betrayal?" she responded as she made it to the landing and followed him to the door at the end of the hall.

Ezra rested his hand on the doorknob and turned to look at her fully before opening it. "You drew the two of cups, didn't you?"

Ana's mouth dropped, and she spluttered at him, crossing her arms over her chest and shaking her head. "I thought those readings were supposed to be *private*?"

"They are! I wasn't listening, I swear," Ezra defended, crossing his heart with his finger and opening the door.

"Then how did you know?"

"Because you and I make a great team, Davenport. And you like me." He winked, then switched the light on.

The room was simple. It was big enough, with two little windows, white walls, and a double bed. A vanity table sat against one of the walls with makeup on the counter and had a huge wooden wardrobe beside it.

"Your mom said this is Abby's room. Who is Abby?" Ana asked as she stepped inside.

Ezra looked around the room, an expression on his face that she couldn't quite read. "She is my sister, a few years younger. Abby is the wild child of the family. We don't know where she is from one day to the next, and she rarely comes home, so you are welcome to this room. She has wardrobes full of clothes if you want to change into something you can sleep in."

Ana nodded as she scanned the room and moved to the wardrobe, opening it and running her hands over the clothes. "And you?"

"I have my own clothes to sleep in." He smirked, then laughed when Ana gave him a frown. "I need to go speak with my mom, then I will go to my place, but I will be back for breakfast and we can go over the next step of our plan."

Ana narrowed her eyes in question. "Why *is* your mom so pissed at you? She was fine until we told her about what happened when I fell."

He shrugged.

"I don't know"

Ezra had never lied to her before. She knew that for a fact when she saw how badly he had done it just now, and it made her frown deeper. Rather than quizzing him about it, she shrugged and walked back to him, taking the doorknob in her hands.

"Well, I shan't keep you, then." Ana said.

Ezra paused, then bit his lip and moved as if he were going to take her hand, but he shoved his hands in his pockets instead. "Yes. Well. Good work today, Davenport."

He walked out of the room and down the hall quickly before Ana closed the door. She stood with her back against it and looked over the room as she chewed her lip.

CHAPTER 15

Sunlight shone through the window as Ana lay in bed at the Sullivan house. It rested on her skin and left her feeling warm and cosy. She stretched, lying against the fresh sheets and watching as little dust particles fell in front of the rays and fluttered in the air. With a smile, she sat up in the sheets and threw her legs over the side of the bed. The night before, she had rummaged through some of Abby's clothes and found a pair of pyjama shorts and a black tank top that read, *I'd curse you, but I don't want to waste the herbs,* in white cursive over the front.

She pulled her phone from where it was resting on the vanity table to check the time. It was after 10:00, and she blinked at the screen, a sense of panic coming over her before she realised she didn't have to be up early anyway. There were no deadlines, no meetings, and no priorities until the end of the month. She never had this amount of time to herself, and as she sat on the chair at the vanity, she recognised how much she had missed a slower paced life.

After putting her phone back on the table, she smelt something sweet drifting under the door, making her stomach grumble loudly.

She stood from the chair and opened the door, walking into the hall and smiling at the soft sound of rock music that came from the kitchen below her.

Coming into the kitchen, Ana smiled widely as she leaned against the door and folded her arms across her chest, resting her head on the wood. Ezra was standing at the stove. His hair stuck out at all angles, and he was wearing a pair of loose-fitting grey sweatpants and a white T-shirt. Cooking utensils and flour covered the kitchen counters and the top of the island, with milk spilled and a bag of chocolate chips tipped over. He was singing to himself and nodding his head to the music, and when he finally turned with a plate in his hands, he jumped in surprise and scrambled to set them down.

"Jesus Christ! Don't sneak up on people like that, Davenport. You gave me a heart attack!" Ezra exclaimed with a frown. He tried dusting his shirt off, but he had flour and batter all over it.

"I wasn't sneaking around. It's not my fault you were in the zone. Nice singing voice, by the way." Ana laughed and pushed herself off the door, walking to him and reaching to wipe the flour caked on his nose. "What the hell are you doing, anyway?"

Ezra shooed her hand away and moved to turn the oven off, then he reached inside with a hand towel and pulled out a tray of freshly baked croissants.

"I couldn't sleep," he said, setting them down and moving to the stack of pancakes and waffles he had made and placed on the clean side of the table.

"So, you opened a bakery?" Ana laughed. She took a seat and lifted a spare plate, looking up at him as he placed a bowl of chopped berries in front of her.

"No. I couldn't sleep after my mom scolded me for a few hours, so I sat up all night doing more research on the next part of the clue from the parchment. Then I couldn't see straight, so I went for a run, and then my legs got tired, but my eyes still weren't, and it was morning, so I thought I'd make you breakfast." Ezra shrugged as he finally sat down opposite her.

"You made me *all* of the breakfasts."

"Well, I didn't know what you liked." Ezra commented, then lifted a waffle onto his plate, beginning to pile it high with cream and honey and chopped fruits.

"Where is your mom?" Ana asked as she pulled one of the hot croissants onto her plate and lifted a knife and fork. She sliced it open to find chopped cherry tomatoes, ham, and cheese, and her mouth watered at how good it looked.

"She left for the shop this morning. I gave her the athame to put in the temple with the box, so it is safe. She told me all about your reading and that I should ask you if you have thought more about what she said." Ezra took a bite of his food and looked up at her with a hopeful look in his eyes. "I don't want to run from this because it might be dangerous. I owe it to Nina to see this through, to get closer to the items and maybe find out who did this to her. If I can tempt them with getting close to me to get to the objects, I could catch her killer. I can't let that go, but I understand if it's too risky for you. I wouldn't blame you if you wanted to go home."

Ana sighed deeply as she thought. She wanted to help him find the objects. She wanted the story and the opportunity to prove herself, but she didn't feel that she was any match for a murderer. Looking up at him and how hopeful he looked, she realised she couldn't let him do it alone, either.

"Well, she drew the two of cups for us, right? Which if I recall correctly, means that we are an equal team. I'm in this until the end if you are. I can't let you go at this alone." Ana smiled, taking a bite of the hot croissant and moaning at how good it tasted.

Ezra grinned at her as he cut up more of his waffle, chuckling a little to himself.

"What?" Ana asked, setting her fork down.

"That's not all the two of cups mean," he said with a small shrug, looking up at her from under his messy hair.

Ana blushed deeply, thinking back to the description that Genevieve had given her. She knew Ezra was waiting on a reaction, but she refused to give him one, and simply took another bite of her croissant.

"What else did your mother talk to you about? Why is she so mad at you?" She asked, reaching for a glass and filling it with the orange juice that sat between them.

Ezra winced and finished off his waffle, then sat back with his cup of coffee and looked up at her from over the rim. "She figured out that I did something I shouldn't have been doing. She wasn't happy and reminded me of a few things I had forgotten. It's fine; she will cool off."

"What shouldn't you be doing?" Ana asked.

"It doesn't matter," he said as she shot him an unimpressed look that suggested he continue. "You wouldn't believe me anyway."

"Fine. I won't pry," Ana said defensively, then sat up in her chair. Her stomach felt wonderfully full, and she stretched her arms to shake out the sleepiness from them. "Can you at least tell me what you found out about the next clue?"

"That, I can do. Come with me."

He stood from his chair and walked around the kitchen island and through the hallways. She followed him to a door that led into a small office. Books covered every inch of the wall, except for a blackboard that was screwed against the wall and had white chalk scribblings all over it. A desk sat in the middle of the room, and it had papers littering the top. Right in the middle of the papers, basking in the sun, lay a large black cat. He stretched and rolled in protest to the interruption, then raised his head up and yawned, looking between them both with an unamused expression.

"You have a cat?" Ana asked, petting his head. He curled into it and jutted his chin out for her to scratch it, and when she did, his ears went flat and his eyes closed happily as he purred.

"Raja is my mom's cat." Ezra said, moving around the table and lifting some papers from underneath the cat.

"Is this her office?" Ana suggested, sitting down in the spinning office chair. The cat moved from the interruption of Ezra grabbing the papers, and he leapt off the table, sauntering out of the door with his tail in the air.

"No, this was my dad's office when he lived here. He left all of his books, so I guess it's kind of my office when I need it." Ezra examined the pages in his hand, walked to the blackboard, and wrote the second of the clues on the board:

The second of us you will learn,
has been the reason of many a witch burned.
Taken from us and hung with twine,
you will find me with one of the Harrow bloodline.

"So, taking it in reverse, the Harrow bloodline is the family and descendants of the original Harrow from the mid-to-late 1500s. Thomas Harrow was a witch hunter. From 1560 onwards, he was responsible for the deaths of countless people over the whole of Europe. He single-handedly started a witch hunt that spread all over the continent and ended in the trial of over 100,000 women and men. As a result, 40,000 people were executed without hesitation."

"He sounds like a grade-A asshole." Ana frowned, bringing her knees to her chest as she spun the chair around and back again.

"Yes, well, what made it even worse was that when someone was accused of witchcraft, their lands and their money and any other valuables went straight to the local mayor and his witch hunter, meaning that Thomas Harrow became an extraordinarily rich man. It is pretty obvious that the majority of the people executed were not witches, but Thomas simply wanted their lands and their money for his own personal gain." Ezra sat on the edge of the table with his arms folded.

"So, he is a murdering thief. Fantastic. I'm guessing whatever the object is that is, he took it when he burned the Marion coven?" Ana asked, stopping her spinning.

"Precisely. I have done a lot of reading and have managed to follow the bloodline all the way to present day, and more importantly, where the antiques and treasures were passed down to. Thomas Harrow had only one son, and in the late 1600s, after his father died, George Harrow commissioned a mansion with his fathers' money. It's one of the biggest mansions in the country. Inside the mansion, he kept all of his fathers' treasures in storage, and it was passed all the way down to a Mrs Cecelia Harrow. She is eighty-six years old and still lives in part of the mansion; the other half is now a museum that is open to the public to show all the treasures and the highly edited history of their family." Ezra said as he turned to look at her with a smug smile.

"You certainly did your research, didn't you?" Ana commented, then stood off the chair and walked closer to the board, examining the scribblings. She reached up and pointed to the verse that spoke about the object that was hung with twine, and she tapped it with her finger, "Have you figured out this part yet?"

"No. That is the only thing I haven't managed to crack. Whatever it is though, if there is any trace of it or if there are any links to where it could have gone, it will be at the mansion." Ezra said.

"Okay, so I guess it's time for another road trip then. Where is the mansion?"

"It's only an hour's drive. It's located inside the Cherry Grove Estate, though I should clean up the kitchen before we leave, and shower." Ezra smiled as he looked down at his batter covered clothes and moved to the door.

"I can meet you outside by the car in thirty minutes?"

Ana followed him out into the hall. "Sure. Do you think I could borrow some of Abby's clean clothes?"

"Yeah, sure. It's not like she will notice. Thirty minutes." He said, then walked out the front door and disappeared down the path.

Ana watched him leave, then smiled and walked back up the wooden staircase.

She moved into Abby's room and closed the door behind herself. Opening the doors of the wardrobe, she began to sift through the clothes inside, running her fingers over the different dresses and shirts and jeans. Everything was black, which she didn't mind, but it was a completely different style than she was used to. She pulled out a plain black shirt that had a lacy collar and held it against her body in the mirror that hung on the door. It looked like it would fit, and she matched it with a pair of jeans that looked like the right size.

Taking off the night clothes, she pulled the jeans up over her hips and buttoned them, then put on the shirt before she quickly fixed her makeup in the mirror and put her hair up in a messy bun. Figuring Ezra was still showering, she grabbed an army-green jacket from Abby's wardrobe, slipped her shoes on, lifted her handbag and rushed down the stairs to the kitchen, where she began to clean the kitchen and put the extra food away.

Ana filled the sink with water, washing everything down and drying the dishes before she started to put them away. Ezra entered the kitchen, freshly dressed in a new white shirt that was rolled up at the sleeves and a pair of jeans, with big clunky black boots.

"Oh, you look like my sister in those. If your hair was dark, I'd be super confused. It's weird." Ezra laughed. "You cleaned?"

"Well, we need to get a move on if we want to get to the mansion, and you were taking your sweet-ass time." Ana smiled, drying her hands on the dishcloth and walking to him after she finished wiping down the benches. "Let's go."

Ezra watched her as she walked past him, looking over her shoulder at him and waiting for him to follow her. "Yes, boss."

CHAPTER 16

"*Y*ou know, it would be a lot safer if you would just let me drive," Ana said as she sat back in the chair of the Beetle, holding onto the handle on the door with one hand and gripping the strap of the seatbelt with the other.

Ezra had swerved into a ditch a few times on the country road on the way to the mansion, trying to avoid the odd pheasant, and miraculously managed to steer the car back onto the road without crashing.

"I will admit I am not the best driver in the world. . ." Ezra started, then shot her an unamused frown when she snickered at him. "It's not my fault! This is an estate in the country, Ana. There is going to be wildlife, and I'd rather not kill something on the way."

"If you have to choose between killing us, or killing a pheasant, I choose the pheasant," Ana said with a raised eyebrow.

They had just turned into the Cherry Grove Estate, and as they drove through the large double gates and high stone walls, Ana was struck silent by the beauty of the landscape. The lane that led them through the estate was covered in huge cherry blossom trees. They fanned out in every shade of pink she could imagine, with some rare ones in white that popped out behind the pink ones.

"Wow, this is stunning! Now I know why they call it Cherry Grove Estate," she said as she pressed up against the passenger side window.

Ezra watched her as he drove, a warm smile coming over his face, and he laughed softly.

"What?" Ana smiled, sitting back again. The lane was getting wider, and less bumpy as it smoothed out onto a tarmacked road.

"Nothing." He laughed. "You are cute when you get excited, that's all."

Ana bit her lip and looked forward at the road. "There just isn't anything this beautiful in the city."

Ezra looked back at her and smiled again, then cleared his throat and pulled into another road that led to a carpark. He parked in one of the empty spaces and turned the engine off, looking out of his window at the building.

It was small for a mansion but still huge in comparison to any house she had ever lived in. It had large stone stairways that curved up each side of the house and met in the middle at the entrance. The building was three stories high, with large windows and tall, beautiful columns.

"It was built in the late 1600s, at least part of it was, then it was finished in the early 1700s. It's a lovely example of baroque architecture, but a little too fancy of a house for my taste." Ezra explained as he got out of the car and walked up the gravel walkway towards the entrance.

"The museum part is in the back in the gardens, according to the map I saw."

Ana was still staring up at the building and had to jog after him to catch up. "I wouldn't mind living here at all. It's beautiful."

They walked together around the stone staircase, over the gravel path, and along the side of the high stone walls of the

Harrow mansion. Around the side of the building, signs pointed over the gardens to a separate building on the estate grounds. It wasn't far, and it didn't take them long to walk peacefully through a massive garden that had perfectly trimmed hedges and beds of roses. A fountain was erected in the middle, featuring a golden saint that stood proudly at its top and watched over his domain.

The museum was positioned at the very bottom of the gardens. Whilst small and simple, it was a very modern build in comparison to the Harrow mansion. It had white walls and a heavy wooden door, with large glass windows and sculptures at its entrance. Upon arrival, Ana realised the door was closed, and she frowned as she tried to push it open. It didn't budge.

"It's closed. Didn't you check the opening times before we left?" Ana asked as she turned to him and shielded her eyes from the sun.

"I did. They said they are open until 17:00." Ezra frowned.

He moved closer to the door and knocked against the wood with three hard *thumps*, then pressed against the window with his hands cupped around his face.

"Hello?!" he called, then sighed before hammering the door with his fist again.

"Can I help you?"

They spun around to see an older man standing on the other side of the building. He wore a suit and had a small pair of glasses on his face, and a steaming cup of tea in his hands. His face held an unimpressed expression, and he was looking at them with a sense of impatience.

Ana smiled sheepishly and stepped in front of Ezra, extending her hand out to the man for him to shake. "Hi. Sorry for the intrusion. Are you closed for lunch?"

"We are closed, my dear, but not just for lunch. We are moving some things around inside for a new display, so we are closed for the week. You will have to come back," he said, hastily shaking her hand and then dropping it quickly.

"That's not going to work for us," Ezra asserted, walking to them and folding his arms.

Ana could practically see his thoughts racing through his head as he tried to think of an excuse as to why they needed to be inside.

"I am with the insurance company that insures the items in this museum. I assume you have been expecting someone to come along and make sure this was all above board and that nothing goes missing in the transit?" Ezra asked. He had a serious look on his face, and Ana was surprised at how quickly he could change character.

The man spluttered and looked around him as if to ask for help from a colleague, but there was no one else, only him. "I was told by your office that all we needed was to take an inventory check before and after we moved things around, and unless we had any problems, you didn't need to send anyone out."

"Yes, well, we reviewed that again and it seems the items inside are too valuable to be so flippant about. I am sure Mrs Harrow would agree that she would rather her valuables be treated with the utmost care. If there is a problem with us getting inside to do the valuations, I can call her myself." Ezra reached for his pocket.

"No! No, please. She is already incredibly stressed about the reopening; this will put her in an even worse mood. I told her this was handled. Please. Do not call her," he exclaimed as he rubbed his forehead.

Ezra gave him a weak smile and returned his hand to his side. "That can be avoided. She doesn't even have to know we came. I'm sure we can help you out by doing the valuations quietly and I can have the office send the paperwork directly to you by the end of the day. Mrs Harrow doesn't need to know about the mix-up."

The man gave a sigh of relief and smiled at Ezra, nodding

eagerly. "Thank you. Give me a moment to get the keys. Stay right there."

As the man rushed off, Ana looked to Ezra with her mouth open in shock. "That. . .That was-"

"Genius? I know." Ezra smiled.

"How the hell did you know that was going to work?" she asked, giving him a playful shove as she laughed.

Ezra shrugged and folded his arms against his chest. "Well, I simply deduced that when a museum is doing a re-work, that maybe they had an insurance company that would need to-"

"You had no idea it was going to work, did you?" Ana shook her head.

"Not a clue, no." Ezra laughed.

The man didn't take long to come back. He was taking fast, long strides across the gravel and was fumbling with a set of keys in his hand. "Just one moment."

Ezra stepped back from the door and mouthed for her to play along. She nodded in reply and moved forward into the building when the door was opened, and the man disappeared inside.

He switched on the lights as they entered, and the large room illuminated in light, revealing white walls and glass cabinets filled with trinkets and items of clothing and jewellery. There was a large painting on the wall of a man who stared coldly and wore a heavy black fur coat and a hat with a feather. The rest of the room was filled with boxes and sheets that covered statues she couldn't see.

"Well, here it is," the man announced.

"Yes. Thank you. Is there anything missing from the collection presently?" Ezra asked as he surveyed the room.

"No, everything should be accounted for," he said, then looked at Ezra suspiciously. "Shouldn't you have the inventory checklist?"

Ezra looked to him a little dumbly, then shrugged, and renewed his smile before pulling his phone from his pocket. "I do. Though everything is done digitally these days, so it's all in here." He pretended to search his phone for something. "My colleague and I will be quick. You don't need to stay if you have things to do."

"Hmm. I think I will stay by the door, thank you," the man said, eyeing him one last time and then walking away from them to hover near the door.

"He's on to you," Ana whispered when she came to Ezra's side.

"Just stay in character. I need you to look over all the cabinet's contents and see if you can find anything with the Marion coven symbol on it. If you spot anything, let me know." Ezra said, then moved away from her to the middle of the rows of displays and began to search.

Ana sighed, looking over her shoulder to the man at the door and giving him another sheepish smile. She then moved to the opposite side of the room to observe the objects behind the glass. There were books, diamonds and some pottery and old plates that were preserved well. Some cases contained folded women's clothing and shackles, and as she moved from one cabinet to another, she came upon one that had a noose hanging from the ceiling. She frowned deeply, then looked behind it to the description.

"The mercy rope.
As our ancestor Thomas Harrow cleansed the lands of witches and their practices, doing God's work in the eyes of his followers, he was not without mercy.
During the burnings, oftentimes winds would blow too freely and would dull the flames, making the deaths of the witches longer and more painful.
In 1595, Thomas Harrow decreed that every person sentenced to the stake would have a rope around their neck that the executioner could pull, giving them a much quicker and painless death."

Ezra came up behind her, thinking she had found an item with the Marion mark, but when he saw the noose, he matched her frown and leaned into her ear. "That's actually true. Though the thing they leave out of that statement is that the rope would burn, and the victim could come back from their dizziness and end up roasting for longer. Like I said, highly edited. Keep looking."

Ana gulped, a hand instinctively going to her neck, and she forced herself to move away from the rope and examined the other cabinets. She could see nothing that bore the mark of the Marion coven, and she was beginning to think that maybe they were barking up the wrong tree.

She came to the portrait of Thomas Harrow and looked up at it with its gilded gold frame. It was big and looked expensive. The man in the painting was hard looking, with deep creases in his face and highly focused eyes that would burn anyone if they were real. His fingers were dripping in jewels and rings, most of them stolen, she figured. Getting closer to it, she realised his coat was made from bear fur and it was clasped around his chest by a gold chain that kept it tight to his body. Hanging from his neck on a piece of twine, she could see a circular pendant that had a large hole in the middle, like a flat decorative hoop. It didn't look as expensive as any of the other jewellery he had on his body. It was simple, flat, and plain, all except for a little squiggle of an engraving at the bottom of it. She tilted her head to the side, trying to see it from another angle, and she gasped, her eyes going wide and looking at Ezra so fast she craned her neck.

"Ezra!" she hissed, waving him over when she got his attention.

He walked to her quickly, ignoring the eyes from the door that were watching him, and he looked at the painting to where she was pointing. He seemed confused for a moment, then his eyes went wide when he spotted the sigil on the pendant. "That has to be it. It's hung with twine."

He turned on his heel and pulled her sleeve to tell her to follow him, guiding her to a glass cabinet in the corner of the room. Behind it stood a mannequin that had the same clothes and cloak on it that

Thomas Harrow was wearing in the portrait, and there, laying against the black bear fur, was the gold pendant. It was bigger than it looked in the painting, and was a little more worn, but it was identical. The Marion coven sigil was etched into the bottom side of it, and it had the large hole in the middle where the twine was tied.

"There it is." Ezra gasped.

"It doesn't look like anything. It's just a gold, flat hoop," Ana said with a small frown.

"Looks can be deceiving, Ana. It's the perfect shape of the missing piece in the athame. I would bet my life on that hoop fitting inside the missing space perfectly," Ezra said as he placed his hand against the glass.

"How exactly are we supposed to get it with him watching?" Ana said, jutting her chin at the man at the door.

"Keep a look out for me?" Ezra asked.

Ana took a few steps away from him to shield his hands with her body.

Ezra pushed his hands against the glass. It rattled, and he frowned when he found it locked. Pressing his finger against the silver keyhole on the glass, he turned to look at Ana with a shake of his head.

"All done?" the man asked.

"For now, yes. Thank you for all of your help. I will send through the paperwork tonight." Ezra said, a wide, fake smile plastered on his face. He turned from the cabinet and walked to the door, shoving his phone back into his pocket.

Ana passed the man and gave him a thin smile, following Ezra out into the sun of the gardens again. "Have a nice day!" she called back, then caught up to Ezra and nudged him. She waited until the man was out of earshot, and then leaned into him closely, "Did you get it?"

"No. It was locked, and he was watching. The security cameras were recording too. If I took it, we wouldn't make it back to the car before the dogs would be set on us."

"Okay so what do we do?" she asked, speeding through the paths between the rose bushes and hedges.

"I'm thinking" He mumbled back.

They walked back the rest of the way in silence, Ezra deep in his thoughts and Ana watching over her shoulder in case someone caught onto their lie and followed them. When they got back to the car, Ana turned to look at Ezra expectantly.

"Well? What are we going to do? You know he is going to check up on the insurance company when they don't send them the information we promised, so he isn't going to let us back in again."

Ezra put the keys in the ignition and started the car, beginning to drive out of the carpark and down the little road that led them through the cherry trees. "I know. That's why we are going to break in and steal it."

CHAPTER 17

"*I* promise we won't get caught!" Ezra pleaded as he chased after Ana into Genevieve's house.

Ana was fuming, shaking her head vigorously before swinging open the door. Genevieve was sitting in the kitchen at the island, sipping her tea and eating some of the left-over waffles that Ezra had made that morning.

"No! Absolutely not! I will not have you turn me into a criminal, Ezra! First, you make me an accomplice to you stealing a rare book from a library, and now you want me to help you with a heist? No way!" Ana shouted, looking to his mother with wide, exasperated eyes. "Your son wants to turn me into a thief!"

Genevieve sighed as she finished her mouthful and took a gulp of her tea, "What *kind* of thief?"

"What?" Ana asked, her shoulders sagging in exhaustion. She had been arguing with him the whole way home and had expected Genevieve to be the voice of reason.

"In my defence," Ezra said, closing the front door and walking into the kitchen with a pant from chasing her, "It was already stolen from the witches so technically, I'm just taking it back from people who shouldn't have had it in the first place. Call me Robin Hood."

"You are not stealing from the rich to give to the poor, Ezra. You are just stealing," Ana snapped as she put her hands on her hips and watched him with a frown.

"Okay, all right, both of you, stop arguing and sit down," Genevieve said as she tapped the space in the middle of the table. "Now."

Ana and Ezra moved without saying another word and sat beside each other at the table. When they looked up at her, she smiled warmly and nodded for Ezra to speak.

"We found the piece we were looking for. It's in the Harrow museum, but it is behind locked glass and in a locked building, with security cameras. I know I can get past the locks easily and I can disable the cameras; it won't be hard to do." Ezra said, looking between Ana and his mother.

"If it's not hard to do, why do you need me?" Ana asked, folding her arms. "I am not comfortable stealing from an old lady."

"That old lady has profited off the torture and deaths of our people to get where she is, Ana. I feel absolutely no guilt for stealing that item. The fact of the matter is, we can't continue this investigation without that pendent. It is as simple as that." He sat back with a shrug and placed his hands behind his head to stretch. "I don't need you to actually steal anything. I will do the stealing, so your conscience will be clear; I just need you to be my lookout."

Ana gave a frustrated whine, then looked to Genevieve for help. "Can you please talk some sense into him? We are going to end up getting arrested."

Genevieve sighed deeply and took another contemplative sip of her tea. "This is how I see it: You both need this item to move forward. Without it you are stuck. I assume there is no way she will sell it to you?"

"Not a chance. It is part of the exhibit," Ezra said with a shake of his head.

"So, we are back to stealing it. Like Ezra said, it was taken from our people a long time ago, and brutally so. Taking it back seems like a fitting response, but my issue is this: If you succeed in taking it, go forward with this investigation, and release the find as you want to, what will you do when they inevitably find out that it was you who stole it?" Genevieve asked, giving her son a frown.

"I have already thought about that. They have it hung on twine on the clothes Thomas Harrow wore. It's being conveyed as a pendant because he wore it around his neck, but I don't think it is a pendant at all, Mom. It's the same shape and size as the missing part in the athame. I would bet my life on it fitting inside that space *perfectly*. When we find the third piece and it fits inside the last space on the athame, then all three pieces will make the athame complete. It won't be a pendant anymore and no one will notice that it is what it is." Ezra showed off a triumphant grin.

"You think you are so smart, don't you?" Genevieve laughed, sitting back in her chair.

"Well. . ." Ezra shrugged with a smile.

"If you think you can get away with taking it, then take it."

"Genevieve, please don't encourage him," Ana begged as she put her head in her hands.

"I am sorry, Ana, but there is no other way. You both need this piece to move on. If Ezra thinks he can take it without being caught, then I trust him." Genevieve stood from her chair and placed her cup in the sink. "I am going to leave you both to figure this out, I have a date. Whatever it is you decide to do, please do it safely."

She kissed her son's head, then pat Ana on the shoulder before grabbing her handbag from the table in the hall and closing the door after herself.

Ezra turned in his chair to look at Ana and smiled at her, reaching to take her hand and squeezing it. "I know you are uncomfortable, and I know it's against your moral compass, but sometimes there is no other choice. Look at it like you are returning a religious relic to its rightful people."

"To *you*. You are not 'rightful people,' Ezra," Ana said as she looked down to her knees, letting him hold her hand. "What if we get caught?"

"I promise I will not let us get caught," he said as he moved his head to try to get her to look at him in the eyes.

Ana finally looked at him and sighed, "How can you promise something like that?"

"I promised I wouldn't let you fall and get hurt in that tower, and I kept that promise. Now I am promising you that I will not let us get caught." He leaned into her, trying to make her smile. "Do you trust me?"

"Absolutely not," Ana said with a laugh.

Ezra laughed at her, then let her go and sat upright in his chair. "Well, you can. I don't need you to steal anything. Just keep a lookout at the door for security, and I can do the rest."

Ana finally relented. She nodded slowly and then gave a nervous sigh, looking at him again in a sideways glance. "How do you plan on opening the lock and shutting down the cameras?"

"I will find a way." He reached for one of the strawberries that were left in the bowl on the table from breakfast.

"That doesn't help my nerves." Ana bit her lip in thought. "Okay, fine. I will help you steal the pendant, but in return, I am going to interview you for my story. Now."

Ezra blinked and looked at her, then gave a nervous laugh and popped the strawberry in his mouth. "What? Aren't you supposed to be doing that on my Mom and the store?"

"I am, but it's not just about her; it's also about the lives of people like her. We have time to kill before we drive back to Cherry Grove. I really need to get some information down on paper if I have any chance of doing the story that Elianna wants in time for the issue deadline."

Ezra thought about it for a moment, seeming a little uncomfortable at the idea. He shrugged, then leaned into her closely and smiled. "I can think of better ways to kill some time, rather than talking about my family."

Ana blushed at how close he was to her face. She gulped, taking a moment to watch his eyes as she felt a bubbling build in her chest before she placed her hand on his face and pushed him back with a small giggle. "Ezra, focus."

"All right, fine," Ezra said as he moved back from her and leaned on the table with his elbows. "What do you want to know?"

Ana reached for her bag that she had dropped at her feet and pulled out her notebook and pen, flipping it open to a clean page.

"I want to talk about what you and your family actually *are*, because I won't lie, I am a little confused." When she saw how confused he also looked, she stuttered and continued, "I-I mean Genevieve calls herself a witch, but aside from the Litha celebrations and the tarot card reading, I haven't seen any actual spells being cast."

"Well why would you? We like you, Ana, but you are not in our circle. You aren't one of us. We wouldn't just openly practice those kinds of things in front of an outsider. No offence, but you just wouldn't understand, and witchcraft is a very private affair. You don't show your craft to outsiders, ever. I got into quite a lot of shit for bringing you to the Litha celebrations, and you didn't even *see* any of the rituals," Ezra said as he reached for another strawberry.

Ana scribbled quickly in her notepad, jotting down everything he had said. She wouldn't admit it to him, but hearing that he considered her an outsider hurt a little. They hadn't made her *feel* like an outsider.

"Okay. So, you consider yourself a witch, then?" Ana asked.

"No, not anymore. I mean, I don't practice anymore. My mother and father and sister all are still practicing, though."

"Why don't you practice anymore?" she asked, looking up at him and watching how anxious his face had grown.

"That's. . .complicated." Ezra mumbled, playing with the strawberry in his hand.

Ana sighed as she nudged him, making him stumble and he had to grab the strawberry before it fell. "Uncomplicate it."

Rolling his eyes, Ezra turned to look at her fully again. "I was banned from practicing any form of the craft. I did something bad, and it had consequences, so the High Council banned me from ever practicing again."

Ana paused and stopped writing as she watched how sad his expression was. Her mind was racing, trying to figure out what was inside his head. "Who is the High Council?"

"The High Council is a group of the high priests and priestesses in our coven. My father is the highest, so, he oversees the rest of the council." He frowned, appearing more and more uncomfortable.

"And what did you do that was so bad you were banned?" Ana asked, moving closer to him, as if his eyes would tell her.

"I can't tell you that. You wouldn't believe me anyway, and it's not something I can tell someone who isn't in our coven. I'm sorry, those are the rules. I didn't make them." He threw his hands up defensively and gave her a forced smile, "But I'd appreciate it if we moved on from this line of questioning."

Ana pouted and sat up straighter, then pulled her notepad closer to her again. "I will find out, you know."

Ezra smirked.

"I have every faith in your investigating abilities."

Ana smiled and looked back at her notepad, beginning to write again. Her mind was going a mile a minute trying to think what it was he could have done to warrant being banned. The witchcraft his family did, from what she saw, was earth religion based. It was offerings and manifestation, but there wasn't any actual magic involved, not that magic existed. She had expected to see more spell work or even a ritual or two by now.

"From what I have seen, the witchcraft you speak of is rooted in religion, not magic. The rituals and offerings you give, what God are they for? Do you have a God?" Ana said as she looked up with a small wince, not wanting to ask the obvious question that had been burning at the front of her mind since she walked into Genevieve's store.

Ezra laughed and folded his arms across his chest, swinging back on his chair a little. "Go on, ask the question, you know you are dying to."

Ana winced again, then tapped her pen on the notepad. "Do you worship the devil?"

Ezra laughed loudly again, almost tipping his chair too far back and having to right it again. "No. The devil, or Satan, or whatever you want to call him, he is a Christian deity. He has nothing to do with our practices. You are safe." He reached forward to poke her nose.

"But for now, our interview is done. We need to gather everything we need before we head back to Cherry Grove."

"One more thing," Ana said as she closed her notebook and looked up at him when he stood up from his chair. "Do you think I will ever get to stand in on a ritual, so I can see what happens behind the scenes?"

Ezra smiled down at her and pushed his seat into the table neatly. "For your sake, I hope not."

CHAPTER 18

he road was quiet as Ana and Ezra sat parked opposite the gates of the Cherry Grove Estate. The gates were closed, but the streetlights that flanked either side of it were off, making the entry way seem even darker than it should have been. The clock on the radio in the car read 00:02. By now, the lights on the grounds should be turned off, security would be hunkered down by their screens instead of doing patrols, and anyone living inside the Harrow mansion should be asleep.

Ana looked out of her window at the high walls and the iron gate nervously. She was gripping a flashlight in her hands, and it was shaking at the idea of breaking into such a heavily guarded place.

"I don't think I'm ready." She gulped.

"You can do this, Ana. All you have to do is stand at the door of the museum, and watch out for any flashlights or security, and I will do the rest," Ezra said as he watched out the window. He had a serious look on his face, and his eyes were focused on the gates as he tried to spot a way inside. "We have parked just out of sight of the cameras at the gate, so if I time it right, I should be able to run up to them and black them out before they see me."

Ana looked down to his hands where he was holding the can of spray paint he had grabbed from his shed at home. "Won't they notice that the cameras have gone dark?"

"Probably. But by the time they notice, we will have been in and out, so long as the timing is right." He reached into his bag in the back seat and pulled out two black baseball caps. He pulled one onto his head and then reached to pass her the other. "Put this on and keep your head down."

"Why do I have the unsettling feeling that this isn't the first time you have done this?" Ana asked, frowning as she put it on her head and tucked her ponytail up inside.

"The less you know the better." He smiled.

Ezra looked over his shoulder and back to the gates, eyeing the curves of the metal, and he finally nodded and opened his door. "I am going to disable the cameras, as soon as I give you the signal, you need to run to me, and I will give you a boost over the gate."

Before Ana could protest, Ezra was already pulling black gloves onto his hands and bouncing out of the car. He hovered at the side lines until he saw the camera above the gates begin to move to scan the area, and when it pointed in the opposite direction, he bolted across the path. The camera was moving slowly, giving him time to reach the gate where it was anchored to one of the posts at the wall, and he climbed. After reaching the top and looping his hand under it, he pushed down on the nozzle, spraying the entire front of the camera in black paint that began to drip. Once he was done, he jumped back down again and looked at the car, waving for Ana to join him.

Ana watched him wave to her with wide eyes. Her feet felt like they were frozen to the floor of his car, and it took everything in her to will them to move. When she was able to, she gulped and opened the car door, closing it quietly behind her and jogging across the deserted road while zipping up the black hoodie he had given her.

"Okay, you need to climb. I will help you up," Ezra instructed as he took her hand and helped her hook her feet into the curved metal of the gate.

Ana held onto the bars, pulling herself up little by little until Ezra was able to stand under her and hold onto her feet. He pushed them up, giving her a high boost that made her wobble, but she steadied herself and reached the top. Then she threw her leg over and lay low against it to pull the other leg over. When she managed it, she smiled in relief and climbed down halfway, then jumped the rest and stood back, looking up at the high gate.

"See? Easy," Ezra said as he jumped. He scrambled up quicker than Ana had, and when he reached the top, he jumped over it without needing to climb down, landing in front of her with a bend to his knees. "We need to get into the trees."

Grabbing her hand, Ezra took off in a jog and guided her off the driveway and into the groves of the cherry blossom trees. In the sunlight, they had looked so beautiful in their hues of pinks and purples, and Ana had loved watching the petals fall delicately when the wind blew through their branches. In the dark, the trees looked sharper. Their branches snapped at odd angles and the hanging blossoms swayed in the breeze in a way that made them look like they were reaching to grab hold of them.

The run towards the mansion was surprisingly quiet. There were no guards or security cameras to worry about among the trees, but when they got closer to the building and the more well-lit the area became, the faster her heart beat in her chest. Ezra pulled her along through the rest of the trees and onto the gravel path, where they both ducked down low and ran to the wall at the far side of the building where the signs that pointed to the gardens were. Standing with their backs against the wall, they both looked to each other, silently making sure the other was okay.

During the research they did on the Harrow mansion grounds, they knew that the only cameras on the outside of the mansion were at the gates, the main doors, and the door of the museum. That left the gardens free of any cameras that may spot them.

Ezra nodded for her to move again. He took her hand and walked along the wall until they made it to the stone steps at the back of the mansion. Then they took off in a run, and Ezra guided her down the steps and into the gardens, past the hedges and rose bushes, and around the side of the fountain. The water pump was turned off now, leaving the water eerily calm. Looking up at the gold saint that sat atop and watched over his domain, Ana almost sensed that he was looking down at them in judgement. In the sunlight, his features had been serene and holy, but tonight, in the darkness of the gardens, they almost looked sharp and angry, like he was trying to warn them from going any further. Since her speed slowed down, Ezra jerked her faster across the gravel of the pathway and pulled her beside a tall bush opposite the small museum building to shield them from anyone who might have been watching them. He was panting, his chest rising and falling rapidly as he gripped her hand.

"I am going to black out the cameras with the spray paint. When I'm done, I will call you over. You need to come as soon as I call you, because when I'm done with the spray paint, I am going to break the lock." Ezra poked his head around the side of the bush. They were just out of sight in their current position, but the mere mention of them made Ana's head feel light.

"Ezra, be careful. . ." She gulped.

He didn't waste any time, simply giving her an abrupt nod and then dropping her hand. When the perfect moment came, he scrambled, his feet slipping on top of the gravel. He was so fast that it took Ana a moment to even realise he was gone, and when she popped her head around the side of the hedge he was already against the wall of the museum and was using the ledge of the window to push up on with his foot and grab onto the camera. He had the paint can in his hands, and after managing to get up high enough, he pushed down on the nozzle and sprayed the camera until it was blacked out. Finishing the first, he jumped down again and moved to the other, using the ledge to push up onto the window again. He blackened the other, finally dropping to the ground with a triumphant grin.

When she heard him call her, Ana's feet moved on their own, bringing her to his side quickly just as he was throwing the spray can onto the nearby grass.

"Keep a lookout. I need to work on the lock."

Ana nodded, her eyes wide and full of fear, but she held strong and placed her back against the wall, surveying the gardens and the mansion. So far, no one was in sight, and no sounds were heard.

Beside her, Ezra had his hands placed flat against the lock, covering it with his palm and closing his eyes. Frowning in confusion, Ana walked closer to his side and looked to his face, noticing his look of concentration.

"You aren't even looking at it. Are you sure you know how to do this?" she said.

"Stop looking at me and keep a lookout!" he hissed, his eyes snapping open to look at her. He made sure she was looking away from him before he placed the palm of his hand over the lock and closed his eyes again.

After a few long moments, Ana heard a loud *click*. Ezra opened his eyes and grinned down at the lock as he took his hand away from it and tried the handle. To Ana's surprise, it was met with no resistance, and the door opened wide with ease.

"How did you do that?" she asked, looking between him and the doorway, her mouth agape.

"Magic." Ezra smirked.

"Very funny. Just hurry and get that pendant."

Ana was left outside on her own when Ezra walked inside the

building. There was a faint beeping coming from somewhere, like an alarm waiting on a code, but it clicked off a few seconds after Ezra got inside. She stood with her back against the wall beside the door, her eyes trained on the areas that surrounded them. The garden seemed quiet, but over the silence she could sense something in the distance to her right near a door at the back of the Harrow mansion. There was movement there, and the more Ana focused her eyes, the more she made out the outline of a figure.

A light switched on, illuminating a man holding a flashlight. He was opening the back door of the side of the mansion and was beginning his rounds of the grounds. Following the path with her eyes, she realised that the route he would walk would take him directly to them. She gasped and forced herself to enter the museum to look for Ezra. He had the door of the glass cabinet open and was holding the golden pendant in his hands.

"Someone is coming!" she whispered as she rushed to his side and grabbed his arm. "We need to go!"

Ezra nodded, shoving the pendant into his pocket, and then took her hand. As they approached the door, they noticed the pathway outside grow brighter from the shaky beam of a flashlight. It was close. Too close for them to be able to slip out and not get caught.

"What do we do?!" Ana hissed, tears pricking at her back of her eyes and her cheeks beginning to feel hot.

Ezra stopped moving; he seemed to be thinking and had a look of panic on his face. He snapped his head back to look at her and gave her a stern nod. "You need to do *exactly* as I say."

Ezra pulled her to the corner of the room and held her against the wall, pressing his body against hers as if he was trying to push her as far into the corner as he possibly could, like he was trying to shield her from whoever was coming into the building. He turned his head away from the door and peered into her eyes, leaning close to her and pressing his index finger against her lips in indication for her to stay quiet.

"Don't say a word. Don't flinch. Don't move," he whispered.

Ana nodded once to show him she understood and tried to relax against the wall as he held her there with his eyes closed. She gulped thickly and tried not to flinch when the door of the museum pushed open, and the room was illuminated by the flashlight in the hand of the security guard.

"Hello?" he called. He took a few steps inside the room and scanned the beam of light over the walls and the glass display cases.

Ana could feel her heart beating faster in her chest as the beam of light travelled over the walls. Her feet itched like they wanted to run, but Ezra kept a firm hold on her and moved his finger slowly from her lips so that he could put his hand over her mouth in case she whimpered, which was exactly what she wanted to do when the beam crept closer.

The security guard took a few extra steps into the room. From the light of the flashlight, she could see that he was an older man with greying hair on his head that was cut neatly and a beard that hung low against his collar.

He moved, shining the beam of light all the way over the room until it came to the corner they were standing in, and the light finally illuminated them.

Ana held her breath and widened her eyes, waiting for him to shout at them and move closer to them, but he didn't. He simply moved the flashlight onwards and circled around to the door he had come through. She gasped behind Ezra's hand, and the security guard flinched and spun back around, shining his light onto them again and making Ana's eyes hurt. She stayed deathly still, holding her breath, and waited until the man shrugged and turned, walking back out of the building and closing the door after him.

Ezra paused for a long moment until they both heard the guard walk away from the building before he finally removed his hand from Ana's mouth and let her go.

She gasped, pulling deep breaths into her lungs and trying to push away the fuzzy feeling of panic that was in her head.

"What the *hell* was that?" Ana gasped, pushing past him and walking to the window where she peeked around the corner of the blinds and watched as the man walked through the gardens. "How did he not see us?"

Ezra ignored her and placed his hand flat against his trouser pocket and felt for the pendant. When he was satisfied it was safe, he walked to her beside the window and tried the door handle. It opened a crack, and he breathed a sigh of relief.

"He must have thought the curator forgot to lock it. Clearly, he didn't have the keys, or he would have locked us in." He opened it wider and looked out the doorway to make sure the coast was clear.

"Ezra!" Ana snapped, making him jump and turn toward her. "How did he not see us? We were right *there*! He had his flashlight shining in our faces!"

Ezra shrugged, looking back out of the doorway. "I don't know. Luck I guess."

Ana gaped at him. "You better start telling me what the hell is going on, or I-"

"I really don't think this is the right time to start a debate, Ana, do you? I'd rather find a way out of here past that guard so we can go home."

Ana bit down on her tongue to stop herself from screaming at him. She clenched her fists and moved to shove him out of the way of the door. "Fine. But we are not done here."

She stormed out of the museum and quickly back to the shelter of the hedges, then crouched down and watched for movement. When she found the surrounding area quiet, she stood again and walked across the stone path. Ezra caught up with her and made it to her side, his long strides making him take the lead.

They made their way to the mansion walls. Placing their backs against the wall and shuffling along them, they poked their heads around the side of the building and looked to the car park. It was still deserted, and the security guard was nowhere to be seen.

"I think we are in the clear. If we run now, we can make it through the trees and back to the gate. Are you ready?" Ezra asked, looking sideways at her and giving a handsome smile.

Ana's anger melted, and she nodded, feeling her nerves alleviate, and she reached her hand out for him to take. "Ready."

Ezra smiled and laced his fingers with hers, then tugged her out from behind the wall, walking quickly over the gravel path and away from the Harrow mansion.

"HEY! STOP!"

Ezra snapped his head to look over his shoulder, and his eyes widened when the security guard shone his flashlight in their direction. He was standing in the doorway at the entrance of the Harrow mansion and was quickly starting his run down the stone steps.

"Shit! Run!"

Ana gasped, dropping his hand and running across the path and through the carpark. She could hear the security guard behind them, the sound of his shoes pounding against the tarmac. Ezra was ahead of her, guiding her into the trees and through the same route they had used when they arrived. It was downhill this time, which helped, but her legs still burned from her feet running on the uneven grassy terrain of the grove.

They were almost there. The gate was just up ahead, and as they came upon it, Ezra stopped running and waited for her to catch up.

"You need to be faster this time, Ana!" he asserted, grabbing her waist when she reached the gate and pushing her up.

Her feet were slipping in her panicked climbing, but she managed it, reaching the top just in time for the flood lights in the trees to turn on, blinding her. She froze, the sound of barking echoing against the trees and into her head.

"Ana, focus! Jump!" he said, scrambling up the gate quickly and meeting her at the top, where he threw his leg over and jumped over the side and onto the road. "I will catch you! Let go!"

The barking got louder, and she trembled while sitting atop the gate. Ezra was saying something to her, but all she could focus on was how bright the floodlights were and how loud the barking was.

"Ana!"

She looked down at him, her focus coming back to her when she saw his face and his outstretched hands, and she nodded, gulping moisture into her dry mouth and finally jumping off the gate.

Ezra caught her roughly, his elbow slamming into her ribs when she fell and she gasped, finding her feet and holding her side. She didn't have time to think about the pain, and instead, she pulled away from him and ran to the car with a limp just as the dogs reached the gate. They were rabid, clawing and biting at the metal.

Ezra opened the car with his clicker, and they both dived inside, closing the doors behind them with a *slam*. "Are you okay?"

Ana cried, holding her side with one hand and ripping his black baseball cap off her head before throwing it at the dashboard. "Just fucking drive!"

CHAPTER 19

*A*na got out of the car the second it stopped outside of Genevieve's house. Tears streamed down her face as she held onto her side where her ribcage met her skin and limped down the paved stone path that led to her front door.

"Wait!" Ezra hissed to her, locking his door and running up the path behind her. "It's too late. You will wake her up if you go inside at this hour. You will have to stay at my place."

Ana wanted to scream, but instead she sniffled and followed him down the second path and around the house. They walked through the garden and around the washing line until he stopped and opened the door to his little house. He walked inside and turned on the lights. Ezra extended his hand to her, but she brushed past him and moved to the kitchen table where she threw her handbag onto it and leaned onto the wood to support herself. She hiccupped in pain as she pulled up her shirt to look at her side.

"Are you all right?" he asked softly, making his way to her and reaching his fingers to grace the skin at her side.

Ana slapped his hand away from her, looking up at him with tears in her eyes. "Don't touch me."

"Ana, you need to let me see it. I need to feel if it's broken." Ezra reached out his hand to her again.

Ana's reflexes kicked in, and before she realised what she was doing, her hand flew to slap him across the face, sending him back as she spluttered, "You are an asshole."

A stifled growl came from deep inside Ezra's chest, like he was trying not to react so he wouldn't make things anymore worse than they already were. He rubbed his reddened cheek, then looked back to her face and shook his head. "Yes. I am. We have established that. Now will you let me take a look at you, please?"

He reached for her again, but Ana raised her hand to slap him again. He caught her arm by the wrist and held it tightly when she tried to take her arm back, and he leaned in close to her face. "One. You get *one*. Now stop being a baby and let me look at your side!"

Ana was breathing deep, angry breaths through her nose as he forced her arm up above her head and pulled her shirt up with his other hand. He ducked down, taking a look at the bruising skin at her ribs and placing his fingers to her ribcage. He pressed on it, making her hiss and flinch. "That hurts."

Ezra nodded, a serious look on his face as he finally pulled his fingers back from her skin and let her arm go. She rubbed her wrist from how hard he had to restrain her from hitting him again. "I don't think it's broken. It's probably bruising. You could get it checked out, but there isn't much a doctor can do other than give you pain medication. It needs to heal on its own."

"I shouldn't have to heal anything, Ezra. I didn't want to even be there tonight! It was dangerous, and we got caught, and I got hurt, and all you care about is that goddamn pendant!" Ana folded her arms across her chest.

"And all you care about is your story, right?" Ezra snapped, watching her closely. Her cheeks were reddening, and she was looking anywhere but him. "Don't throw this on me. I am doing what I need to do to get the result we are both searching for. This is the whole reason we are doing this, to find out the truth, so I can have my find, and you can have your story. I am willing to go to whatever lengths I need to so that we can finish this. You need to ask yourself if you are, too, because I can't do this alone. If you can't commit to what it takes, Ana, then go home."

Ana frowned and looked at her feet. She didn't want to go home. She wanted to see this through, to find out what all this was for, to get the story she needed to prove herself. Even as mad as she was at him, she wanted to be near him, too; she just didn't want to have to ignore her morals to do that. She gulped and set her jaw, then wiped her cheeks of her tears and looked up at him.

"Fine. But for your information, I am never breaking into anywhere with you again. Don't even ask, because the answer will be a *no*. I can't believe I let you talk me into it in the first place." She sniffled.

"It didn't take *that* much to convince you." He shrugged, a small smile curving at the edges of his mouth, "And I have a feeling you were only easily convinced because you want to solve this mystery just as much as I do."

Ana bit her lip and looked him in the eyes. They were kind again and had lost their anger from when she had hit him. "Maybe."

Ezra reached into his pocket and pulled out the pendant, holding it in the palm of his hand. He sat down on a chair at the wooden dining table and placed it on top to inspect it more closely. "It's beautiful. Solid gold, it looks like, with only one inscription," he said, running his finger over the Marion coven sigil.

Ana sighed and moved to sit beside him, holding her ribs with a wince as she did. Looking down at the pendant she noticed how it appeared more like a flat ring than a pendant, and the hole in the middle was more an oval in shape rather than circular.

"So, you think this piece fits inside the ringed hole that is missing from the athame we found at the tower?"

"I would bet my life on it," Ezra said as he leaned in closer, "It's decorative, which is possibly why Thomas Harrow thought it was a piece of jewellery."

Ana reached into her bag on the desk and pulled out the small digital camera and turned it on. After fixing the settings on the screen, she pulled it up to her eye and focused it, snapping a few close-up pictures of the pendant, the flash reflecting off the bright gold. She took a few more of him holding it.

Ezra jumped when he saw the flash and heard the click of the camera, and he reached his hand to grab it and pull it away from her face. "You can't show that to anyone, remember? Until it becomes part of the athame, we could get into deep shit if anyone knew what this was, and that it was stolen."

He took the camera from her as she pouted and looked at the screen, deleting the pictures she had taken, then smiled and turned it around so that the lens was facing them. "Though, we can document our find in another way."

"No! No, I am a mess. I'm tired, and I'm sore and I really don't want my picture ta-"

"Ana. Shut up." Ezra laughed, then turned so that they were side by side and held his arm out with the camera in his hand. "Say cheese."

Ana groaned, then leaned into his side so their heads were together, and she gave a smile for the camera when it flashed. Little light spots hovered in her eyes after he pulled the camera back down and passed it to her, and she took it back, looking down at the screen. It was a nice photo, she guessed, and it made her smile softly when she glanced at it.

"Okay, well, now you have your pendant and a selfie, I think it's time for me to go to bed," Ana said, looking at the clock on his wall. It read 02:22. She stood with a wince, using his shoulder to steady herself, and walked across the room towards his bedroom with her camera in her hand.

"That's *my* room." Ezra smirked as he stood from his chair and walked after her when she reached the door and opened it.

"Well, you only have one room, right? Where am I supposed to sleep?" Ana asked as she looked back at him after she flipped the light switch. The room was just as neat as it had been the last time she had been here. The bed looked fresh and cosy, and her legs ached to be off them and underneath the sheets.

"There is a perfectly good sofa out there. This is my room," he said, leaning on the doorway as Ana turned to face him with an unamused look on her face. He grinned cheekily, wiggling his brow at her and leaning in close, "Or we could always share?"

Ana smiled as he leaned in close to her face, and she tilted her head as she watched his eyes. She bit her lip gently and grinned when he leaned in even closer before she grabbed the door handle quickly and closed the door between them. "Nice try."

There was a groan on the other side of the door, and Ana laughed as she locked it and looked around his room. There was a large wardrobe and a full-length mirror in the corner that faced the bed, a desk filled with books and papers, and a little window with the curtains open that let the moonlight through. She sighed tiredly, then kicked her shoes off and pulled herself from her clothes, leaving them on the floor where they dropped. She stepped out of them, quickly turning the lights off and walking in her underwear to the bed, where she placed the camera on the bedside table. Pulling back the sheets, Ana got into the bed with a wince, pulled the sheets up to her chin and sunk into the mattress with a happy groan. Her body felt tired, and her feet throbbed in a dull ache, but she was warm now, and content, and she could feel the threat of sleep begin to sting the back of her eyes.

She must have fallen asleep quickly, and when she opened her eyes thinking it would be daylight outside, she was confused to find that the room was still plunged in darkness and the moon was still shining through the window. She groaned and rolled onto her back, looking to the clock and camera that was sitting on the bedside table. The clock read 04:47. Sitting up in the bed, Ana noticed how cold it was in the room. She could see her breath leaving her body in small clouds, and her skin had goosebumps, making her shiver and pull the sheets up around her tighter. That was when she noticed it.

The full-length mirror in the corner of the room was rocking on its legs, making the hinges squeak lowly. Her eyes widened, and she leaned forward to get a better look as to why it was rocking when she realised that she couldn't see herself in the reflection. There was no reflected bedroom, no sheets, no walls, no her. Instead, someone else's figure was standing there, swaying from side to side.

No. Not standing. Hanging.

She gasped, her breath catching somewhere in her throat as the light changed inside the mirror. The room she could see in the reflection wasn't Ezra's. It was the room of the Harrow museum where they had stolen the pendent from, and the person who was in it looked awfully like the security guard. He was hanging from the wooden beam by a rope around his neck, and he was clawing at it as he swung, his feet inches from the floor. Something moved behind him, and she realised that what she thought was the security guards shadow wasn't a shadow at all. It was a person, and they were stalking towards the mirror.

Ana tried to scream, but no sound came from her mouth. It just faded out into a soft croak in her throat as the shadow drew closer and closer, and reached for the mirror. It had no features, like it was a black void in the shape of a person. Its hands seemed longer than they should, like they had an extra knuckle on the end, and the tips of its fingers were pointed in black claws that pushed through the glass of the mirror like it was made of water.

It's just a dream. You are dreaming, Ana. Wake up!

She could hear her own voice in her head, but her body did not comply. It shook harder, and her breaths became more and more rapid as the full-bodied shadow gripped onto the edges of the mirror and crawled its way through the watery glass and into Ezra's room. It cracked its neck and reached to hold onto the wooden bedpost of the bed, crawling over the top of it and laying its black hands on top of the white sheets at her feet. Her legs wouldn't move.

There was a sound somewhere in the room. It was loud and it rang in her ears, and after a few seconds she realised she was screaming. Loud banging came from the bedroom door, like someone was trying to break in, but the figure just tilted its head at her and crawled further to where she was laying back against the pillows.

Think, Ana, think!

Light. The last time this happened, the last time she saw this shadow, it disappeared as soon as Ezra had turned on the light. She couldn't move to reach the light switch; it was too far on the other side of the room. She could move her eyes to look at the bedside table, where her camera lay, and she managed to fight through the fear that was radiating through her skin and push her hand out to grab it. She lifted it, pulled it back to herself and held it up against her face, where she closed her eyes and pushed down on the button. The camera turned on, and she heard the flash. A scream in the room that wasn't hers pierced the air, and when she opened her eyes, she could see the shadow retreating from the light like it had been burned. When the flash died away, it came for her again, so she held it out in front of her and kept pressing the button until the shadow screamed and thrashed, scrambling back to the mirror.

Finally, Ana felt her body again, and how raspy and sore her throat was from screaming. She was drenched in sweat, and tears were streaming down her face.

It wasn't a dream.

Ezra finally burst into the room, having to break the lock to do so. He turned on the light and rushed inside just as Ana noticed the mirror was reflecting the room again. Ezra was standing in his boxers, his eyes wide and his hair at all angles like he had woken up with a start.

"What's going on? What happened?!" he asked as he sprinted to her and sat down on the bed.

Ana was hysterical. She threw her camera aside and lunged on him for a hug with trembling arms, looking over his shoulder at the mirror. She couldn't explain what happened. Logically, that couldn't happen; shadow people don't just crawl out of mirrors. But it did happen, and she was terrified.

"The mirror! Someone came through the mirror. It was like a shadow but a person a-and the security guard was there, and he was hanging in the museum and I think the shadow person did it, a-and it came for me a-"

"You need to calm down," Ezra said as he held her tightly. He cupped her head and let her rest against his shoulder, allowing her to calm down as he rocked her. "It's okay."

"It's n-not okay!" she stuttered. "I think that security guard is dead! He looked so scared." She sniffled, pulling back to look at him. Her nose was running, and her eyes were puffy and red as she sat on the bed in her underwear. She was so glad to have him there she didn't even care that she was half-naked.

Ezra looked her over when she pulled back from him, checking her over for any marks, "Did it hurt you?"

"N-no, I don't think so," she sniffled, "What was that thing?"

Ezra sighed and reached to wipe her cheek dry with his thumb. "It's hard to explain, but tomorrow, I will do my best to help you understand. For now, you are safe. You should try to get to sleep. It won't be back. This place is supposed to be protected, it shouldn't have gotten in, but I forgot about the mirror. I'm so sorry."

"Have you seen one of those things before? It was huge and had long fingers and was completely black."

"I am very familiar, yes." He stood from the bed, moved to the full-length mirror and reached for the cloth that was hanging beside it. He gave it a once over, then put the cloth over it, covering all of the glass. "They are messengers who do the bidding of a witch or warlock. They can travel through mirrors, and since they are made from the shadows, they are allergic to light. Usually, when I'm in here, I'll have this covered just in case. I will explain more tomorrow, but you should sleep."

Ana's breathing was finally level again, and she had stopped crying long enough to pull the blanket up over her chest. Her head felt fried, like it didn't know what to think or believe. "Do you promise it won't come back?"

Ezra smiled softly and looked over his shoulder with a nod. "I promise." He walked to the door. "Get some sleep."

"Sleep with me?" Ana spluttered when he made to leave, and he turned to look at her with a raised eyebrow. "In the bed, obviously. Sleep with me in the bed. I mean, sleep *beside* me in the bed."

"I know what you meant." Ezra chuckled. He closed the door over and reached for the light switch.

"Leave it on?" she asked, shuffling over in the bed.

Ezra nodded patiently and dropped his hand, slipping in beside her and laying back against the pillows. He looked sideways to where she was laying, and how she was staring at the ceiling and trying not to cry.

"Come here," he said, opening his arm for her and waving her in.

Ana sniffled and looked sideways at him as she held the sheets to her skin and bit her lip as she thought about it. For once, she wasn't thinking about how good he looked in his underwear, how warm his smile was, or how green his eyes were. She just wanted his comfort. She nodded quickly and shuffled to him, coming into his side and wrapping her arm around his waist as she rested her head on his chest and he held her close to him. He was warm, but more importantly, he felt safe.

"Thank you," she mumbled against his chest.

Ezra smiled as he snuggled down with her and closed his eyes, giving her a comforting squeeze. "You're welcome."

CHAPTER 20

She had a restless sleep. Throughout the night she had awoken periodically to make sure the mirror was still covered and that Ezra was still there. Ezra had been patient, tucking her back into his side and telling her it was okay, and she was safe, and she would fall back to sleep again, only to repeat the process over again. When she awoke for the final time, she found herself wrapped around Ezra's middle with her head on his chest. He was awake, his eyes open and looking at the ceiling as if he was waiting for her to wake up on her own.

"Morning," he said, looking down at her as she raised her head.

"Hey. How long have you been awake?" She sat up on her elbows, blinking until her blurry vision righted itself.

"A while. You didn't sleep well, which means I didn't sleep much either. I figured it would be best not to wake you when you finally slept," Ezra said as he wiped his chest where Ana's head had been and moved his hands behind his head so that he could stretch. "You drool in your sleep, by the way."

Ana blushed deeply and wiped the corner of her mouth in embarrassment. "No, I don't."

"You do." He laughed. "But it's cute."

Ana blushed, looking away from him and internally cringing. To save herself from any more embarrassment, she turned from her front to lie on her back beside him and looked at the ceiling, so she didn't have to look in his eyes.

"Thank you, for staying with me all night," she mumbled, holding the bedsheets in balled fists so she could keep them close to her chest.

"It was really no big deal." Ezra smiled, looking sideways at her. She had the sheets clamped around her, now more aware of her modesty, and he recognised it. He let her have the blanket, then moved to get out of the bed. "It's after 10:00. We need to get changed so that we can get the pendant to my mom's temple for safekeeping."

Ana watched him. Now that her heart was at a steady pace and she wasn't crying or terrified, she let herself glance over his body as he stood in the room in his boxers. He was trying to fix his hair and didn't seem to notice her watching. To stop herself from letting her mind wander, she cleared her throat and looked up at his face instead. "You said you would explain to me what happened last night, about what that thing was that came for me."

"And I will," Ezra said as he walked to the door slowly, pointing to the mirror that was covered in the sheet in the corner. "When we are away from prying ears and in the safety of the temple. I will meet you outside."

He smiled as he left, and Ana noticed how he was careful not to look at her for too long to save her embarrassment. She was thankful for that, and when the door closed, she gave a deep sigh and groaned to herself.

"I don't drool in my sleep," she whispered to herself, placing her thumb to the corner of her mouth. "Do I?"

She pouted, and instead of thinking about it and growing more self-conscious, she got out of the bed, lifted the clothes she had worn the night before, and pulled them on. Surprisingly, the simple pair of jeans and black shirt were remarkably clean, considering she had run through the trees and climbed gates in them. Her side ached, and it hurt to bend over to pull her jeans on, but she managed it and turned back to the bed where she re-made it and reached for the camera that had saved her the night before. Frowning down at it in her hands, she glanced to the cloth-covered mirror and gulped thickly, a feeling of cold sweat coming over her in remembrance. She shivered, then pulled on her shoes and moved out of the room and into Ezra's little living room.

He was standing at the table, fully dressed in a pair of black jeans and a smart white shirt with the cuffs rolled up to his mid-forearm. He had the pendant in his hand and was looking over it again with a smile.

"You look like a proud parent." Ana smiled as she walked to him.

Ezra nodded and held the pendant between his fingers. "We are *so* close, Ana. One more item and we will have all three, then we can put them together and see what happens."

Ana frowned in confusion as she watched down at the pendant, then up at his face. "What do you mean? It's just an athame. The whole story was finding the old relics of witches, right?"

"Half-right. It's a major find, for the both of us, obviously. These were thought to be lost to time, and this find alone will be enough when we complete it and take it to publication, but don't forget that it is a magical tool. Remember, the parchment said that the objects are the source of the Marion coven's power. If we complete the athame and it works, if we find the right ritual, we will have access to all that power," Ezra said, a flash of excitement in his eyes.

Ana shuffled on her feet. She wasn't sure what she thought about that. She didn't believe in magic or witches, but after what happened the night before, she was left feeling shaky in her beliefs. She just wasn't at the *magic is real* part quite yet though.

"We should get going. We have three days to find the last item before my deadline," Ana said as she grabbed her bag from the table and walked to the door.

She knew that going against Elianna and writing this story was going to come back and bite her in the ass. Elianna was probably going to fire her if she didn't hand over the story that she wanted, but it was worth the risk. This would make her a credible journalist, and she wouldn't have to write the story that Elianna wanted on the weird witches of the country, which would hurt Ezra. It was the best option. It was the *only* option.

IT WAS RAINING TODAY, but it was still warm and sticky, making her hair cling to her face and her body feel damp. As they walked through the doors of *Strange and Unusual Curiosities and Wonders*, they were affronted with the sweet relief of the shop's air conditioning. It came down from the ceiling and filled the room, rolled over their bodies, and relaxed their shoulders.

"It's coming down heavy out there, my loves," Genevieve said as she leaned on the heavy wooden counter with a strained smile on her face. "I assume you both got back very late last night. What on earth happened out there?"

"What do you mean?" Ezra asked as he walked to his mother quickly and kissed her cheek. "We just got in, got the pendant, and got out."

"Do not lie to me, Ezra. I know when you are lying. What else happened?" Genevieve asked, frowning at him.

"Nothing, he's telling the truth. We got away," Ana said as she walked to the counter and leaned on it, a look of confusion coming over her face. "Why?"

Genevieve tutted and shook her head. "The news is on in the back. Find out for yourselves."

She went back to doing her paperwork, leaving Ezra to look at Ana with a frown. He guided her around the back of the counter and through the curtain that separated the shop from the backrooms and walked straight to the television that was playing. It was small and the picture was hazy, but the sound was perfect and the images were clear enough to make out.

On the screen was footage of the Harrow mansion and Cherry Grove. Crime scene tape was cordoning off the entrance of the little museum, and from what they could see from inside, it was completely trashed. The windows were broken, and the glass show cabinets were smashed, their contents sprawled all over the floor. The footage changed to the forensics team, who was wheeling a trolly out of the building, a black filled body bag strapped onto it. The policemen and the forensics team were surveying the damage, and then the footage changed to the reporter, who was standing a short distance away from the scene.

"In the early hours of last night, the Harrow family were alerted to the sound of crashing and came upon this scene. All the security cameras were blacked out with spray paint, and the Harrow museum had been broken into. As of yet, police tell us nothing was stolen, but unfortunately, the body of the security guard who was working the ground last night was found hanging from the ceiling of the building with one of the ropes that were in the exhibit. The police expect foul play, but they have no current suspects. The security guard was a Mr Gerard Towley, age 52. His family has been notified."

Ezra switched off the television and ran his hands through his hair, pulling it in anger as he began to pace. "No, no no, this is not good."

Ana was beginning to hyperventilate. Her breathing came in short pants, and her eyes couldn't move from the black screen. She

209

had completely forgotten about seeing the security guard in the mirror. All she had focused on was the figure that had come through the glass.

"W-we were there, Ezra; we did that to the security cameras. They are going to know it was us–"

"We didn't kill him. We didn't do that to him, Ana. This wasn't our fault," Ezra said as he dropped his hands.

"Of course it's our fault, Ezra!" Ana exclaimed. "Whoever killed him was following *us*. If we didn't go there, that man would still be alive! We need to go to the police."

"No. We can't," Ezra said as he walked to her and took her by the arms, forcing her to look at him. "If we go to the police and tell them we were there, they are going to ask why and they will know we stole the pendant. After that, they won't find any physical evidence of anyone else there no matter what we say, and they will pin this on us. That's one count of murder. Then they are going to check our last movements, and they will see we found Nina. They will put two and two together and pin that on us as well. That's two counts of murder, Ana. Right now, we are safe from this; we just need to keep going."

"Keep going? Ezra, what if they find evidence we were there before we tell them? They won't believe a word we say!" She started to shake.

"They aren't going to believe us anyway, Ana! What are we going to tell them? That a witch or a warlock used a shadow messenger to kill that man and attack you because he was looking for an enchanted dagger? They would never believe that. *You* would have never believed that if you didn't see it for yourself." He let her go and sighed. His face was pale, and she could tell he was freaking out just as much as she was. He was just better at containing it.

"Then what do we do? Whoever did this is going to keep coming for us, and once we find the last item, they are going to come take it and do the same thing to us. We aren't safe. No one attached to that athame is safe." Ana sniffled.

Ezra rubbed his head like it hurt. He thought to himself in silence for a long moment, then gulped and sat down on one of the chairs heavily.

"We keep going. We can't involve anyone else in our plans from now on. The only thing we can do to get justice for Nina and that security guard is to keep going and draw this person out from hiding. He is going to come for the athame when it is whole. He has clearly been trying to find its location by using the paths we have been, and once we stop, he will be there. We can use his obsession to our advantage and draw him out. Then we can give the police his name once we see his face."

"What the hell makes you think we will survive that?" Ana asked, pacing the floor in front of him.

"We might not. He could come at us and take the athame and kill us before we have a chance to get away. But what is the alternative? We cower away and let him come to us anyway for information, kill us, and take it?" Ezra asked, biting his lip as he thought. "It's the only way. He is going to follow this until the end; that's what my mom read in your cards, right? I know it's hard and that you are scared, but I *promise*, I won't let anyone hurt you."

"How can you promise something like that?"

"I just can. I know you are confused and that everything inside that head of yours must be scrambled, but deep down somewhere, whether or not you want to admit it to yourself, you *know* I can keep you safe," he said, reaching to take her hand when she walked past and pulling her to him so that she was standing in front of him. "Do you trust me?"

Ana squeezed his hand and wiped her cheek with the back of her other hand. "N-no, absolutely not," she said with a small spluttering laugh.

Ezra smiled at her and stood, then reached to tuck some of her hair behind her ear. "Put all of this out of your head, and let's keep going, hm? We have work to do."

He held her hand close to his chest before walking her around the table and down the steps into the private temple. The room was dark as always, but the candles gave them enough light for them to walk directly to a chest of drawers that lined the wall beside the book stand where the Book of Shadows still lay open. He opened the drawer and pulled out the athame he had stashed inside. He delicately held it in his hands before he walked to the desk and sat down, laying it on the wood.

Ana moved to the table and sat beside him, looking down at the athame. It was shinier than she remembered. The markings were clearer now, and the gold and silver had been shined and cleaned, bringing it back to its former glory.

Ezra pulled the pendant from his pocket and held it in his fingers carefully, then looked up to her with a small smile. "There is a polish cloth in the drawer. Will you grab it for me?"

She nodded and stood, quickly grabbing the used cloth from the drawer where the athame had been and handed it to him before returning to her seat. He took it and cleaned the pendant, rubbing away any scuffs of dirt that were on it, and then set the cloth aside.

"Okay, moment of truth. Let's see if it fits," Ezra said as he reached for the athame.

At the bottom where the hilt met the blade, there was a round hole. It was a semicircle going inwards and was the same rough size as the pendant in his hand. He reached forward and hovered it over the hole, then lowered it slowly until he finally let it drop into the missing space. It fit perfectly, but as he lifted the athame with the gold pendant inside, he realised it wasn't secure. When he lifted it so that the point of the blade tipped upwards, the pendant fell back out of the hole.

"Hmm. Okay. That wasn't what I expected to happen." Ezra frowned, picking it back up again.

"What did you expect to happen?" Ana asked, looking over it.

"I thought it would stay in. It's a perfect fit," he said in confusion.

"Maybe we need to find the third object, the one that goes inside here," she said, poking her finger through the oval space in the pendant, "and then it will be complete and stay inside."

"I guess so. It's just a little disappointing." He pouted. "Anyway, onwards and upwards. Let's figure out what this last piece is."

Ana nodded and stood as Ezra wrapped up the athame and the pendant in a cloth and put it back into the drawer safely. She walked to where the Marion Book of Shadows was sitting on the book stand. It had the map they had found sitting on top of it, and she lifted it with her fingers, looking over it in thought. The first circle was the little town of Blackrock where they had found the athame. The second was around an old house that Thomas Harrow had lived in before the mansion was built, so it had been no help in finding the pendant. The third circle was huge. It encased the whole area of a dense forest to the west, spanning a hundred miles.

"How exactly is this supposed to help us with the location of the last object?" Ana inquired as she bit her lip in thought.

"Well, like we said when we found it, it's not a direct map," Ezra said as he came up behind her. "It's just the general locations of where they left them. I guess they had to keep it vague in case someone outside the Marion family bloodline got their hands on it. Someone of the bloodline would have decoded that original parchment in seconds and knew exactly what the riddles meant. We are at a disadvantage that way."

"Then we need to turn the tables into our favour. Have you got the last riddle here?" Ana questioned.

"I do." He grinned as he reached in front of her and lifted the back of the book, where he had stuffed a photocopy of the parchment. He flattened it out and laid it on top of the map, running his finger down it and pointing to the last clue.

The last of us you need to acquire
is so beautiful and rare than any other prior.
Red as blood and hard as stone,
You will find me below where the banshee moaned.

"Red as blood and hard as stone," Ana said as she read it over and over again. She tilted her head and looked back over her shoulder to the drawer where the athame and pendant were. "It goes inside the space that's left in the athame, in the centre of the hole in the pendant. What would be red as blood and hard as stone, is carved into a perfect oval shape to fit into that empty hole of the golden ring, and is missing from a decorative dagger?" She smiled, looking back at him.

"Well traditionally, athames were covered in–"

"Jewels," Ana announced, bouncing with excitement. "Either a red diamond or a red ruby, something along those lines. We are looking for something shiny and beautiful!"

"Oh god." Ezra laughed, moving away from her to sit at the desk again. "You know you can't wear it, right? It's a sacred piece."

"Oh, but I can dream, right?" Ana said as she looked sideways at him, biting her lip.

Ezra shook his head with a small laugh and pulled some books on the table. He opened them, flicking through titles on folklore and mythical creatures.

"So, what is a banshee?" Ana asked as she folded her arms over her chest and looked over him as he studied the texts.

"A banshee is a female spirit that is sometimes seen as an old, craggy lady with hollow eyes. Sometimes she is a beautiful red-haired maiden who washes blood off items of clothing. But regardless of her appearance, she is the messenger of death. You see her when you or a loved one is near death, and when she screams, it's the sound of her recognition that a soul has left a mortal body."

Ana shivered and sat down beside him again, rubbing her arms to bring heat into them. It was cold down here in the basement now, but she wasn't sure if that was the cause of her chill or his story.

"Is there any mention of a story or a sighting of one somewhere in these woods?" Ana inquired as she pointed to the place on the map that was circled.

"It's called the Westwood Forest, and no, not that I know of, but magical creatures and folklore are not really my area of expertise," Ezra said as he turned the page of his book.

Ana bit her lip in thought. They had three days to find the last object so she could type up the story and rush it off to Elianna. If it was good enough, she wouldn't fire her, and she wouldn't have to write that other story.

"Well, if I remember correctly, it's your dad's area of expertise. We could call and ask him?"

"No," Ezra said sharply, not looking up from his book as he read.

Ana sighed and rested her head in her hand on top of the table. "But Ezra, we have three days to find the last object, and we have no clues, he could really help us–"

"Ana, I said no," Ezra said again as he finally looked up at her from his book. "I would rather scoop my eyeballs out with a rusty spoon than have that man anywhere near my investigation. And *you* have three days. I have as long as it takes to get there on my own. Now you can either sit there pouting at me or you can lift a book and help, but we are not calling my father."

Ana sighed at him and folded her arms across her chest, leaning back in her wooden chair and looking around the temple. She knew they had a rocky relationship, and that his dad had stolen his work before, but they needed help even if he was too stubborn to accept it. Ezra wouldn't ask his father, but maybe she could. If she could find him and get his help without Ezra knowing, she might have a chance to solve this in time for her deadline.

"I'm not much of a reader," Ana said, looking sideways at him and trying not to look suspicious, "but I could go to the library and use the computer. I'm sure I could find some good leads online. Can I borrow the car?"

Ezra frowned in confusion as he turned to look at her, smirking. "You are a journalist. What kind of journalist doesn't read?"

"One that's too busy writing and running after strange men into strange places to steal things." Ana frowned. In truth, she *was* a reader, but she needed an excuse to get away. She held out her hand and wriggled her fingers. "Keys."

Ezra shrugged, reached into his pocket, and handed them to her, then looked back to his book. "Fine. I can't read with you yapping in my ear anyway."

"Thanks. I will be back later," she said as she stood from the chair and walked to the door.

"Lettuce, tomato, onions, and mustard," Ezra muttered as she walked away.

"What?" she asked, looking over her shoulder at him when she got to the stairs.

Ezra looked up at her with a grin from where he was reading, leaning back in his chair. "The dressing I want on my burger that you are going to bring me for lunch when you get back. Lettuce, tomato, onions, and mustard."

Ana rolled her eyes and started up the stairs, pulling her phone out of her pocket and walking into the backroom of the store. She typed *Alexander Sullivan: Professor* into her search engine and read down the list of results. She found the university he taught in and where his office was, mentally taking down the address and then putting her phone back into her pocket. Going behind Ezra's back like this made her feel bad, but what Ezra didn't know couldn't hurt him. Right?

"You need to go home, miss. I will not warn you again."

Ana turned quickly from where she was standing in the backroom of the store. The old lady from before was standing behind her on the steps that led down into the basement.

"Go! Get out before you get yourself into trouble you cannot get out of! Shoo!" she snapped, waving her cane at her as she stumbled forward.

"I am leaving, I'm leaving!" Ana staggered through the shop and out the front door with a blink.

CHAPTER 21

*A*na sat parked inside Genevieve's car, opposite the university. The drive was short, and when she arrived, she had sat inside the car holding the steering wheel so tightly her knuckles were white. She had a gnawing feeling in her stomach that tugged at her conscience, making her head throb and her skin feel cold. Ezra would be furious if she knew she was here, but she couldn't let his stubbornness ruin their chances of finishing this investigation before her deadline. She took a deep breath as she contemplated her options, then before she had a chance to talk herself out of it, she pulled the keys out of the ignition and jumped out of the car with her handbag over her shoulder.

The history block of the university was large, but not so huge it was hard to navigate. It was a new build, with grey pebble-dashed walls and big glass windows. Students were filing out of the doors after their lectures, running down the steps and over the lawns to freedom. She pushed her way through the exiting bodies and into the main hall, where she checked the list of professors and the corresponding map to their lecture rooms. She ran her finger down the list until she found his name.

History of witchcraft and lore, Professor Sullivan, lecture room two.

She smiled, then turned and followed the signs that took her down the long winding halls. She passed display cases filled with history memorabilia and pages of explanations pinned to the walls. After arriving at the lecture room, she poked her head through the doorway. A few stragglers lingered, but for the most part, the lecture room was empty. The seats swooped from high up near the wall and to the floor where the huge chalkboards lined the walls. A large desk sat in the middle of the room, and beside it, flicking through his stack of papers, Alexander stood. He looked so different dressed in a normal brown suit as opposed to the black fur cloak and white shirt of the Oak King that he had worn the last she saw him.

She cleared her throat and walked down the steps, giving him a sheepish wave to catch his attention. "Professor Sullivan, do you have a moment?"

"I already told everyone, there will be no extension," Alexander said without looking up, but when she cleared her throat again, he pulled his glasses from his face and looked up at her, blinking. "Oh. My apologies, Miss Davenport."

Ana smiled as she waved and walked closer to him. The closer she got to him, the more she was reminded of how much like his son he looked. They had the same eyes and the same jawline. The similarity made her think of Ezra, and her stomach twisted in a guilt so strong that she had to talk over it to make it disappear.

"Good afternoon, Professor. I don't know if you remember, but the last we talked, you said if we came to a point in our investigation where we couldn't progress ourselves that we could come to you for advice. If that offer still stands, I have a few questions I would like to ask you. Do you have time?" Ana asked.

Alexander smiled and set his stack of papers aside before sitting on the edge of his desk and folding his arms over his chest. "Of course it does. I hope I can help you." He tilted his head, giving a small laugh. "You look nervous. My son has no idea you are here, does he?"

Ana gave a sheepish smile and slowly shook her head. "No. To be honest, when I asked him to call you, he was very direct on the fact that you weren't involved."

"And yet you came anyway." Alexander shrugged, sighing as he looked to the floor. "Did he tell you why he hates me so much?"

"Yes. I can understand his reasoning. I wouldn't be your biggest fan if I were Ezra either," Ana said honestly as she set her bag down and sat on one of the lecture chairs.

"I can see how his version of events would make you feel that way, Ana. I didn't do it to spite him, you know. I didn't steal it from him to make a name for myself; I already had my name. He was lazy and prioritised his drinking and partying over being rested for his interview. I took his research and the coins he found to his meeting for him, and I guess they made a mistake. Ezra was new to the job and didn't clearly state the find as his, and they misread it and assumed Mr Sullivan was me. So, they documented it as such because it was me who took it to them. I thought I was helping him, but it blew up in my face. I corrected the mistake as soon as I found out about it. You can check." He sighed, looking down to his feet awkwardly.

Ana chewed her lip as she listened to him. It sounded plausible. Maybe Ezra *was* overthinking it and feeling sore about it, but something told her that Alexander wasn't being completely sincere. She just couldn't put her finger on what it was.

"With all due respect, Professor, I'm not here about the coins or the relationship with your son," Ana said, reaching into her bag and pulling out her notepad.

"Ah, yes. The Marion coven mystery. The box, the parchment. It's a very fascinating find for you both, though I assume if you are here, it is not going well? What do you need from me?" Alexander's smile renewed, and he looked at her, opening his hands.

"Well, one of the objects pertains to banshees. You know of them, yes?" Ana asked. He had an eyebrow raised at her, and she blushed and stuttered, "Course you do. Sorry. Do you know if there have been any sightings in the Westwood Forest area?"

Alexander pushed himself off his desk and moved around it to the stack of mythology and folklore books he had stacked neatly at its edge. "There have been banshee sightings all over this land, dating back as far as anyone can remember. They are an interesting entity. In appearance, they can be quite menacing, but they are harmless."

"Aren't they the bringers of death or something? That's what Ezra told me." Ana said as she watched him where he was flicking through one of the books.

"No, not quite. They do not bring death to those who see or hear them. They are an omen. Their scream does not kill you, but they can feel death. When they feel that someone has died, their scream confirms it for all around to hear. But mostly, banshees are blood-bound," he said, flipping through the pages of his book and settling on one.

"What does blood-bound mean?" Ana inquired as she scribbled it down in her notebook.

"Nowadays, a family may have pets like a dog or a cat, but the old families who settled here long before anyone else, had banshees. They are tied to a family line, one per family name, and they stay with them forever. They howl loudly three days before a member of that family is to die, then two days before, then one day, until finally, their scream pierces the air for miles around. That's how the rest of the family can know about it and prepare themselves. The Marion name is a very old one, and to my knowledge, it was said that they had a banshee attached to them, too." Alexander approached her and placed the book in front of her.

Ana looked over the browned pages of the book. The writing was faint, like it had been in the sun too long. The writing spoke of banshees and their appearance, their traits, and their screams but nothing she hadn't already been told. Looking up to his face from the pages, he walked back to his desk to sit down as he continued his story.

"There are no sightings that I know of, but there is one story of a banshee in the Westwood Forest. Just before the burnings at the monument in 1588, the Marion coven's magic was waning. After a long time of a bounty of power, the gods' patience for their children was wearing thin. They demanded a sacrifice to restore the power to the coven, and so they complied. There was one catch: the sacrifices had to be of Marion blood, and there needed to be three. A child, a man in his prime, and an old crone. The coven took the chosen deep into the forest and began the ritual. It was simple; they laid the child, the man, and the old lady together on the ground of the forest and covered them in the corresponding ointments, summoned the gods who they had made the deal with, and slit their throats. They collected the blood of all three sacrifices in a golden chalice, and each member of the coven consumed it, restoring their power to what it always had been."

"That's horrible. How could they do that to their own family?" Ana asked as she looked down to the notebook and kept scribbling down the information.

"It had to be done. Sometimes, the evillest of things must be done to the few for the goodness and wellbeing of the whole. That is the way of the coven. That's the ways of witches." Alexander shrugged as he watched her write.

"And what of the banshee?" she asked.

"Yes, throughout the ceremony, the banshees of the Marion Coven were weaving themselves among the trees and screaming until the people of the coven could barely hear anything else. They cried and cried with each death. It was confusing for them, because with each death, there would have been a feeling of more on the way. Watching the ritual through the trees were spies, who told the magistrate what had happened. The result of that was the death of the coven at Monument Hill. If you give me your notebook, I will give you the coordinates to the ritual site. There is a marker left there now, so modern-day witches can pay homage. It's a statue of an artist's rendition of the banshee. It's quite the place."

Ana breathed a small sigh of relief. That was exactly what she needed. The place where the banshee moaned. She stood quickly from the table and walked to him, passing him the notebook and the pen. "Thank you for all of your help. This is a good lead."

"You are welcome," Alexander said as he took it and scribbled the coordinates on it, then closed it and passed it back to her. "Though, perhaps I could give you a little advice before you go on your way?"

"Sure," Ana said as she took the book back and walked to her bag.

"If my son is still angry with me and insisted you do not come here, I suggest you do not tell him you came. He will not take it well." He said with a forced, sad smile.

"I didn't intend on telling him. I told him I was at the library, so I'll say I got my information there. Thank you, again. You are helping him, even if he doesn't know it." Ana smiled, then pulled her bag up over her shoulder and walked back up the steps.

"Good luck, Miss Davenport," Alexander called after her up the stairs, stroking his beard back into place.

Ana looked over her shoulder at him when she got to the top of the stairs, watching him as he cleaned up from his lecture. Talking to him, she never would have guessed he was capable of stealing Ezra's work. His excuse seemed plausible, and it seemed reasonable that Ezra's anger would have clouded him from the truth of the matter.

The only truth she knew for certain, though, was that if Ezra ever found out she went behind his back to talk to his father, he would never speak to her again.

~

"BURGER WITH LETTUCE, tomato, onions, and mustard," Ana called as she walked down the steps and into the temple where Ezra was still sitting at the table. His hair was at all angles, like he had been gripping at it in frustration, and empty wrappers and cups of coffee were scattered across the surface.

He turned in his seat and looked up to her when she made it to the table and set the paper bag on top of his work. He smiled weakly at her, looking tired and drained.

"Thanks." He sighed, reaching to open it and pulling out the box that was inside. "I am afraid you have come back to nothing. I can't find anything in any of my books about a banshee in the Westwood Forest. I found sightings of druids, of fairies, and of witches, but no banshees." He opened the box roughly and took a bite of it with a small groan of happiness.

"That's unfortunate." Ana smiled as she slid to sit on top of the desk beside him and looked down at him with a tilted head. "So, you are saying you have gotten nowhere, then?"

"You don't need to rub it in; I'm pissed off enough already, thanks." Ezra frowned as he took another bite and leaned back in his chair.

Ana leaned back on the table on her hands and swung her legs happily, smiling at him with a raised brow and laughing when he rolled his eyes and put his burger down.

Ezra wiped his mouth with a napkin and gulped down his bite, then folded his arms across his chest. "Why are you looking so smug? You were the one who was panicking that we were not going to find the last item in time for your deadline, and I'm telling you, we just hit a brick wall. Why are you so happy?"

"Oh, I don't know." Ana leaned forward again and reached to poke him in the chest. "Maybe because I know where the last item is."

Ezra reached for his burger again and took another bite. "Very funny."

Ana pulled her notebook from her bag, then pulled open the page she had written in and read, "In the Westwood Forest, the Marion coven held a ritualistic sacrifice of its own people, and at this ritual, a chorus of screaming banshees was heard echoing in the trees. Nearby people heard the screams and told the local magistrate who discovered the sacrifices and executed the coven at the Raven Hill Monument in 1588. The spot has a marker in the shape of a sculpted banshee by a local artist."

Ezra's mouth dropped open, and he set his half-eaten burger aside. "Where the hell did you find that?" he asked, jumping to his feet.

Ana laughed. "The World Wide Web is a marvellous place; you should try it sometime. I even have the exact coordinates. If we leave tomorrow morning we can–"

Ezra pulled Ana from her feet and close to him, spinning her as he laughed. "Yes! I *knew* you would come in handy!"

"Ow! Be careful! My ribs!" Ana laughed weakly with a wince as he held herself to him as he spun her. She tried to dull the ache of guilt in her stomach, but no matter how much she tried to convince herself that she had done the right thing, she couldn't help but feel like she had betrayed him, even if he was happy about the outcome.

Ezra set her down again and kissed her cheek, then moved to take his burger again. "Tonight, we will rest. Tomorrow, we find the last piece. It's almost over, Ana!"

Ana gave him a weak smile and nodded to herself as he sat back down again to finish his burger. "Yeah. Yeah, it is."

She walked away from the table slowly to distract herself from the guilt that was building in her stomach, looking over the trinkets that lined the walls and the bookcases. Sitting on one of the small tables was a frame with candles and rose petals all around it. She walked to it and examined the face in the picture, the face of the old lady who kept shouting at her.

"That's weird." Ana smirked. "I didn't think she had the ability to smile."

"Who?" Ezra asked from around his burger, looking over to where she was standing and frowning in confusion as he glanced at the photo. "My grandmother? What do you mean?"

"She's your grandmother? That makes sense, actually. Is she always so rude, or is it just me?" Ana laughed, looking back to him with a smile.

Ezra blinked, nearly dropping his burger. "What? My grandmother has been dead for eight years."

Ana's face fell, and she looked back quickly between the picture and his face, her eyes going wide and her hands flying to her mouth. "But she . . ."

"What?" Ezra laughed, lifting his burger again.

She raised her hand to her head, rubbing the pain from it and gulping dryly. "Nothing, doesn't matter."

CHAPTER 22

*A*na blinked awake when her alarm rang from her phone that was sitting on the bedside table of Genevieve's spare bedroom. She stretched, wiping the sleep from her eyes and reaching for the phone to switch the buzzing off. The screen read 8:00.

After getting back from *Strange Curiosities and Wonders* the evening before, they had spent the night at the island in Genevieve's kitchen planning the route they would take through the dense forest of Westwood. Ezra had been excited, darting around the island and marking points of interest on a map in bright red pen. It was a beautiful area, he had said, and as much as they were supposed to be going on a mission, he wanted to make sure they appreciated the magnificence of the area while they were there. They had spent hours plotting and planning, drinking and laughing together, that by the time her eyes began to sting with tiredness and she finally managed to crawl into the bed, it was nearing 1:00.

She yawned tiredly and scrolled through the most recent updates that were added to her online calendar by Elianna. She was checking up on the news of the morning when her phone vibrated in her hand.

Text message: Bexley Matthews

Ana opened the message, and staring back at her were two simple words. Call me.

She groaned and pressed the call button beside Bexley's name, pressing the phone to her ear and rolling onto her side to curl up under the sheets again.

"Guess who is back from her holiday and is planning the engagement party to end all engagement parties?" Bexley's voice sang through the phone and into her ear.

"I don't know. Is her name Bexley Matthews?" Ana mumbled with a smile. Bexley's voice always made her smile, no matter how tired she was.

"For now, yes!" Bexley squealed. *"So, I'm thinking on Monday, the first, in the afternoon, we go for drinks at Che Bon, then over to Baby Jane's for dinner in the evening, then City Blues when the sun goes down for a party. What do you say?"*

"I say that sounds like a lovely evening, but unfortunately for us mere mortals who have to actually *work* for a living, I will be at *The City Herald* until five. I can meet you all for dinner afterwards, though." Ana finally sat up in her bed and rubbed the blurriness from her eyes.

"Ew, no. You are coming, and that's final. I bought you the perfect dress for it in France and everything! Please?" she whined.

Ana sighed, but she was smiling. "Fine. I will see if Elianna will let me go early. What kind of dress?"

"Oh Ana, it's to die for! You are going to love it! I can bring it over. Are you in?"

Ana winced. She had forgotten to tell Bexley that she had made up with Ezra after he had pulled the story. "No . . . I am still with Ezra," she said, cringing when she heard Bexley gasp.

"What?! You told me he was a toe rag!"

"No, I didn't. Those were your words!" Ana laughed as she moved to get out of the bed. "He apologised, and we made a new arrangement. The story is back on."

"New arrangement, huh? What happens after the story has finished? What's the arrangement then?" She had a tone of playfulness in her voice that made Ana's cheeks blush.

"I don't know," Ana said, moving to the wardrobe to flick through some of Abby's clothes and trying to find anything that would be suitable for a hike.

Bexley sighed from the other end of the phone, and there was a sound, like she had moved to sit down. *"Yes, you do. You like him."*

Blushing, Ana lifted out a cute white tank top and a black cardigan. "Yeah. I do," she finally admitted. She groaned and threw the clothes onto the bed, slumping down to sit beside them. "But I can't do anything about that, Bex. He's a source."

"Not after your story is submitted, Ana. After that, he's just a guy." Her voice was soft now, like she was hugging her with her words and sitting right beside her. *"You know, you could ask him to come to the party with you. Take him as your plus one?"*

Ana chewed her lip in thought. She wanted to, of course, but the idea of it made her stomach twist in knots and her cheeks feel hot. "Maybe. I'll think about it."

"Well, don't think too much about it or you will talk yourself out of it. I will drop your dress off at your apartment when you get back to the city. Call me when you get home, okay? I love you." Bexley said, a smile lighting up her voice.

"I love you too, Bex." Ana smiled.

The line went dead after Bexley hung up, and she pulled the phone from her ear to look down at the screen and Bexley's name and photo. She pouted a little at her photo, then ran her thumb over it. She missed her.

After dressing in a pair of jeans, the white tank top, and the black cardigan she had picked out, Ana made Abby's bed and set everything the way it was when she had got there, then walked out of the room and downstairs into the kitchen. Ezra and his mother were already sitting at the island, going over the map again and drinking coffee.

"Good morning, my dear, come join us," Genevieve said, patting the seat beside her and pushing the cafetière of coffee towards her.

Ana smiled as she sat down beside her and lifted one of the mugs on the table. She filled the cup with steaming hot coffee and poured in a little milk and sugar before she stirred it and brought it to her lips with a smile. "How is the final planning going? Do you have a rough estimate of how long the hike will take us?"

Ezra was halfway through eating a bacon sandwich. He swallowed and passed her the plate with the other half as he pointed to the red lines he had made on the map that marked the trail. "It should take just over an hour if we keep a steady pace, but knowing you, we won't." He smirked as he looked up at her playfully.

Ana tilted her head at him and reached for the other half of his sandwich, shrugging. "You aren't wrong, but still, rude." She smiled as she took a bite.

"Well, I am going to open the shop. I hope you find everything you need today. Be careful. Have your wits about you," Genevieve said, more so to Ezra than Ana.

"We will, Mother, thank you. I will call you when we get home." Ezra stood to kiss her cheek. She hugged him and left the house, leaving them to finish the coffee together.

Ana lifted her coffee cup to her lips as Ezra folded the map into a perfect rectangle, which he then shoved into his rucksack. "Ezra," she said, her face flushing red.

"Hm?" he hummed in response as he busied himself filling bottles of water for them and putting them into the bag, along with snacks and a compass.

Ana bit her lip. She knew that after they found this last object that she would have no reason to see him. As much as she didn't want to admit it to herself, she didn't want to leave him and never see him again. "I, um . . ." she started, then took a sip of her coffee to distract herself.

No. It was a bad idea. "Never mind."

Ezra stopped what he was doing and turned to face her, his eyebrow raised and a smile tugging at the edges of his mouth. "What? You can't just start to say something and stop. What is it?"

Ana blushed again and set her cup down on the table, clearing her throat. "I . . . Well, Bexley called this morning when I woke up. She's home, engaged, happy, and in the mood for a party."

Ezra smiled at her and folded his arms patiently as he waited for her to get to the point. "And?"

"A-and she told me she is throwing an engagement party on the first, and I'm going obviously. She's my best friend, so it's kind of my job, and she said I could have a plus one." She finally looked up from her cup to his smiling face. "I figured, you know, when we find the last item and we have solved the mystery of the box and I have sent my story to Elianna, perhaps we deserve to celebrate? If you wanted to go with me, I mean . . ."

Ezra smirked and moved from where he was filling his rucksack to sit beside her at the island, leaning on the top of it with his elbow and watching her closely. "Did you just ask me out on a date, Miss Davenport?"

Ana's face was red up to her ears now, and she shrunk back from him out of embarrassment when he leaned closer to her. "No," she said, shaking her head quickly, then gulped dryly when he didn't say anything back. "Okay, maybe I did."

Ezra tilted his head and kept his eyes on her, even as she took her coffee cup in her hands and looked away again. "I'd love to be your plus one to Bexley's engagement party, Ana."

She looked up at him quickly, chewing on her lip and taking a small breath. "Okay."

"Okay," Ezra said with a laugh.

A beat of silence passed between them before Ezra stood from the table and held out his hand for her to take. "But first, let's finish what we started, hm?"

THE WESTWOOD FOREST was an hour-and-a-half drive from the house. Ezra had been humming along to the radio softly to himself as he drove, making Ana feel sleepy as she lay back in her seat and rested her head against the door of the car. She watched as the road gave way to beautiful rolling hills and tall, towering trees. It was drizzling today, and the clouds hung low in a blanket of mist that weaved its way over the valleys and through the treeline, giving the scenery an old mystical feeling that made her skin tingle. She stretched sleepily and turned her head to look at Ezra as he concentrated on driving. They hadn't passed another car for miles now, and it seemed that they were perfectly alone in the middle of the wilderness.

"We are here," he said as he turned his head to look at her, catching her staring at him.

Ezra smiled and pulled the car into a little gravel area and parked the car. He lifted his rucksack from the backseat and set it on his lap, then reached inside and pulled out the map and the compass. "Are you ready?"

"I think so," Ana said as she got out of the car and closed her door, looking up at the trees that towered over them. They were dense, and as she moved closer to the pathway, she found that it was dark inside the forest. She paused in her walking and looked back over her shoulder at him, waiting for him to join her.

"Don't look so scared." Ezra smirked, placing his hand on the small of her back and pushing her forward gently so she would start walking again. "There hasn't been a wolf sighting here in years."

Ana blinked as she walked with him, pulling her cardigan closer around her and folding her arms against her chest. It was humid, but somehow her skin still felt cold, like the atmosphere of the place was lingering on her skin. Ezra pulled the map open and checked his compass, then righted his path and laced between the trees.

"You never did explain to me what that thing was that came for me in your bedroom," she said, staying close to his side and looking over her shoulder.

Ezra frowned as he walked, shrugging. "I will be honest. I find it hard talking to you about these things when I know you think it's bullshit."

"That's fair. I know I am not the most open-minded of people, but what I saw that night was not normal. I'm starting to think either I was sleep-deprived or I dreamt it, but either way, it felt real and I was scared." Ana said, looking to him as they walked. "I'm *still* scared, so even if I don't believe your explanation, it's not because I don't want to. I am just scared that if I do believe you, then it makes it real, and if it's real–"

"It's real, Ana," Ezra cut her off. "The shadow messengers are simple creatures. They are not evil or good. They are not sentient enough to make judgements at all, actually. When someone who practices the craft needs something done, but they cannot do it or get there themselves; they can cast a spell to create a shadow messenger. It can be for anything, but the stronger the witch, the further they can send their messenger and the more they can make them do. When we were kids, Abby used to make them when she was just learning. There were no other kids around to play with, so she would make one with the purpose of playing games with us, and when its purpose was complete, it faded away. They can't think and don't have feelings, and they can only have one reason for being. This person who is after the objects we are looking for obviously either can't get close enough to us to get them from us or they don't want to reveal themselves by coming in person. Obviously, the best way for them to scare us into giving them up, would be to terrify the one who didn't know what she was looking at into giving up the location of the objects, or handing them over to make it stop."

"It almost worked. If you hadn't been there . . ." Ana started, but she stopped herself from finishing her sentence. "If you didn't come in when you did, do you think that thing could have hurt me?" she asked, the image of the hanging security guard flashing into the forefront of her mind.

"Yes. If the goal that the witch instilled into the shadow messenger was to kill you, it would have killed you. Luckily, you think fast on your feet. That was a good trick, with your camera by the way." Ezra smiled.

"Thanks, I guess," Ana said as she shrugged and kept walking, trying not to trip over fallen trees and moss-covered rocks as they worked their way through the forest.

They walked for what seemed like hours, jumping over stumps and rotten wood, over boulders and through wet moss that seemed to sink far into the ground. The mist was thick inside the forest, making it hard to see through the trees ahead, and even harder to read the land to tell where they were on the map. Finally, when their legs burned and their breath was ragged, Ana looked ahead to a small clearing that came upon them out of nowhere. Right in the middle of the clearing was a stone statue, whose features made her flinch and duck behind Ezra's shoulder and point in its general direction.

"The banshee." Ezra smiled, blinking widely at it.

He shoved the map and the compass into his rucksack and took her hand, walking with her into the misty clearing and to the statue, where he looked up at it in awe. The old craggy lady wore a cloak of frayed fabric and had her bony hands gripping it in what looked like agony. Her face was skyward, and the holes where her eyes should have been were completely hollow. Rainwater collected in the holes and dripped down her face like tears as she screamed her silent scream, her face awash in torment.

"That's not creepy at all," Ana said sarcastically as she gulped and held onto his shoulder, trying to shield herself from the image of her.

"She's perfect," Ezra said as he reached to run his hands over the stone, admiring the craftsmanship. "Do you know how long this would have taken to sculpt?"

"Ezra, it's modern. It wouldn't have been here during the time we are looking for, it's not where the object is," Ana said, beginning to look around the clearing for any other markers that *would* have been there in 1588.

"That's not the point. Whoever made this is extremely skilful." he said as he gazed at it.

"Ezra!" Ana snapped, giving him a shove to shake him back to their task. "Focus, please? This place is freaking me out. People were *sacrificed* here."

"Oh. Yeah, I guess that would be creepy to some people," Ezra said as he backed away from the statue and looked at her. She was frowning at him, and he held his hands up. "What? I find it peaceful, that's all."

"You are so weird," Ana said, not being able to stop the smile that curled at her mouth at the dumb smile he had on his face.

"Thank you. Now, look around the edges of the trees for any marker that may have the Marion coven sigil on it. The last two items had the sigil, so it would make sense that this one would be marked, too," Ezra said as he moved away from her and to the edge of the trees on the opposite side of the Banshee.

Ana watched him walk away from her, smiling after him. She walked to the edge of the trees on the other side and wove in and out through them, using her hand to brush away some of the low-growing weeds and shrubs. As much as Ezra felt at peace here, it didn't quell the heavy nauseous feeling that had settled in the pit of her stomach. The atmosphere was heavy and left her chest feeling like she couldn't get a full, clean breath. She spent a while walking around the edge of the trees, and when she felt like she had exhausted all the areas around her, she gave up and looked for Ezra, wondering if he had had any better luck.

Ezra was gone. At least, she couldn't see him from where she was. He wasn't in the clearing or beside the banshee, or anywhere near the lining of the trees where she had left him. Her heart beat faster, and she stumbled forward.

"Ezra?!" she called out, her breath coming from her in small clouds from her mouth.

Out of the corner of her eye and just behind her, she could have sworn she saw something move. She whined where she stood, her feet frozen to the ground and the hair on the back of her neck standing up and tingling.

Something moved again to her left, and she snapped her head backward, looking around frantically to find what was watching her, but there was nothing. Nothing but mist and trees.

"Ezra!" she called again.

Fear gripped her heart when she heard something move behind her again, a rush of leaves and a snapping of twigs as if under someone's foot. The sound echoed like a bullet, and it brought the feeling back to her feet and she bolted as fast as she could back to the clearing, trying to ignore the sound of the running feet that chased her. In her haste, she didn't see the rock that was covered in moss, and her foot slammed into it. She fell, skidding into the clearing with a painful scream as she scrambled onto her knees and looked back into the trees for whatever was chasing her.

There was nothing.

"Ana!"

Ezra was calling to her, coming up behind her and sinking to his knees where she was holding her foot and shaking, her eyes focused on the treeline.

"There was someone in the trees!" Ana yelled, rubbing the pain out of her foot.

He stood and walked into the treeline, searching for any movement, but if anything *was* there, it wasn't any longer. "It's okay. No one is there."

"Where were you?" Ana asked as she moved slowly to stand, putting pressure on her foot to make sure she could still walk on it. A dull pain shot up her leg, but it died away quickly.

"I was in the trees. I heard you calling, but I couldn't see you. Are you okay?" Ezra asked as he turned to look at her.

"Yeah, I'm fine. I tripped over a rock," she said as she pointed towards a moss-covered rock. From the force of her foot colliding with it, the moss had partly been torn off, and looking closer at it, she could see some small markings on it. She blinked, snapping her eyes from the rock and then up to his face. "The rock!"

Ezra looked confused, but when he looked down to where her finger was pointing, his eyes widened, and he sunk to his knees beside it, running his hand over the moss on the rock and pulling it away in bits. The more he pulled, the more the rock revealed its markings, and after a moment, he sat back on his knees and panted in shock. It was the Marion coven sigil.

He scrambled to where his rucksack was resting on the ground beside Ana and opened it quickly, pulling out a small shovel that had a pickaxe on the end. Crawling back to the rock, Ezra reached to grab onto it with his hands and pulled it. It took a moment to come loose from where it had sunk into the ground, but after a few grunting pulls, he managed to lift it free and roll it aside into the foliage.

"Wait," Ana said, raising to her knees and coming to his side as she held his shoulder, surveying the edges of the trees.

Ezra looked up and followed the path line of her eyes but saw nothing. "Nothing is there, Ana, okay? Whatever it was is gone, and even if it wasn't, I'm not leaving without this last item."

Ana gulped and looked back to him when she was sure the trees were quiet, and she nodded to him slowly to continue.

He nodded back and took the pickaxe side of the shovel before he hit it into the ground. The more he hit it, the more the rocky soil chipped away and revealed softer soil. He smiled, then turned the pickaxe around to the shovel side and dug, pulling the soil up and away frantically. Soil covered his knees and dirtied his hands as he used his free hand to pull up the soil more quickly, finally coming upon an old, rotting canvas bag. His hands were shaking in anticipation. Throwing the shovel aside and positioning himself on his knees, he reached inside the hole and pulled up the bag, grinning up at her. "Ready?"

Ana smiled at how excited and bright his face was and how softly he was cradling the bag. "Ready."

Ezra nodded and opened the bag as gently as he could, reaching inside. When he pulled out his hand, she saw something red between his fingers and resting in the palm of his hand. He reached out to her and opened his fingers, revealing a beautiful red jewel. Its facets were sharp, shaping it into a beautiful oval shape that fit snugly in the middle of his palm.

"You found it!" Ana gasped, reaching forward to run her finger over its smooth surface with a laugh. "You *found* it."

"*We* found it," Ezra said as he watched her with a grin. "We wouldn't be here if it wasn't for you opening the box in the first place or finding the information to get here. Thank you." His hand closed around hers, holding her hand and the jewel in his before he laughed and pulled her close to him so that he could bring his face in to hers and kiss her.

Ana blinked against him, but she relaxed quickly, smiling softly against his lips. Her heart slammed against the walls of her chest and thudded in her ears as he pulled back from her and opened his mouth to say something, but she cut him off by placing her fingers against his lips to silence him.

"Shut up?" she asked, then when he tilted his head in confusion she laughed and let her finger move from his lips. She dropped the jewel between them and moved her hands to grip his shirt and pulled him to her before she had too much time to think about what she was doing and kissed him fully.

Ezra wrapped his arms around her to steady himself on his knees and pulled her close to him, covering her white shirt and black cardigan in his muddy hands until she finally broke it and pulled back from him. He opened his eyes and smiled at her dumbly, blinking a few times and giving her a smile, "That was nice."

Ana laughed and slowly unclenched her hands from his shirt and sat back. Her lips tingled, and her cheeks were flushed. "Yeah." She cleared her throat. "We should go, though, before whoever was chasing me finds us and murders us."

Ezra pouted in protest, but he nodded, then leaned in to kiss her cheek softly and took the jewel. He stood, then reached his hand down to help her to her feet and began brushing down the dirt from his knees, but the more he wiped, the muddier they became, and he gave up. He grabbed the shovel and put it back into his rucksack, then placed the jewel inside safely and zipped it up.

"Ready?" Ana asked as she helped him with the straps so that the rucksack was secure on his back.

Ezra smiled at her warmly and took her hand in his, looking down at her face with a nod. "Let's go home."

CHAPTER 23

$\mathcal{T}$he drive back to Genevieve's house was quicker than the drive to the Westwood Forest. Ezra had been excited to get back as quickly as he could so that he could look at the jewel more closely. They had decided against looking over it in the car in case they got pulled over and had it taken from them, or the person who was hunting them down would use the distraction of driving to get their hands on it.

When they pulled up in front of the house, Ana lifted the ruck-sack from where it was resting against her legs and got out of the car, pulling it over her shoulder and walking up the footpath. The door was unlocked, and she wasted no time in opening it and entering the hallway, then moved into the kitchen to place the ruck-sack on the island.

Ezra breathed a sigh of relief when he closed the front door and walked up behind her, placing his hand on her shoulder and looking down to the bag. "We made it. I told you no one would follow us."

"Just because you say something is not going to happen doesn't make it so," Ana said as she looked up to him, leaning with her hands on the island and biting her lip. "Can I hold it now?"

Ezra laughed to himself and opened the bag. He reached inside and lifted out the old rotten rag before laying it on the table and walking to the kettle. "Just be gentle," he said, lifting the kettle and beginning to fill it with water, then placed it back onto the counter and flicked it on.

As the water began to boil, Ana pulled the old cloth away from the stone and cradled it in her hand. It was beautiful, brilliantly red, but dull from being stuck in a rotten bag in the earth for so long. She walked quickly to lift one of Genevieve's cleaning cloths from the drawer, turned on the tap to dampen it, and returned to the table to take a seat.

As Ezra made the coffee, Ana cleaned the edges of the stone with a delicate, cloth-covered finger. She wiped at every facet, all the dirt and smudges that had settled there over all those years until it was clean and mark-free. Setting the cloth aside, Ana held the jewel up against the light of the window so that the sunlight would shine through it. As she looked over the gem, she noticed how the inside seemed to be moving. She frowned and narrowed her eyes, watching as the redness in the middle swirled, like a little red glitter storm that was trapped inside.

"What is it?" Ezra asked as he walked back to the island and set the two large mugs of coffee down.

"Something is moving inside it," Ana said as she handed it over to him and took her coffee mug, blowing the steam from the top of it and taking a sip.

Ezra lifted the jewel up against the light. "That's strange. This is a solid gemstone; it's not hollow inside. At least, I don't think it is. We will have to get it checked out at the lab to be certain, but perhaps there is some sort of liquid inside," he said as he placed it on top of the old cloth and lifted his own mug to his lips. "What do you want for lunch?"

"Anything. Everything you make is amazing." Ana smiled.

Ezra moved to the kitchen cupboards and lifted eggs, milk, and bread from them. As he set about beginning to mix the eggs and milk together, Ana sat happily staring down at the stone, tilting her head at it, and thinking deeply.

It was almost over. Once they went to the shop to collect the other items and fit them all together, the investigation was done. She was sad that it was almost over, but she felt proud at what they had achieved, and a ball of excitement built in her chest at the idea of writing up their story. She knew Elianna would be angry with her for turning in the wrong story, but if she just gave it a chance, if she just read it and understood how special it was, she would fall in love with it just as much as she had.

She stroked the stone. "I can't believe we found it. It was exactly where he said it would be."

Ezra turned his head to look at her as he started dipping the bread into the eggs and placing it into a pan. "What?"

Ana paused, snapping her head to look at him and taking her finger back from the jewel. "Nothing. I said I can't believe it was exactly where we thought it was."

"That's not what you said." Ezra turned to face her fully, his brow furrowing as he studied her expression. "Who is *he*?"

"N-no one," Ana said, turning away from him so she didn't have to look in his eyes when she lied.

"Ana," Ezra said sharply, setting the wooden spoon down on the counter roughly and walking to her. "Don't lie to me. You told me you got your information online. Who told you we would find it there?"

Ana squirmed in her seat and turned to look up at him from under her hair. "Ezra, we were stuck; you said so yourself. We were getting nowhere, and I was on a deadline. You were too stubborn to see that we needed help!"

Ezra slammed his fist down on the counter, making the jewel topple over and Ana jump in her chair. "Who did you go to, Ana?" his voice was hard and his brows were furrowed.

She gulped thickly. "Your dad."

Ezra let out an angry breath and turned away from her, reaching up to hold his head with his hands. He paced as the French toast began to burn. "I knew it. I knew there was no way in hell you found that information online, but I talked myself out of it because I trusted you, Ana! I can't believe you would do this!"

Ana was on her feet and moving to him quickly. "Ezra, calm down! He is your *dad*! He loves you and just wanted to help! He said he knew you wouldn't accept any help, so that's why I went myself!" she said as he reached out to touch him, but he flinched away from her hand like she had burned him.

"Don't touch me," he snapped and stepped back. His eyes were angry, and his voice was shaky, like he wanted to scream at her but was holding it in. "I specifically told you that I didn't want him involved. I told you what he did to me the last time I worked with him, and you still–"

"Ezra, he said it was a mix-up! I asked him about it, and he said they thought it was his find because they assumed Mr Sullivan was him, not you. He didn't betray you! Please, Ezra . . ." Ana sniffled, trying to open her hands to him to calm him down, but he was too angry to even look at her.

"You are so fucking naïve, Ana!" Ezra shouted, making her wince and take a few steps back from him. "It shouldn't matter if he didn't do it or not. The point is I told you I would rather not investigate this *at all* than have him help me. Do you know what you have done? Actually, I think you do know. You just don't care about anyone or anything, so long as you get your goddamn story done in time, right? Tell me I'm wrong!"

Ana sniffled and wiped her cheeks as he shouted at her, then slowly sat down at the table again. "You know how hard I am working. You know I need this too, right, Ezra? Please. You must admit, his information is the only reason we have this." She said, nodding to the jewel.

243

Ezra had to look away from her so he could calm himself down. He lifted the pan from the cooker and threw it into the sink roughly, the metal sizzling when it hit the water. "I told you I would have solved it if you gave me the time I needed, but you betrayed me. I asked you to do *one* thing, and you couldn't even do that for me. I worked so hard on this, I have gotten in so much trouble over you already, things you can't even imagine–" he said, stopping himself from finishing the sentence. He shook his head and cleared his throat before finally looking at her. "You have your story. Get out."

Ana tilted her head like she didn't quite hear him right and wiped at her cheeks again to try and stop her tears from dripping off her chin. "What?"

"You heard me," Ezra said as he walked to the table and rolled the jewel back up into the cloth, then shoved it back into his rucksack and threw it over his shoulder. "You got what you came for, didn't you? Then you have no reason to be here anymore." His eyes finally met hers, and he leaned in closer to her, making her shrink back from how angry his face was. "I have already asked you once to leave. Don't make me ask you again."

Ezra watched her for a beat longer, then stood back from her and walked around the island and out of the house. The door slammed after him, and Ana was left in his mother's kitchen, staring down at the surface of the island in shock. Her throat felt tight, and her chest was rising and falling faster and faster until she finally forced herself to stand. She clenched her fists into balls at her side and tried to stop herself from crying as she staggered up the stairs that led to the bedroom.

She reached Abby's room and found her bag, where she made sure all of her things were still packed away. Her clothes were hanging over a chair at the end of the bed, and she lifted them, folding them and putting them inside the bag through tear-filled eyes. She would have to wash and mail Abby's clothes back to Genevieve in the morning. Sobbing, she walked out of the room again and down the stairs. She had to force herself out of the door and into the sunlight, trying to gulp down the knot of guilt in her throat, but it wouldn't move.

The purple Volkswagen Beetle was gone from the driveway. She took a deep breath in through her nose and out her mouth, steadying herself and pulling her phone from her jeans pocket where she opened the internet browser and searched for a local taxi number, then started the call and pressed it to her ear.

"H-HELLO? I need a taxi to the train station, please."

CHAPTER 24

*L*ight streamed through the blinds of Ana's room. She was back in her own bed, in her room, in her apartment in the city. It had taken her hours to get home the night before when Ezra told her to leave Genevieve's house. By the time the taxi arrived to take her to the station and she journeyed two hours by train back to the city, it was already past dinner time. When she arrived home and observed her cold, dark apartment, she had gone straight to her bed, pulled the covers up over her head, and cried herself to sleep.

It was 14:00 now. She had been awake for hours, staring at the ceiling and listening to the couple above her arguing and having angry make-up sex, then arguing all over again. Her phone had been ringing all day from where it was stuffed inside her bag at the bedroom door, but she didn't have the energy to get out of the bed and reach for it. She suspected it was Bexley. She had called her from the train ride the night before to tell her she was on her way home, and she had offered to come straight over but she asked her not to. All she wanted to do was hide. She didn't want to have to explain it over and over again, picturing his angry face and having to relive the guilt.

Her phone buzzed again and again, and finally, it stopped, leaving the room quiet again save for the muffled arguing from the couple upstairs. It was then that the knocks on the door of her apartment filled the air, and she snapped up in her bed, looking out through her bedroom door into the hallway. The banging came again and again. She groaned and pulled the covers off herself, then stood up on weak legs and pushed her feet into her slippers.

"I'm coming, I'm coming!" Ana shouted as the banging came once more. She walked along her hallway and to her door, where she unlatched the chain lock and pulled the door open wide.

Bexley stood on the other side. She had a black duffle bag that was bursting at the zip looped through her arm, a dress bag hanging over the other arm, a bottle of wine in one hand, and a large pizza box in the other. She was panting, her eyes wide and looking like she might buckle under the weight of everything she was carrying.

"I've been calling you *all day*," she said through gritted teeth and pushed past her into her living room, where she set the pizza box and the large designer duffle bag down.

Ana closed and locked the door, following her into her living room and taking the bottle of white wine from her friend's hand. "Sorry. I just woke up," she said. She walked into her kitchen and grabbed her bottle opener, unscrewing the cork and pulling it out roughly before throwing it aside on the counter. She took a large swig of it as she walked back into the living room.

Bexley was watching her, her face full of concern as Ana walked past her and slumped down onto the sofa. "What happened? Talk to me? Please?" she said as she sat down beside her and tucked her messy hair behind her ear.

Ana shook her head and took another swig from the wine bottle as she thought over the events of the previous day and how to explain them to her friend. She gulped down the taste of wine and looked side-ways to her, her eyes filling with tears again. "I messed up, Bex. I messed up *really* bad, and Ezra kicked me out of his house. I don't think I'm going to ever see him again." She sniffled, wiping her cheek.

"What the hell did you do to make him kick you out?" Bexley asked as she opened the pizza box and pulled it closer to them. She lifted one of the large triangle-shaped pieces and passed it to her. It was topped with mushrooms and peppers and so much cheese it was dripping off the sides.

Ana grabbed it from her and took a hungry bite. She hadn't eaten since the day before, and her stomach grumbled loudly when her tongue tasted the cheese. She moaned, lying back against the sofa. "Ezra doesn't speak to his father. He stole some of his work he did when he was first starting out, so he doesn't trust him. We were stuck on the location of the last thing we had to find, and I said we should ask his dad because he offered me his help before. But Ezra said no. I know I should have listened to him, but my deadline was so close! If I didn't go to him, we would have never found it in time. So, I went behind his back, and I met with his dad." she sniffled, taking another hungry bite.

Bexley sighed deeply through her nose and lifted her own piece, taking a smaller bite of it than Ana had done and kicking her shoes off. "Babe, I've told you before, you shouldn't get involved in family drama that isn't your own.'" she said as she crossed her legs under her.

"I wasn't! W-well, I didn't think I was. I didn't think Ezra would ever find out! But I let it slip, and now he won't speak to me. I tried calling him to apologise when I was on the train, but he wouldn't pick up," she said as she took another gulp of the wine.

Bexley snatched the bottle from her when she finished her swig. "This isn't just your wine," she said, taking a sip of it herself and then tilting her head. "Just because you didn't think he was going to find out doesn't make it right."

"I know that now, Bex. I just . . ." she started, then sighed and finished off her slice, throwing the pizza crust back into the box. "I let my ambition for my story take over, and I hurt him. I would never usually have done something like that. I feel s-so bad, but he won't even talk to me," she hiccupped. "I really liked him."

Ana flopped over and laid her head on her friend's lap, and Bexley stroked her hair to comfort her. "I know you did, babe. I know. But if he doesn't want to speak to you after this, you can't make him. Maybe once he cools down, you can try calling him again, hm? What about your story? Can you still write it?"

Ana laid on her back and looked up at her friend with her head on her lap. She shrugged, shaking her head and wiped her cheeks dry as she stopped crying. "No. I mean, he didn't say I couldn't, but he implied it. So, after all this, I am back to square one, and I have to write that original story *slandering* them. I don't want to have to do that. I was trying *so hard* so that I didn't have to do that."

"Well, you don't have many options left, Ana. Ezra has kicked you to the curb, again, and like you said, you are never going to see him again, right? Write your story, get it all out of your head, and send it to Elianna. Once you send it, it's over. The story is over, Ezra is gone, he probably won't ever see it anyway. Then you can move on," Bexley said as she rubbed her head, smiling down at her. "In the meantime, to help you get over this almost-breakup, we have pizza, lots of wine, chocolate and snacks, movies to watch, and the best part: a brand-new, French couture dress, just for my best friend." She poked her nose gently.

Ana finally smiled, looking up at her through a small pout. "Have I told you how much I love and appreciate you lately?"

"Not lately, but you don't need to. I know I'm amazing." Bexley laughed.

Ana smiled weakly and sat up again, sitting side by side with her friend and reaching to take the bottle from her and taking a large drink. "Okay. Let's party, then."

"That's the Ana I know and love!" Bex grinned, nudging her as she stood from the chair and turned the television on. She flipped through the channels until she came to one that was showing reruns of a 90s TV show they loved. "Perfect. Are you ready to see your dress for my party?"

Ana nodded as she set her bottle aside on the table and renewed her smile. The idea of a beautiful new dress pushed her guilt over Ezra out of her head. "I am *so* ready."

Bexley bounced in excitement as she set the remote down on the table and reached for the dress bag. She opened the zip and pulled out the hanger, letting the bag drop off the dress, and then turned it around for her to see.

Ana gaped at the dress. It was a long, stunningly beautiful lace dress that flowed in layers of light rose gold fabric. It swayed beautifully, and when it did, the light reflected off the glittery parts of the bodice that continued all the way down the dress to the hem at the bottom. The neckline was heart-shaped, and it had thin straps that connected to the back near the waist, leaving the back exposed. Bexley moved the hanger in a swaying motion so that she could see how it flowed in the air, and Ana jumped to her feet, her face in awe as she walked to her and extended her fingers to touch the fabric, but Bexley slapped her hand away.

"No! Not until you wash your hands from pizza grease! Hold it by the hanger until the party." She grinned, holding it out in an extended arm. "I saw it in the window of a designer's store that I absolutely *adore*, and I had to get it for you. It screams Ana Davenport, don't you think?"

"Bex, I can't take this from you; it's too much!" she said, but she took the hanger from her anyway before rushing to the closest mirror and holding it up against her frame. It was her size, obviously, and as upset as she would still be by the time her party came, she knew this dress would make her feel a lot better. "Thank you, Bexley."

"You are welcome." Bexley laughed. She walked up behind her in the mirror and hugged her tightly, resting her chin on her shoulder and looking at their reflection in the mirror. "Now, hang it up and meet me on the sofa for 90s reruns and wine, hm? Let's drink this day away."

"Yes, Mom." Ana smiled. She leaned to nuzzle her friend's head, then rushed off down the hallway to her room to hang it up over the edge of her door. When she returned, Bexley was pulling all the snacks and other bottles of wine from the bag and fanning them on the table.

She joined her just as she was opening the second bottle of wine, and they curled up together, drinking and eating until the feeling of dread and guilt Ana had in her stomach melted away.

By the time the clock struck 23:00, Bexley had passed out on the sofa, snuggled up in a pair of Ana's pyjamas, and Ana reclined with her laptop on her lap and the last bottle of wine in her hands. She had been watching her laptop screen for a while now, staring at the half-finished article she had to write for Elianna. The deadline was tomorrow, and she knew if she didn't have it finished and sent to Elianna's inbox by the time she arrived at the City Herald tomorrow, she was screwed.

She didn't want to slander Genevieve and Ezra. She cared for them both deeply and had taken every step she could *not* to do that to them so she could look Ezra in the eye and feel everything she did for him without feeling guilty, but Bexley was right. She was never going to see Ezra again; he had made that perfectly clear. The only thing she *did* still have was her job, and she wasn't about to lose that too over someone who didn't want her back.

Anger fuelled up inside her head in a drunken haze, and she took another large gulp of the wine and set it aside roughly, then typed with fast fingers. She finished the article in less than an hour, then proofread it to check for any drunken typos before she attached it to an email and sent it to Elianna. The second she pressed send, she felt a huge weight lift off her shoulders. Her head felt lighter, and her chest felt like she wasn't holding a breath anymore.

"Feel any better?" Bexley asked as she yawned and stretched on the sofa beside her, looking up at her friend's face and then to the screen of her laptop.

"Yeah. I do actually. It's over, at last." Ana smiled drunkenly, pushing the screen of her laptop down to close it, and then stood with a stumble, crashing into the table in front of her with a loud laugh.

"Okay, you are really drunk," Bexley said as she sat up and held her head. "Shit, *I'm* really drunk." She stood slowly and took Ana's arm, pulling her away from the sofa as they stumbled together. "Time for bed!"

Ana felt her head swimming as she held herself to her friend all the way down the hall and into her bedroom, where they both fell into the soft sheets. They laughed together as they lay back and watched the room spin, holding each other's hands and closing their eyes. "Thank you, Bexley. I don't know what I'd do without you. I love you," she mumbled, drifting into sleep.

Bexley hummed as she cradled her friend's hand. "I know. I love you, too."

CHAPTER 25

"*I* am going to be sick."

Ana groaned as she felt movement beside her in her bed. Bexley was scrambling out of the bed and was making her way out of the bedroom so she could run to the bathroom, her hands covering her mouth and her bare feet slapping against the wooden floor. She had been up and down all night, running to the bathroom to throw up the alcohol from her stomach and then crawling back into the bed, swearing to God that she would never drink again.

Ana, on the other hand, didn't get hangovers the same way Bexley did. She didn't throw up or feel nauseous, but she did get extremely horrible headaches, and she could feel one beginning to work on her as she rolled onto her back in the bed, opening her eyes and looking up at the familiar white ceiling of her bedroom. She listened for Bexley to return, but when she flushed the chain of the bathroom and walked into the living room instead, she got out of her bed with a moan and threw her legs over the side, slipping her feet into her slippers and dragging her feet all the way into the hallway.

Bexley was standing in the little kitchen, looking down at the phone in her hand and waiting on the coffee machine to finish brewing. She was frantically typing and moving her fingers across the screen. As Ana got closer to her to lift two cups from the cupboard, she realised it wasn't Bexley's phone that she had in her hand; it was hers.

"What are you doing with my phone?" Ana asked as she grabbed for it.

"Nothing. Just checking the weather," Bexley said as she waved Ana's hand away. She finished what she was doing and handed it back to her, then turned back to the machine and poured the freshly brewed coffee into the two cups that Ana had set down.

Ana narrowed her eyes suspiciously at her and looked down at her phone. There was nothing recent on her call list or in her messages or browser, so she set it aside and reached into a drawer to pull out a little packet of pills. "Aspirin?" she asked, and when Bexley nodded, she pushed two out of the little silver packet and handed them to her.

"Thanks," Bexley said as she popped them into her mouth and washed them down with her coffee. "I really need to go. I have so much planning to do for the party tomorrow, and it's already past 11:00." She checked the watch on her wrist, sipped her coffee, and looked up at Ana with a small grin over the rim of her cup. "What are *your* plans for today?"

"Nothing, really," she replied, rubbing her temples and walking out into the living room. Wine bottles still littered the coffee table, and the pizza box lay open with the half-eaten crusts still inside it, along with piles of discarded chocolate and snack wrappers from their feast the night before. "Maybe clean this mess up. It's my last day off before I have to head into the office tomorrow, and I fully intend on spending most of it in bed."

Bexley grinned at her as she followed her into the living room and sat down on the sofa among the toppled over pillows and crimped blankets. "Good. You deserve a nice day after everything that's happened."

"I guess." Ana sighed, slumping down beside her and resting her head on her knees as she pulled her legs to her chest. "I just want to get back to normality. *The Herald*, my job, my life. It may not be as exciting as treasure hunting in the countryside–"

"Or as handsome," Bexley said with a tilted head.

"Or that." Ana pouted. "But it's mine."

Bexley nodded and sipped her coffee until the cup was dry. After putting the cup on the coffee table, she rested her hand on Ana's and leaned in to kiss her head. "I need to go. I am only a phone call away if you need me." She stood from the sofa and reached for her black duffle bag and looped it over her arm.

"You are still wearing my pyjamas." Ana smirked.

"I know. My car is just outside, I'll bring them back tomorrow. Throw my clothes in the laundry for me?" she asked as she made her way to the door and opened it wide. "*Ciao!*"

The door closed, and Bexley was gone, leaving Ana alone in her apartment again. The room seemed instantly colder and duller when she left, like she had taken all the heat and the colour from the room when she went. Bexley had always had that kind of personality, one that shone bright in any room that she was in, and when it was gone, it seemed to affect the literal atmosphere of the room. It was something she had always wished she could mimic, but never did. It was some sort of magic that was uniquely Bexley.

She finished her coffee and stood from the sofa, grabbing a black bin bag and filling it with the empty bottles, the pizza box, and the wrappers that littered the table. Once it was cleaned, she took the wine glasses to the sink, wiped down the table, fixed the sofa and its pillows, and started to hoover the floor from the crumbs that had fallen from the pizza. As amazing as Bexley was for bringing her wine and food to cheer her up, she was extremely messy.

After she finished cleaning and hoovering, Ana walked into her bathroom and filled the bath with steaming hot water. Her skin felt grimy, and her hair was greasy, making her feel sluggish and sticky. As she waited for it to fill, she brushed her teeth and examined her tired expression in the mirror. Her face was pale, and she had red skin around her eyes.

"Give yourself a shake, Ana," she mumbled from around her toothbrush.

She spat the excess toothpaste into the sink and washed it away, then undressed and slipped into the hot water of the bath. It was scorching, and it stung her skin as she stood in the bath and lowered herself inch by inch into the water, her skin getting used to it the further she got in. The hot water should sweat out her hangover, she thought, and purge her skin of whatever lingering sadness was caked there. She scrubbed and scrubbed until she felt clean, then washed her hair and sunk back into the water, closing her eyes and trying to relax her tense shoulders. By the time the water was starting to go cold, the knots in her body seemed to have finally ironed out, and she felt brand new when she emerged from the water and into the steam-filled bathroom.

After brushing and drying her hair, she slipped on a new set of underwear and a long baggy T-shirt that hung down to her knees. It was her dad's t-shirt. It was a deep charcoal grey with large white writing on the front that read, *World's Best Dad*. It was very old and had holes near the bottom where she had used to grip at it when she was a kid and the hem of the shirt was starting to fray, but she couldn't help but wear it when she needed a little extra courage or comfort. It didn't smell like him anymore, but every time she wore it, she felt like she could almost feel his arms hugging her inside it.

She sighed to herself, walking into her living room and looking around her empty but now clean apartment. Thankfully, her head wasn't pounding anymore, and she felt lighter, like she was beginning to feel like a kind of normal again. She slumped down on her sofa and lifted the remote control from the table, turning the television on and flipping through the channels. She passed murder documentaries, home improvement programmes, daytime talk shows and the news, and just as she was about to change it again, she heard a knock against the door.

Ana frowned, sighing deeply and throwing her remote aside before standing and making her way across the room. It knocked again, and she clenched her fists in frustration. It was a Sunday. She never had visitors on a Sunday.

"Okay, okay, I'm coming!" she snapped, walking up to the door and pulling it open roughly. "What?"

Ezra stood on the other side of the door, leaning lazily against the wall with his arms folded against his chest. He looked up at her from where he was watching his feet, giving her a small frown. "Is that how you greet everyone who comes to visit you?"

Ana gaped at him. He was the last person she expected to be standing on the other side of her door, and she cringed internally as she tried to stand up straighter. "Sorry, I didn't know it was you." She gulped. They stood in silence for a long moment until Ezra raised his eyebrows. "Oh! Sorry, do you want to come in?"

She sidestepped from the door and looked up at him as he walked through the threshold and into her apartment. She watched his back as he made it to her living room and turned around to look at her just as she was closing the door. "What are you doing here, Ezra? How did you know where I lived?"

Ezra frowned as he watched her, one of his eyebrows raised and his hands in his pockets. "You sent me it? This morning? You texted me last night, something about being 'super sorry' and that you wanted to talk? Any of this ringing a bell? How drunk *were* you?"

"What? I didn't . . ." Ana trailed off, her heart beating faster in her chest as she glanced in the direction of the kitchen where Bexley had set her phone down after she had caught her using it this morning. "Damn it, Bexley. She was using my phone; she must have texted you from it last night and this morning when I wasn't near it." She placed her hand to her forehead with a groan and closed the gap between them so that she could stand in front of him.

"That explains why you kept calling me *babes*," he said, a small smile curling at his lips, but he stopped it before it reached his eyes. "So, you aren't super sorry and don't want to apologise? Should I leave?"

"No! No, please don't go," Ana said as she reached to take his hand so that he wouldn't turn away from her. His hand felt warm in hers, and as she held it, she sensed just how much she had missed him building in her chest.

Ezra sighed and nodded, taking his hand back so that he could fold his arms against his chest again and look down at her, waiting for her to break the silence.

"I'm so sorry." Ana sniffled. She could feel tears stinging the back of her eyes, and her cheeks were getting hot as she tried not to cry. "I feel awful. I should never have gone behind your back. It was a really shitty thing to do, and I'm sorry."

"You should be," Ezra said. His face softened, and he gave her a weak smile, rocking onto his tiptoes and back onto his heel like he was uncomfortable. "But I should be sorry, too. I was harsh with you. My mom talked some sense into me when you left. She made me see that as much as it was a *really* shitty thing for you to do, we did get what we needed, and my dad . . ." He trailed off, sighing deeply as if he hated what he was about to say. "I guess he did help, and maybe I *was* being stubborn. I talked to him, too, we hashed out some things, blew the cobwebs from between us, so I guess I should be thanking you for that."

"That's great. He loves you, you know; you can hear it in his voice when he talks about you," Ana said as she looked up at him.

"I know. He seemed sincere, and I told him if he promised he wouldn't stab me in the back again, I would show him the items we found. I haven't pieced them together yet. He said if they are magical items that they deserve a ritual to put them back together. He's the high priest, so I guess it's important for them to do it right. He is excited about it; it's endearing, actually." He laughed. "I was going to show them to him tomorrow if you want to come along?" Ezra said, finally uncrossing his arms and reaching for her hand.

"I can't. I am working tomorrow morning, and it's Bexley's engagement party in the afternoon," she said with a blush. It was the same party that he was supposed to join her as her date.

"Then I will reschedule with him. I can't put the pieces together without my partner in crime," Ezra said, reaching to tuck some of her wet hair behind her ear. "Do you still need a date for the party?" He leaned down into her.

Ana smiled at him widely as she looked up into his eyes and shrugged her shoulders. "Would you still like to go with me?"

Ezra smiled and pulled her into him, leaning in close to her face. "Yes, I'd still like to go with you."

He kissed her, and Ana felt her heart leap into her chest. She melted into it, and held his shirt in fistfuls, pulling him down so that she could stand on her tiptoes to match his height. His hands were on her waist, working their way down to the hem of her shirt at her mid-thigh. He deepened the kiss and pushed her shirt up over her hips to hold his hands against the bare skin of her back.

"I like this shirt," he uttered.

"Yeah," Ana mumbled in between kissing him. She had his face in her hands and her fingers were working their way into his hair, keeping him as close to her as possible. "It was my dad's." She said, having to stop talking when he bit her lip gently and pushed her T-shirt further up her body, then let her go to pull it up over her head and threw it over his shoulder. "I got it for him for Father's Day . . ."

She was nervous and rambling, she knew, but she couldn't stop herself talking as he pressed his lips to her neck and she gulped, her knee buckling a little where she stood. "It's old, a–"

"Ana." Ezra laughed, leaning back to look her in the eyes as he reached to pull his shirt up and over his head. "Please stop talking about our dad's."

"Sorry," Ana said breathlessly. She grabbed onto his arms, pulling him to her and kissing him more passionately, then moved her arms to loop around his neck. As he lifted her, she wrapped her legs around his waist. "Take me to my room?" she mumbled.

"Absolutely," Ezra spoke against her neck. He held her under her thighs securely and walked down the hallway with her and to the door that she indicated with her finger. He walked through the doorway, kissing her lips again with a small moan, and kicked the door closed with his foot.

CHAPTER 26

*A*na was awoken by a gentle kiss to her shoulder as she lay in her bed. They had spent the whole evening and night together in her bedroom, the door closed and the curtains drawn until the candles died away and the light peeked through the windows. They wasted hours away, talking about their investigation in between the many times they melted into each other. When she fluttered her eyes open to his kiss, they still stung from the want of sleep. The alarm clock on her bedside table read 6:45, and she groaned, rolling onto her back and pulling the sheets up over her chest.

Ezra was sitting up against the pillows, his elbow under him as he held his head in his hand and smiled sleepily down at her. "Morning."

"Morning . . ." Ana stretched. She blushed deeply and tilted her head to lie beside his chest, feeling how warm his skin felt against her cheek. She felt so safe inside the sheets and against his chest, like nothing bad could reach out and grab her from there. She wanted to stay this way forever. "I feel like I haven't slept." She yawned, closing her eyes again and relaxing into the sheets.

"We didn't. Not really." Ezra smirked down at her as he watched her try to keep herself awake. He leaned down to gently kiss her lips, then rolled away from her and got out of the bed, searching her room for wherever his clothes had ended up the day before.

Ana blinked her eyes open again when she felt the weight leave the bed, and she sat up on her elbows, watching him as he found his boxers and pulled them on, then his jeans and his shoes. "Oh come on . . . don't be that guy."

"What guy?" Ezra asked, looking up at her as he tied the laces of his shoes and looked for his T-shirt before he remembered he had taken it off in the living room. He moved to her mirror instead and started to fix his hair, running his fingers through it so that it didn't stick up at the ends.

"The kind of guy who swoops in all charming and forgiving, spends the night, and then leaves super early and never calls," Ana said with a raised eyebrow and a small smile as she watched him. He looked good shirtless and sleepy. "Please don't be that kind of guy."

Ezra gave a small, tired laugh and shook his head as he walked back to the bed and sat down on the edge of it beside her. "I'm not that kind of guy. I *am* the kind of guy who is going to go out to get us some breakfast, though, because, *no offence*, considering how little time you spend here, I don't think you are the kind of girl to have much stuffed in the back of her cupboards."

Ana rolled her eyes and smiled at him as she sat up, wrapping the sheets around her chest to scoot closer to him. "You would be correct," she said, then leaned in to kiss him softly. "There is a bakery just down the road. They should be open."

"Then to the bakery I go."

He kissed her forehead and then stood off the bed again before opening the door of the bedroom. Ana could hear him walking down the hall, and then a few moments later, her front door opened and closed after him. She sunk into her sheets when he left the apartment and stared at her ceiling like she did every morning when she woke up, only this time, she felt like her chest was going to burst. Her heart felt full, and her body felt weak in the best possible way. She squealed to herself, shaking the covers and grinning to herself before she let the duvet go and covered her face with her hands.

Ana laughed at herself, then quickly got out of bed and ran naked into her living room so that she could find her dad's T-shirt and pull it over her body. Once she was covered, she walked into the kitchen and lifted her phone, checking for new updates to her calendar for the month, and then flicked the screen to Bexley's name. Ana pressed the phone to her ear.

"You are not seriously calling me before 7:00 on a Monday morning, are you? I better be dreaming." Bexley's tired morning voice came over the phone.

"You are ridiculous, do you know that?" Ana said as she chewed on her thumb with a giddy jump. She shuffled out of the kitchen and back into the bedroom, where she slumped down on the bed and crossed her legs under her.

"I'm not the one calling at this ungodly hour." Bexley sighed. There was movement behind her, like she was sitting upright in bed, then her voice changed, like she was talking through a grin. *"Is he still there?"*

"No . . ." Ana smiled, bouncing on the bed slightly in excitement. "He just left to get us breakfast."

Bexley squealed into the phone, making Ana laugh and join her, giggling into the receiver with each other until Ana had to flop back on the bed to calm herself down.

"So? What happened? Tell me everything! Was he amazing?" Bexley asked. There was the sound of someone talking tiredly behind her, but Ana couldn't hear what they said. All she could hear

was a muffled, *"I'm talking to Ana, shhh!"* through a hand that covered the speaker on the other end.

"Bex, you have *no* idea." Ana grinned. "He's so gentle, and strong and . . . God, I'm so tired!"

Bexley laughed loudly at the other end of the phone. *"I'm really happy for you, Ana. I told you things would work themselves out, didn't I?"*

"They didn't sort themselves out. *You* sorted things out," Ana said with a sigh, rolling onto her side and resting her phone on her ear. "Thank you . . . for being my best friend. I love you more than anything."

"I love you more than anything, too, babe. But it's officially 7:00, and I have a fiancé to wake up. I will see you later. Make sure to try to get out early! Please don't be late!"

"I won't be late. I promise. Bye." Ana ended the call and looked down at her phone with a happy sigh, then stretched again contentedly.

She lay among the crumpled sheets of her bed, rolling onto her side and hugging the pillow as she stared out through the blinds and waited for Ezra to return. The pillow smelt like him, and it made her smile as she fought the sleepiness behind her eyes. Just as she was starting to fall asleep again, she heard her front door open again and close loudly, and she smiled widely, jumping off the bed and making her way down the hallway.

"So, I was thinking, I still have to go to work this morning, but you can stay here if you want while I'm there, and when I come back, maybe we can find you something to wear to Bexley's party?" She said, looking for him as she entered the living room.

On the coffee table sat two tall cups of takeout coffee and a large box of pastries. Ezra sat on the sofa, a dark frown on his face as he held a large newspaper in his hand, open in the middle. His hand was shaking a little as he held it, and when she neared him, he looked up at her, his eyes narrowed. "What the *hell* is this?"

Ana looked confused until her eyes spotted *The City Herald* logo on the front of the paper, and her mind flashed back to when she had sat on that same sofa with Bexley, drunk out of her mind and angry. Her face paled as she stared at him, a cold blanket of sweat draping over her shoulders as she realised what he was referring to. "E-Ezra . . ."

Ezra stood from the sofa roughly and folded the paper so that he could hold it at arm's length, pacing the floor and reading aloud. *"Genevieve and Ezra Sullivan's little store stands in the middle of a sleepy hamlet, and as unassuming and quaint as it seems, my experience of their store is anything but. Beneath the wonderful smells and bright colours, there is no escaping the deluded and dangerous beliefs that Strange Curiosities and Wonders provides for their patrons."*

"E-Ezra, please stop, just put it down!" Ana said as she rushed forward to reach for the paper, but he held it back from her, and the look he had on his face made her stop in her tracks.

"It is hard to tell if these people are conning the impressionable people they serve, or if they are truly convinced that they do indeed have mystic powers, but either way, the practices and beliefs that they follow is nothing short of a kind of devil worship."

"Are you fucking kidding me, Ana! There are three full pages of this shit! You know that's not true!" he shouted, the paper now wrinkled in his hands.

"H-how did you find it? You weren't supposed to see it!" Ana sniffled. Her chest felt tight, and her legs started to shake as she tried to reach out to him, but rather than let her come to him, he threw the paper at her feet.

"I thought it would be nice to see your name on your paper, but *this*? These are lies! It shouldn't matter if I was going to see it or not; the whole fucking city has a copy, Ana! Do you know what this could do to my career? Do you know what this will do to my *mother*? Do you even care?!" he screamed at her, making her back away from him.

"I'm sorry!" she shouted. Tears were streaming down her face again. "I had to! You threw me out, I had nothing to give to Elianna, and this was what she demanded! I didn't have a choice, Ezra!"

"There is always a choice, Ana!" His chest was rising and falling in angry pants as he stared at her. "My mother and I welcomed you into our world with open arms, we cared for you, we *loved* you, and you rolled over us for a fucking story! You've *ruined* us over three fucking pages. Do you know how pathetic that is?"

"I can make this right . . ." Ana sniffled as she walked to him, reaching to take his arm. "Let me make this right, Ezra, please."

Ezra looked down at where she was holding his arm, then looked up at her face. His eyes were angry, like he held nothing but hatred for her inside them. "Get your hand off me." When she complied, he turned and reached for his jacket that was lying on the sofa and pulled it on, then grabbed his keys from the table. "Whatever we had, whatever *this* was," he said, indicating to the space between them. "It's over."

Ana hiccupped and hugged her arms around herself. She knew there was no use apologising, that he was never going to forgive her after this. His body was tense with anger, and he was watching her with so much hate that she knew there was no point in pleading with him.

"I am going home to try and console my mother," he said as he walked back to her again and leaned in close to her ear, his breath hot on her neck. "If you even *breathe* in my town again, Ana, I'll fucking end you. Do you believe me?"

Ana flinched and nodded quickly once, shrinking away from him and looking to the floor to avoid how dark his eyes had become.

"Good." He moved away from her quickly and stormed out of

the apartment, slamming the door after himself so hard that it rattled on its hinges.

When she was sure he was gone, Ana let out a spluttering breath and gasped for air, but the harder she cried, the harder it was for her to bring any air into her lungs. She ended up on the floor on her hands and knees, trying to make her head stop spinning and her world cease from crumbling down around her.

Ruined.

Everything was ruined.

CHAPTER 27

A loud buzzing filled Ana's head as she stood in the elevator of *The City Herald* building. She couldn't remember picking herself up off the floor, cleaning her face of tears, and putting her makeup on over red-ringed eyes. She didn't remember pulling on a black pantsuit and her white shirt that frilled at the neck, fixing her hair into a high ponytail, or slipping on her black heels. She didn't even remember getting onto the bus into the centre of the city and coming into the building, but somehow, she must have. She knew she must have because when the doors pinged open, she was standing in the lobby.

She stood for a long moment, the people behind her pushing past her and joining the crowd of rushing people who darted up and down the halls to get ready for their first of the month meetings. Ana looked down at her feet blankly, having to force them to move her out of the elevator and down the hallway, into the side offices, and finally to her little desk in the centre of the room. Setting her bag down on her desk, she observed the pictures of her mom and dad staring back at her from where they were hugging each other inside the frames, secretly judging her from under the glass. After slumping into the chair, she lifted a picture frame of her as a child running in a race with her father, who shouted after her proudly. He would be so disappointed if he was here and knew what she had been doing. As a kid, he was always there, cheering her on from the side-lines, yelling, "Run, run as fast as you can" during sports games. She could hear him from behind the glass, silently screaming at her.

"Morning. You look like shit. Where have you been?" Ted, Ana's cubicle mate, looked down at her, standing behind her and looking down at the frame in her hands. "We are going to be late for the monthly meeting. Come on, stand up."

He was waving his hands at her for her to stand, and seeming to be on autopilot, she did. She set the frame down and lifted her bag, then followed him down the hallway. She didn't say anything, her body feeling numb as she walked. She watched everyone rushing around them like worker bees, stumbling into each other in a panic as they readied themselves for Elianna. *Run, run as fast as you can.*

Ana walked into the conference room and followed Ted to their seats around the oval table. The seats were beginning to fill with people. They were taking their briefcases and placing them on the table, lifting out their folders, notebooks, and pens. She sat there, staring at their robotic movements.

"Hurry up, everyone sit down, Elianna is in the elevator!"

Run, run as fast as you can.

A few seconds later, Elianna strolled through the door of the conference room. She was smartly dressed, as always, wearing a crisp white pantsuit, a white shirt, and a bright pink silk scarf. Her greying white-blonde hair was styled in a perfectly crafted bun at the top of her head, and she was looking over the rim of her black cat-eye glasses at everyone in the room. She swayed as she walked, making her way to the head of the table opposite where Ana was, and sat down in her chair as everyone instantly quieted down, watching her expectantly.

"Good morning, everyone. Let me start by saying that everyone did a fantastic job yesterday on the end-of-month issue. To the teams who are working on the daily and weekly issues, keep up the good work. I know your workload is unimaginable, but you all do a stellar job and it shows. I am going to delegate the titles for the monthly issue now, then after we will move on to the weekly issue working titles, the daily; well, you all should have what you need by now." Elianna said, looking over all of their eager smiling faces.

Ana gulped and looked down at her hands on the table where she sat, the only one with no notebook or pen in her hand. She loved this job, right? She *knew* she loved this job, but as she sat listening to Elianna, the only thing that seemed to be in her mind was how much she wanted to slap her.

"It is fashion month in the city, so this is going to be a major month for this department. We have stories that need to be fleshed out on the designers, their current work, the celebrities they are working with, and the scandals that are associated with said celebrities. If one of them starts a fight after drinks in a bar, I need to know about it. If there is a mishap on stage with a model, I need photographs of it. If a new designer gets too excited in their first fashion month and gets behind the wheel drunk, I need to have it on my desk instantly. Everyone knows, fashion month is less about the items of clothing and the art that is created and more about the public displays of scandal, and that's what I want from you all."

Run. Run as fast as you can.

Ana felt her body heat up and her head begin to cloud further. Her hand was shaking, and the tears that lingered behind her eyes were threatening to break loose again.

"Georgie, you take the photographer sex scandal I told you about," Elianna said as she threw him the file from where she sat in her chair without even looking at him. He caught it and rushed out the door with it, his face buried in the pages.

"Rana, you take the rivalry story between House of Fashion,

Inc. and Couture France, Inc. I hear their legal battles are getting nasty. Make it spicy," she instructed, throwing the file to a girl at the edge of the table to her left.

"Ana, your work on the countryside witches was very amusing." Elianna laughed, then placed a file on the table and held it with her index finger. "Good job. You will be working on the models and their eating disorders. You are a pretty little thing, so dress yourself up and go to a casting to see what quotes you can get. Learn their habits and report back." She pushed the file across the table.

The file stopped in arm's reach in front of Ana, and she stared down at it with sad eyes. She felt sick. Her stomach twisted, and her brow sweat as she pulled her hands back into her lap without taking the file.

Run. Run as fast as you can.

"Ana?" Elianna asked, trying to bring her attention into the room, but she didn't move when she said her name. "Ana!"

Ana jumped and looked up at Elianna, biting back tears and trying to keep the redness from her face, but it was no use. "I . . . I . . ."

"Did you hear a word I just said to you?" Elianna asked as she watched her through narrowed eyes. "Take your story and get to work."

"I heard you," Ana said as she gulped, feeling the eyes in the room burning through her. "But I can't. I'm sorry."

"Excuse me? There is no discussion; this is the story you are assigned. Get to it." Elianna looked back to her files and lifted the next one to move on.

Run, run as fast as you can.

"I . . . I quit . . ." Ana murmured, sitting back in her chair. She pushed her chair out from the table and stood quickly before she changed her mind, pulling her bag up over her shoulder.

"What?" Elianna asked, sighing as she removed her glasses

271

from her face, her brow furrowed and her face unamused. "What did you say?"

"I said, I quit," Ana said louder as she finally turned to look at her, her jaw set and her face sad. "I can't do this anymore." She turned quickly and headed for the door without looking back, but the sound of Elianna rising from her chair stopped her dead in her tracks when she reached it.

"If you leave this room now, Ana, there is no way back into it for you. You do realise that, don't you?" Elianna yelled as she watched her. "Think about this carefully. No one just quits *The City Herald.*"

Ana gulped, her face red and her hands in tight fists at her sides. "I understand. Thank you for the opportunity, but I'm done." Without looking back at her, she cleared her throat and moved out of the room.

Run, run as fast as you can.

THE LONG ROSE gold dress sparkled as she pulled it from the hanger and held it against herself in the mirror in her bedroom. The sheets of the bed were still unmade, and the pillows still smelled like Ezra. She couldn't bring herself to flatten out the sheets and risk losing his smell, so she had left them exactly the same way they were when he left. Instead, she slipped off her clothes, unzipped the dress to step into it, and pulled the straps up over her shoulders. Reaching behind herself, she pulled up the zipper again and smoothed out the fabric down her legs. The dress was stunning, with a glittery rose gold bodice and a low back that showed off her skin. She would have looked perfect if not for her red-ringed eyes and sad expression, but if there was one thing she knew she was good at, it was putting on a happy face when she needed to.

She sat down at her vanity table and brushed her long blonde hair, then watched herself in the mirror blankly and curled it until it bounced around her shoulders. She ran her fingers through it to untighten the curls, then took two bobby pins and pushed them up behind her ears to keep her hair from falling around her face. Once she was done, she pulled out her makeup bag and reapplied her makeup, using the eyeliner to place delicate flicks at the corners of her eyes, now that they were covered in concealer and no longer red. She almost looked normal as she stood from the stool and slipped her heels on, then lifted up her sparkly black bag and placed her phone inside. It was after 15:00, and she knew Bexley would be halfway through a bottle of champagne and already waiting on her.

Walking out of her apartment and into the hallway, she locked her door and slipped her keys into her bag, then rushed down the stairwell and out into the bright afternoon sun. The day was hot again, and she raised her hand to hail a taxi. When a yellow taxi pulled up beside her, she bounced inside and pulled her dress up so it wouldn't get wrinkled under her. "I need to go to Che Bon, quick as you can," Ana said as she sat back in her seat and gazed out the window as the buildings passed.

Che Bon was a beautiful little afternoon cocktail bar on the outskirts of the city, right on the rooftop of a swanky hotel that Bexley's parents owned. The rooftop had been decorated beautifully since the last time she had been there. Bexley had hundreds of bouquets of flowers decorating the tables and the walls, all in white and pinks, and there were fairy lights dripping over the walls and overhead. As she walked across the rooftop, Ana could see Bexley standing beside her fiancée and her parents, wearing a beautiful cherry red dress that hugged her hourglass figure and fanned out behind her in a long fishtail train. Her hair hung loosely in bouncy black waves to the middle of her back, and as she raised her champagne glass to her lips, Ana could see her engagement ring sparkle in the sunlight.

"Ana! Ana is here! I will be right back," Bexley said to her parents and shimmied towards Ana with her arms open wide, bringing her into a hug when she met her. "You made it! You look stunning! I *knew* that dress would be perfect for you, didn't I tell you?! Where is Ezra?"

Ana shrugged and gave her a half-smile. She didn't want to tell her what had happened just yet. This was Bexley's day, and she didn't want to ruin her happy mood. "Ezra can't make it; he had to go home. He sends his apologies, though. You look beautiful, Bexley. Everything looks amazing."

"I know, right?" Bexley said as she took her arm in hers and guided her towards the bar, where she lifted a tall glass of champagne and handed it to her. "Elianna gave you the afternoon off, hm?"

"Something like that," Ana said with a forced smile. "So, how is Marcus handling the engagement? Is he freaking out yet?"

"Look at him, of course he is." Bexley laughed as they both turned to look at her fiancé as he talked to her parents. He had a sheepish look on his face, like he was scared of saying the wrong thing. "He is very handsome in his suit, though, isn't he?"

"He is. You will make beautiful babies." Ana smiled.

Bexley wrinkled her nose and shook her head, then downed the rest of her glass and pulled her with her across the rooftop to where Marcus and her parents were talking. "My maid of honour has arrived, finally."

"I am your maid of honour?" Ana asked with a laugh and juggled her champagne glass and her bag so she could open it and lift out her camera. "I mean, I would love to be, but you never mentioned it."

"Of course you are!" Bexley said as she let her go and leaned into Marcus, resting her head on his shoulder.

"Then I think my first act of maid of honour should be documenting your party, hm?" Ana smiled, stepping back and turning her camera on. "Okay, everyone get in close, big smiles!" she said.

She waited until they all lined up together, and Ana took the picture of their smiling faces. "Perfect. I will go take some more for your scrapbook. I'll be right back"

Ana walked away from them, finishing her glass off quickly and setting it aside before she looked down at the screen of her camera of the photo of Bexley and Marcus she had just taken. They really were a beautiful couple. She pressed onto the next one, and the camera took her back to the first photo on the memory card: the day she met Ezra and Nina. The picture showed Nina kneeling in the dirt, showing where she found the box, and Ezra was looking over her shoulder to get a better look.

She passed photos of the parchment and the box when he had taken her to The Daria Research Lab, and she smiled softly at how pissed off he looked in the photo. She flipped through the photos until she saw Ezra at the table in his house after they had just gotten back from the Harrow mansion. They had just stolen the pendant, and Ezra had wanted to take a picture of them in their black outfits. She was smiling in the picture, but it was strained, probably because of how sore her ribs had been.

She pouted and ran her finger over his face on the screen, and as she did, her thumb pressed down on the button, and it flicked to the next picture. She gasped and looked away quickly, her heart beating faster in her chest, having not expected to see the giant black figure crawling over her in Ezra's bed. She gulped and forced herself to bring the screen back up to her face. She had completely forgotten she had taken it.

The figure was huge, with black taloned fingers and no features. It was a blur, really, and the closer she looked at it, the more she realised that it was not a solid form at all. Instead, it seemed like it was made of black swirling smoke. That was when she noticed it. The mirror it had come out of, the one she saw the security guard hanging from when she was laying in that bed; she could see him plain as day in the background of the mirror in the photo. Standing beside the dying guard was a man. He was tall, and the flash of the camera illuminated his features so when she zoomed in as far as she could on screen, she could see exactly who it was that sent that shadow messenger to hurt her. He had a peppered beard, green eyes, and features like Ezra's.

Ana's knees buckled under her, and she had to sit down on a chair nearby as she stared down at Alexander Sullivan's face in the photograph. He had his hand extended out, the same arm of the shadow messenger that was also extended, like he was controlling it, forcing its arms to reach out and grab her. "No . . ." she mumbled. If Alexander was the person who attacked her and killed that security guard, then it was he who killed Nina and was trying to get the athame from them this whole time . . . and he was with Ezra right now.

Ana jolted to her feet and looked around at the faces in the room, searching for Bexley. She had to warn Ezra about his father before he gave him the athame.

"Bex!" she called, rushing through the crowd and finding her. "I need to go! Give me your car keys."

"What? You just got here!" Bexley whined, looking over her face. "You look like you have seen a ghost. What's wrong?"

"I don't have time to explain! I am so sorry, but I need to go. It's an emergency. Give me your keys!" Ana said as she stuffed the camera back into her bag.

"All right, all right! Marcus, do you have my keys?" Bexley asked, taking them from him when he offered them to her. "Will you be back, at least? We are going for dinner now."

"I'll try. I love you! I'm so sorry!" Ana called as she snatched the keys from her and ran in her heels towards the door.

Run, run as fast as you can.

CHAPTER 28

*a*na pushed her foot down hard on the accelerator, making the car engine rev and growl as she ploughed down the road with Ezra in the forefront of her mind. It all made sense now. All the carnage that had happened only started after she met Alexander at the Litha celebrations, when she told him that Ezra had found the box. He hadn't known Ezra had found it before then. That was the same night Nina was found tortured to death at the monument. He was the one who offered her his help, knowing she wouldn't tell Ezra of his offer, knowing they would stall in their investigation and that she would have to come to him eventually, and he was the one who sent the messenger to hurt her through the mirror and killed the security guard. The photo of him proved that.

It was he who managed to patch things up with Ezra and convince him to let him see the completed athame so that he could bless it in a ritual, bringing it straight into his hands without his son ever knowing it was he all along, so he wouldn't lose him again.

All roads led back to Alexander Sullivan.

And Ezra was clueless.

Ana's knuckles grew white the longer and harder she gripped

onto the wheel of Bexley's black BMW. The journey from the city to Genevieve's store was usually a two-hour drive, but at the speed she was driving, she managed to race into the town an hour and a half after leaving the party. It was coming close to 18:00 now, and as she pulled the car down the cobbled street where *Strange Curiosities and Wonders* stood, she saw that the sign on the door read, *Closed*.

She pushed down on the brake when she pulled up outside, bringing the car to a screeching halt and opening the car door. She rushed around it and to the door of the shop. The lights were on inside, and she could see movement. "Ezra! Genevieve!" she shouted, bringing her fists down hard on the door and making it rattle on its hinges. "Hello?!"

More lights switched on inside the shop, and after what seemed like ages, Genevieve finally came through the curtain near the till and rounded the counter. She had a sour look on her face as she came to the door and looked through the glass at her, folding her arms like she was trying to protect herself from her. "We are closed."

"Genevieve, please let me in!" Ana said as she pushed at the door, but it didn't budge. "Listen, I know you are mad at me, and you should be, I'm a horrible person, but it's an emergency. *Please*, Genevieve, I need to see Ezra."

Genevieve sighed and watched her for a long moment suspiciously, then nodded once and reached to unlock the door and walk back into the middle of her shop.

"Thank you!" Ana gasped as she opened the door and burst inside, looking around the room frantically for any sign of Ezra. "Ezra!" she called, her eyes wide and her hands shaking at her sides. "Where is Ezra?"

"He is not here, and even if he was, he does not want to see you, Ana," Genevieve said with a dark frown on her face and her jaw set like she was biting her tongue.

"Where is he, Genevieve? I told you, this is an emergency. If it wasn't important, I wouldn't be here!" Ana said, beginning to get impatient as she walked to her, extending her hands out to her and resting them on her folded arms. "Please. I think he might be in trouble. Where is he?"

Genevieve sighed and looked away from her, like she couldn't look at her in case she said something she shouldn't. "He is not in any trouble; he is fine. He is with his father."

Ana's face paled and she whined in frustration. "Oh, God." She hiccupped, pacing the room. "Do they have the athame with them? Where did they go?"

"Yes, they took it to the monument about half an hour ago to place it back together and bless it in a ritual. You are not invited, Ana. Stay clear of my son," she said firmly.

So Alexander had it. He had it in his hands and Ezra was oblivious of his fathers lies. She had to go and warn him, she knew, but she didn't know how well she would fare in a dress and heels against a murderer on a mission.

"I need your shoes," Ana said as she snapped her head back to Genevieve. She could barely walk up that hill in walking shoes, never mind heels. "Now, I need your shoes!"

"I am not giving you my sh–"

"Genevieve, please! Give me your goddamn shoes!" Ana shouted, making Genevieve jump and flinch.

She gave her a shaky nod and held her hands up defensively, using her feet to kick them off without having to bend over. "Ana, tell me what is going on."

Ana rushed forward after kicking her heels off in the middle of the shop and slipped Genevieve's much flatter pair onto her feet. They were a size too big, but they would do. "I don't have time to explain, but Ezra is in trouble and I need to warn him. Stay here, please, I will send him back to you." She nodded, then rushed back to the open door.

She jumped back into the car, pulling her dress around her legs tightly so that she could drive without obstruction. The car revved again and growled as she pulled out fast from the edge of the path and hammered down the cobbled streets. The way to the monument was signposted with little brown signs that pointed the way, and she followed them as quickly as she possibly could without damaging the wheels of Bexley's BMW. If she remembered correctly, the monument was only a fifteen-minute drive from the store, and if she was fast enough, she could make it while the sun was still in the sky.

When she pulled into the car park, she could see that the only other car that was there was Genevieve's purple Volkswagen Beetle. She sighed in relief as she pulled up beside it and got out of the car, leaving the keys in the ignition and looking in through the other car's window to see if she could spot Ezra. When she saw that no one was inside, she looked up the high hill to where the white rounded monument was and started to run towards it, past the willow trees at the bottom, through the maze of gravestones, and to the statue of Mary Marion. She looked up at her briefly. If it were possible, Ana could have sworn she could see copper tears dripping down her face, but she shook her head and focused on her ascent up the steep hill.

The sun was lower in the sky now, and she could see that the half-moon was out early today, hovering just above the monument in the dimming, misty blue sky. Her legs burned as she scrambled up the hill, her hair beginning to fall out of place as the bobby pins loosened. Her dress was fanning behind her, and as much as she tried to hold it up out of the mud and grass, it didn't stop the hem from picking up dirt along the way. Bexley was going to kill her.

When she got to the top without stopping, she put her hand to her chest and gasped for air, bringing thick gulps of air into her chest and trying to push the ringing from her ears. Looking directly to the little doorway that led into the one-room ceremonial tomb,

Ana saw candlelight flickering inside illuminating the hallway. She edged close to the entrance and poked her head around the corner, looking inside and trying to listen for Ezra. She could hear someone talking, and laughing softly, but who it was, she couldn't tell. Taking a deep breath to steady her nerves, she tiptoed into the little stone hallway and made her way down it quietly until she could see the room. Alexander was standing at a low wooden table with candles all around it. The pieces of the athame lay on a purple cloth side by side, waiting to be assembled as he anointed them with an oil and herb mixture inside a bowl.

"It was much easier this way, my boy. After you took each piece and kept them in your mother's temple, I knew there was no way I was going to actually get to them. She blocked me from that place a long time ago; my skin would melt off if I stepped within an inch of that place." Alexander mumbled.

Ana thought he was talking to himself until she heard a painful moan and moved to stand beside a pillar in the hallway so that she couldn't be seen. When she moved her head around it, she saw Ezra sitting in a chair with his arms behind his back and his head drooped forward like he was sleeping. Her eyes widened when she saw that his arms and legs were tied to the wood of the chair, and his head was bleeding, staining the back of his neck and his shirt collar. He was waking up, and he blinked a few times as he looked up at his father from under his hair as he worked at blessing the items.

"If you wanted the find that badly, why didn't you just steal it like you did my coins? You didn't have to kill Nina." He groaned, his head falling forward again.

"I didn't mean to kill Nina. I was trying to get information from her about where you took the first piece. She didn't give me anything I could use. I guess the stress of torture was just a little too much for a human body to take." Alexander shrugged. "And I never wanted these things for an article or a find for the museum, Ezra."

281

He laughed and lifted the red stone before holding it up against the light of one of the candles. "No, this is much more than that."

"It's just an athame, Dad. A very valuable one, yes, but it's just metal. It's not worth killing people over." Ezra sat up straighter now, wiggling against the ropes that bound his wrists.

Alexander gave another laugh and shook his head. "You have had this all this time, and you had no idea what you were actually holding. You are a fool, Ezra. This is no ordinary ceremonial athame. This is the *Marion coven* athame. This stone was enchanted, back when the coven ruled supreme! When they knew their lives were most likely going to end, they cursed themselves and this athame so that all the power of every witch in the coven would return to *this* stone when they died. So, a descendant, or I guess anyone who knew how to use it, like me, could access it and take all of that power back into themselves." He watched as the energy trapped inside the stone swirled, colliding against the inside of the red stone like it wanted to get out. "This is the most powerful magical item in existence, and soon, it will be inside me."

Ezra was watching his father with widened eyes, pulling at the bindings and trying to set himself free. "You did this for power?"

"Of course I did this for power!" Alexander shouted at his son, holding the gemstone in his hand carefully and placing it in the hole at the bottom of the hilt where it met the blade. "I may be high priest, but our magic is weakened these days. The more power one has, the less we must bow down. I will bow down to no one anymore. With this, everyone will sink to their knees. *Everyone.* We have spent too long in the darkness, Ezra. We have dumbed down our abilities so that we can fit into a human world. That is not how it should be. They should bow to *us*. With this, I will make sure they will. This is *our* time, my boy."

He grinned as he lifted the gold pendant and placed it over the gemstone. It fused to it perfectly, and she heard a metallic *click*, like it was magnetized when all three of them were placed in the correct places. When he held it up against the light, it stayed together in his hands, a golden glow emulating from it.

"It is beautiful!" He smiled, then brought it down to his side. "Much like your little girlfriend in the hallway. You can come out now, Ana. I can sense you lurking."

Ana's heart leapt into her throat and beat loudly in her ears when she heard him say her name. She gasped, looking between them and standing up straighter. He knew she was there, there was no point in hiding now, so she straightened out her dress and cleared her throat. She rounded the corner of the hallway and stood in the doorway, clenching her fists at her sides. "You won't get away with this."

"That's cute," Alexander said as he shrugged and turned back to the table where he wiped the dagger one last time. "But I think I have this under control. Thank you for your concern, though."

"My concern? You have killed people, *innocent* people! What is your plan now? Kill me? Kill your *son*?" Ana asked as she looked at Ezra. He was watching her with wide eyes, like he wasn't sure if she was really there or if he was hallucinating from his head injury.

"Oh, please. I am not going to kill my son. With the magic from this stone, I can wipe his memory of this, of you, and we can go back to being happy families. Then, I will be the most powerful witch on this planet." He walked around the marked-out circle on the ground with the athame in his hand and then looked up at her sharply. "You on the other hand . . ."

"Ana, run!" Ezra shouted.

Ana gasped, and just as she tried to step back away from him, Alexander's hand shot out in front of him. He clenched his fist, and she found that she couldn't move her feet, no matter how much she tried to shift them.

"The ritual needed to do the magic transfer requires blood. I was going to use my own, but I guess now that you are here . . ."

Alexander trailed off and opened his hand gently, holding it out to her. "Come here, child."

Ana whimpered. She wanted to cry, she wanted to run, she wanted to scream *something*, but she found that her body no longer complied. Instead, her feet began to move on their own, walking her forward and into the circle. She watched her hand raise in confusion and terror as it took Alexander's gently and was tugged in close to him.

"Dad! Dad, stop! Let her go! She doesn't need to remember any of this. We can let her go! I will even help you do this ritual if you just *let her go*!" Ezra shouted at his father.

Alexander's eyes never left Ana's as he grinned and leaned in close to her. "Now, where would be the fun in that?"

The athame in his hand suddenly thrust out in front of him, pushing through her beautiful rose gold dress, and clean through her stomach just below her rib cage. Ana was frozen in pain in the middle of the circle and gasped when Alexander suddenly started shaking. His hand clamped around hers like he was being electro-cuted, and as he shook in front of her, she found she was able to get control of her body. Looking down at the blade in her stomach, she could see blood pouring down the sides of the blade and over his hand. His hand was fused to the hilt, like he couldn't let go of it, and it was beginning to turn black, his skin wrinkling and falling from the meat of his arm. It spread all the way up to his elbow before he could finally let go of her and stumble back, cradling his ashen arm as it withered away in front of his eyes.

"No! No, what's happening?" Alexander growled. He was in pain; she could see it all over his face as he cradled what was left of his arm against his chest. He panted, looking up to Ana as she stood frozen and bleeding in the middle of the circle, and before his arm got any worse, he spat at her and turned, rushing out of the stone chamber.

The second he left and her body was returned to her, pain rushed through her like she had never felt before. She collapsed onto the stone floor of the room and looked down at the blade that was still lodged inside her stomach, her hands shaking on either side of it as her eyes began to blur from the tears that filled them. Ezra was screaming something at her, but she couldn't hear him over the loud metallic sound that was invading her ears as she lay back on the ground, her chest rising and falling as she started to go into shock.

"Ana! Ana, stay awake!"

She heard the wooden chair snap and Ezra's weight hit the ground. "Ana! Keep your eyes open! Look at me!"

Ana cried out in pain once she heard his voice again, and he was suddenly over her and laying shaky hands beside hers where the blade was still lodged inside her stomach. "M-my dress. Is m-my dress r-ruined? B-bex is gonna be so m-mad," she stuttered. She was in the throes of shock now, her face wet with tears and her hair sticking to her forehead in sweat and panic. She looked down at her stomach and gagged, trying to reach her bloody, slippery hands to the hilt so that she could pull it out, but Ezra's hands stopped her.

"You can't take it out, Ana; you need to keep it in so we can stem the bleeding. I am going to lift you now, okay? Take a deep breath," he said as he brought her into his arms and cradled her, lifting her as she screamed in pain. "It's okay! It's okay, you need to hold on, it's going to be okay."

Ana's head lolled back as she began to feel lightheaded, and she tried to hold on to his shirt to keep her upright, but she was just too weak now. Instead, she watched his face as he grunted and tried to keep her steady. He carried her quickly out of the chamber and down the hill, where he slipped a few times in the dry grass.

"It's okay, Ana. Are you awake? Talk to me, you need to stay awake!"

Ana could barely feel the pain anymore. She just tilted her head back and watched the moon and how high it was in the purple sky as he carried her past the gravestones and Mary Marion. He carried her through the willow trees and into the car park, and when he searched for his car, he found it was gone. His father must have taken it when he was trying to get away with his disintegrating arm. Instead, he pulled open the door of the black BMW and placed her inside, laying her down in the backseat and trying to belt her in with bloody hands.

"Ana! Ana, are you awake?" he spluttered. He had tears in his eyes now as he checked her over.

Ana lolled her head, weakness taking over her whole body. She forced her eyes to stay open, watching as he closed the door and rushed into the driver's seat, turning the car on with the keys that were left in the ignition. When he was on the road, she could see him reach inside her bag and lifted out her phone, pressing it to his ear in panic.

"Mom! Get the temple ready! Ana's dying!"

CHAPTER 29

"*A*na? Ana, can you hear me?" Ezra asked, his voice panicked and his eyes wild with worry.

Ana whimpered from his arms. Her face was pale, and her hands were barely able to keep hold of his shirt.

"Mom! Mom, where are you?!" Ezra shouted as he carried her through the threshold of his mother's shop. She was bleeding heavily, and it dripped onto the wooden floor as he rushed across the room and behind the curtain. "MOM!"

Genevieve rushed up the stairs of the basement and met him in the backroom, gasping loudly when she saw Ana in his arms. Her skin was so pale, like her body was drained of all her blood. "What the hell happened to her?!"

"Dad happened to her. You need to help her. Please," Ezra said. He didn't wait for his mother to reply, and he rushed past her and down the steps into the temple.

Genevieve followed him and watched him as he walked straight to the white circle on the floor in the centre of the room near the altar and laid her on the floor in the middle of it. He held her face in his bloody hands, slapping at her cheeks.

Ana groaned, lolling her head from side to side as she opened her eyes again as fully as she could, but they only opened halfway. Ezra was hovering above her, his face pained and his eyes full of fear as he stared down at her. "Where am I?"

"Shh. Don't speak, you need to save your energy, okay? My mom is going to help you, just try to stay awake." Ezra stroked her hair back from her head.

"Ezra, I'm so s-sorry," Ana started to say, but as she did, she felt something fill the back of her throat and found she couldn't breathe. She spluttered and coughed, and when she pulled her head back from his chest, she realised she had coughed blood all over the front of his shirt. She whimpered in panic, her hands shaking as they tried to grip at him, but she was just too weak. "A-am I going to die?"

"No, no, you are not going to die, Ana!" Ezra said as he looked down at the blood on his chest and he began to shake, looking back over his shoulder to find his mother. "Mom! Mom, hurry!"

"I am coming!" Genevieve said as she rushed around the room, bringing an armful of swabs and books and jars of strange-looking ointments. "We need to take the athame out of her stomach." She sunk to her knees beside them.

Ana looked down at the dagger that pierced her. It was no longer glowing, and the stone that had the swirling energy inside was now just a simple solid stone, like it never contained anything at all. Her head lolled again as Ezra moved to sit behind her, bringing her head into his lap as he cradled her.

"Do it quick, I'll hold her down." Ezra nodded.

Genevieve set down the items she was carrying beside her and reached her hands out to the athame, placing her fingers around the hilt, and in one swift movement, she pulled it out of her stomach. Ezra placed his hand over Ana's mouth as she screamed loudly into his palm. Genevieve then pushed down on her wound to try to stop the bleeding, but it just kept seeping through her fingers. "Open the book! Page fifty-four," she said as she got to work undressing Ana.

She ripped the dress open to expose her stomach and pressed down on the wound with the cloths, looking to Ezra when he found the page and laid it out in front of her. "Good, now get to work with the sigils."

Ezra nodded and pulled the straps from her shoulders, taking the dress clean away from Ana and leaving her in her underwear, then reached for the pot of oily ashes that was sitting beside the book. He drew symbols Ana didn't recognise on her skin.

"Ezra . . . I c-can't keep my e–" Ana hiccupped, her body losing all feeling.

"Keep them open, keep looking at me, Ana, you can't fall asleep," Ezra pleaded. He didn't stop drawing on her, even as she began to lose consciousness.

From where she was laying, she could hear Genevieve beginning to chant over her stomach, her hands pressing down on her wound as she rocked back and forth on the ground beside her. Her hands felt like they were vibrating on her skin, and when she fluttered her eyes open to look at her, she saw Genevieve had her head pointed skywards, and her eyes were no longer her own. They were glowing white and shining so brightly that it was hard for her to look at them. Weakly, Ana looked up a final time to Ezra's face as her eyes closed and her heartbeat slowed.

"Ana, stay with me! You are going to be okay. Do you trust me?" Ezra panted, finishing his sigils, leaning down to kiss her forehead, and stroking her hair back from her pale face.

A small curve of a smile reached Ana's lips. "Absolutely," she mumbled as her body finally gave up and her world went black.

CHAPTER 30

*S*he never thought about what death would feel like. She never pondered about where she would go if she died, or what awaited her if she slipped away from the land of the living and floated into the abyss that was death. What was worse was the confusion and pain of drifting in the in-between, being powerless to pull herself closer to the white light of life as the darkness of death magnetized her downwards into its void. As she chased the sweet, warm comfort of the light, the darkness chased after her just as fast.

Run, run as fast as you can.

Fluttering her eyes open, Ana looked up to a familiar ceiling, though as she lay there for what seemed like an age, she couldn't quite place exactly where she was, the memory just beyond her reach in the fog of her mind. She groaned and turned her head, Abby's bedroom coming into view as she slowly sat up against her pillows. She was wearing a black t-shirt with a band slogan on it she didn't recognise, and as she looked down to her stomach, all the memories that had seemed so far away rushed back into her mind.

Alexander. The athame. Ezra.

"Ana?" Ezra was sitting in an armchair, looking like he had just woken up. He had an old book open on his lap and was wiping the sleep from his eyes as he closed it and set it aside. He stood from the chair and moved to the bed, sitting down beside her and reaching for her hand. "Hey . . ."

Ana gulped thickly, the bite of thirst thick on her tongue and her head spinning. Her body felt different, like it wasn't completely hers somehow, like there was so much of herself that didn't sit in the same places as it had before. Something in her veins tingled and vibrated; colours seemed brighter, and smells seemed sweeter. "What happened? How did I get here?"

"I brought you here," Ezra said as he watched her face behind eyes that were searching for something. "How are you feeling?"

"I . . ." Ana started, then looked back down at her stomach. She didn't feel like she was in any pain, and in confusion, she reached her hand down to the T-shirt she was wearing and pulled it up quickly. There was no bandage there, no blood, and no wound that invaded her. There was only a thin, white scar that knitted her skin together where the blade had been. "How long have I been here? I thought I died . . ."

"You did. A couple of times, actually." Ezra sighed with a frown as he took her hand and laid it in his lap, stroking the back of it gently. "You have been unconscious for three days."

"That doesn't make any sense, Ezra. I'm healed. It doesn't even hurt. The human body doesn't heal that quickly," Ana said as she lay back against the pillows again and looked up at his face.

"A human body doesn't, no." He sighed, opening and closing his mouth like he didn't know which words to choose next.

"Ezra, what is it? What is going on? Why am I healed? Why do I feel so different? Where is Alexander? Did you find him?" She was rambling questions, desperately trying to reach for answers that he seemed so reluctant to give her.

"No one has seen him since he left the monument after he stabbed you. There hasn't been one sighting of him. We tried to track him, but he is gone with the wind." Ezra looked down at the floor and gulped. His eyes seemed heavy, like they were yearning for sleep.

He bit his lip in thought, then held his finger out and reached into the drawer beside the bed, lifting out the long silver and gold athame with the dulled stone inside. Ana instinctively flinched when he pulled it out in front of her and turned it over in his hand, then offered it to her. "I have a lot to explain to you, and you aren't going to like it."

"Ezra, if you don't start talking, I'm going to show you exactly what this blade feels like," Ana threatened as she took it from him in a shaky hand. It felt light, and looking at it closer, she was confused at how such a simple blade could have done so much damage.

A small curve of a smile tugged at the corners of his mouth, and he tilted his head. "After my mother managed to heal you, we washed you and laid you down here so you could rest. Afterwards, I went back to the monument to find my father. He was gone, obviously, but he had left all of his ceremonial tools and his spell book there. This was so much more than just an athame, Ana. I had no idea. My father had been looking for it for a while, that's where I got the idea to find it before he did, but he wanted it for a much darker purpose." He took it from her again and ran his finger over the stone at the hilt, his expression tortured in trying to explain to her in words she would understand.

"Do you remember when you told me there was something moving inside the stone? My father was right. It was linked to every Marion coven witch; they linked their souls and their magic to it so that when they died, all of their collective power was kept inside of it safely. My father was going to do a ritual to take the power out of the stone and inside himself, but he didn't read the spell clearly. I don't know if he misread the translation or he was too busy with knocking me out, but he made a mistake. The person who wielded the athame was supposed to be the sacrifice, not the person at the end of the blade. That's why his arm disintegrated. The person who the blade entered, the person whose blood travelled up the athame and tainted the stone, that is who it then became linked to. So . . ."

"So, what, Ezra?" Ana asked, watching him. Her heart was pounding in her ears louder, like her panic was affecting the atoms in the air around her. The bed began to vibrate and the trinkets on the vanity shook. She gasped. "What is going on!"

"You need to calm down. You can't let your emotions get the better of you anymore," Ezra warned as he ignored the vibrating in the room and took her hands again, making her look at him. The longer she looked into his eyes, the more the movement stopped and returned to normal. "That's better." He smiled.

"Ezra, what's happening to me?"

"Everything." Ezra smiled. "When the athame linked to you and your blood, the spell was already cast, and the power of all of those witches left that stone and entered you, Ana. *You*. Not my dad."

Tears pricked the back of her eyes as she watched him, and she started to panic again. The bed under her began to rise off the ground and wobble, causing her to whimper. She hugged his chest and watched as the bed started to right itself when she tried to calm herself down. "It's real? It's all real?"

"Every bit of it," Ezra said as he pulled back to look down at her. "But it is a lot of power, Ana, and if you don't control it, it will consume you. But I can teach you."

Ana sniffled and looked around the room as she tried to comprehend what he was saying. She searched her memories, thinking back to when she had fallen in the tower and woke up on the ground under him safely, to the Litha ceremony when she thought he killed his father, but he hadn't, then to the Harrow mansion when he had unlocked the door with his hands and when the security guard didn't seem to see them standing right in front of him. "You . . . you . . ."

"Yes. I mean, I couldn't tell you the truth. You would never have believed me," Ezra said as he sighed and looked down into his lap. "As overwhelming as I am sure all of this is for you, you need to trust me. My father might be back to finish what he started, and the High Council won't be happy that a human has the power of the whole Marion coven. So, we need to move you somewhere safe, for now, until you can control it and defend yourself."

He was speaking in words she didn't understand, but when she looked up into his smiling face, she smiled back weakly.

"Do you trust me?" Ezra asked, taking her hand close to his chest.

Ana gulped and nodded once slowly. "Absolutely."

She looked down at her free hand, and her eyes found her vein that pulsed with blood. She could see it, she could feel it, all that power that rushed through it like new life. It felt clean and refreshingly cold, like nothing that would have plagued her before could touch her now. She didn't know how many witches' worth of magic was trapped inside that stone, but she could feel each one inside there somewhere, their hands on her shoulders, ready and waiting. A magnitude of power . . .

And now, she had all of it.

A LITTLE BIT OF HISTORY

Unfortunately, all of the strikingly horrific stories that Ezra relays to Ana in *Whisper of Witches* are true. The names have been changed, but the woman who was burned to death while in labor was true.

The women who died in spiked barrels, was true. The useless invention of the mercy rope was true. The astonishing numbers of those accused of witchcraft and subsequently murdered, also true.

The exchange of the money and lands from accused witches into the hands of those in power, true, true, true.

It never ceases to amaze me what humans can do to each other over fear of the unknown, and the fact is, these things continue to happen in our modern world.

To those men and women accused of witchcraft: no one can change the sins of the past, but I hope with this book, a few more people will know your stories.

Blessed be.

ACKNOWLEDGMENTS

Firstly, this book would never have happened had I not stumbled into the musings of a little group of fellow writers. Maddie Cowan, Kristin Sargent, Marie Freeman, Kassi Parsons, Eurydice Noelle Perkins, Emma Reinhart and Heather Coy; I can't thank you girls enough for our special little creative group that got me started.

To my best friend, who has been writing with me for over fifteen years, Lainie Elizabeth. We may be a whole ocean apart, but you mean more to me than most people on the planet.

To my amazing BETA readers, Corri Clarke, Amy Dunlop and Shauna Browne, whose enthusiasm and love for these characters kept me going. You guys are the reason this novel was finished in the first place, and I love you all.

To one of my closets friends and proofreader, Joanna Magill, who has been with me though all of my nerdy phases, you are amazing, and I am so lucky to call you a friend.

To my sister, Shalana Hegarty, the person who knows when I need a hug and a shopping trip to clear my head, even before I do. I love you so much.

Most importantly, to my wonderful husband, who gets just as excited as I do about my stories, who has been there for me with ideas, and plot twists. The man who brings me coffee, love and support when I am on a writing roll: I love you more than anything.

And finally to my beautiful step children, who distract me from my writing with jokes and funny videos, hugs and smiles; thank you for pulling me back into the real world, where your magic shines the brightest.

ABOUT THE AUTHOR

 Nikita Rogers lives in a little rustic village in Northern Ireland. She lives with her husband, Lee Rogers, an insanely talented musician, her wonderful step-kids, and their cats, chickens and pygmy goat.

She has been writing for 16 years (as of 2021).

During the day, Nikita spends her time working in her tattoo studio where she has etched designs on her customers since 2008. At night, you will find her curled up on her sofa with a good book, creating sketches and designs, or writing in her pyjamas with a cup of coffee.

She is currently working on book two of *Whisper of Witches*, and a completely different untiled Fae series that will be released sometime 2022.

Come say hi on her socials, she promises she doesn't bite.

Instagram: @Nevermoreink

Tiktok: @nikitarogersauthor

Email: nikitarogersauthor@hotmail.com

Find her husband's music:

Instagram: @leerogersmusic

Facebook: Lee Rogers Music

Twitter: leerogerstweets

Made in the USA
Monee, IL
14 July 2022

99641167R00167